Waves Take Your Bones

Waves Take Your Bones

Athena Giles

Space Wizard Science Fantasy
Raleigh, NC
www.spacewizardsciencefantasy.com

Cover art by MoorBooks
Editing by Courtney Brooks
Book Layout © 2015 BookDesignTemplates.com

Waves Take Your Bones/Athena Giles.— 1st ed.
ISBN 978-1-960247-43-8

Author's website: https://www.athenagiles.com/

To Book Club and Amos, for reading this when it was barely a book. And to my family, who told me I needed a real job in addition to writing. They were right, of course.

CONTENTS

SERPENT RIVER
KING'S HA
THE WESTERN WILDS
OKAESA
WESTHAM
FOGGY RIVER
THE NIGHTMARE BRIDGE
SE
Waves take their bones

Giant's Isle
Sabutia
Isles of Kereth
Mouth
Bloody Shoals

CHAPTER ONE

Lion Rampant

"Keep up, Finn!" Tallis called over her shoulder to her friend. At her sides, Aiven and Osind, her younger siblings, were also running. "We'll miss it!"

Finley Tyne and Tallis Larke had spent years together, romping through the woods past their curfews and returning home to scoldings and violent scrubbings to get the mud off their legs and twigs out of their hair. Finn quickened his pace to catch up with the three siblings. He didn't have their long legs and struggled to keep up with them when they really meant to run.

Together, the four hurried away from the Larkes' farm, toward the center of Westham. Their feet slapped against the hard-packed dirt of the road. Neatly planted rows of trees separating the farms on the outskirts of Westham flashed by, leaves the deep green of midsummer. The farmer's fields beyond were golden with wheat, or green with corn.

They crested a hill, panting with the effort and sweating from the summer sun, and the village of Westham spread out in the river valley below them. The buildings crowded in on each other around the main road, as if vying for the best spots. Beyond the cluster of buildings, the blue-green Foggy

River flowed, one bridge crossing the river where the main road met its bank. The bridge was barred with barricades.

"Look!" Osind pointed east down the main road with childish excitement. At just past ten, he often pretended he was ready to be a man, but his older sisters and parents knew better.

The three others followed Osind's outstretched hand. Tallis could not help an audible gasp. She'd visited the harbors providing trade with Okaesa's capital, Giant's Isle, often enough to see the King's soldiers, but she'd never seen anything like the lines of infantry marching down the road now.

Rows of men and women in sea-blue uniforms marched in formation down the road that led out of Westham. At the head of the line, a bannerman bore the standard of King Leander Adamaris: a white lion, rearing upon a field of the same blue as the soldiers' uniforms. From this distance, Tallis could not make out the insignia upon the breasts of the uniforms, only blurred outlines, but she knew that they would all bear the lion rampant, as well as the sigil of the captain they served under.

Tallis glanced over at Finn, whose dark eyes were fixed on the soldiers, shining with wonder. Unlike her, Finn had never been outside of Westham. Tallis' father would bring her to the harbor, the Serpent's Mouth, where the Foggy River and the Serpent flowed together into the ocean. There, they would sell crops to be brought to the capital.

"Told you it'd be worth it," Tallis told Finn.

He looked back at her, a grin spreading across his face. "Glad you convinced me."

"There's so many of them," Aiven spoke up, the same wonder in her golden-brown eyes. "It looks like more than all of Westham!"

Tallis laughed, smoothing a stray lock of curly black hair away from her sister's face. "Maybe next year, we can convince Papa to let you come with us to the Serpent's Mouth. Then you'll really see more people than all of Westham just in one marketplace."

"Come on!" Osind grabbed his sisters' hands and pulled them down the slope of the hill toward the main road. "I want to be right there when they pass through!"

They reached the bottom of the hill just as the bannerman in the lead came abreast of the smaller road they'd come down. He kept his posture, holding the king's banner high, but he turned his head to give the four a smile. Tallis imagined what he saw in them: just a handful of farm children who'd known nothing but the simple life of Westham. As far as the kingdom of Okaesa was concerned, even the lowest ranking of these soldiers was far above Tallis and her family.

It seemed to take ages before the entirety of the battalion had passed them and made their way into the center of Westham. Most of the group broke off to make a camp along the riverbank, as Westham's inn could not fit them all. Likely, only the senior officers would be staying in rooms tonight.

"No way the Shriekers will get past all of them!" Osind said with a confidence that almost convinced Tallis.

The Shriekers were what the barricades on the bridge were meant to keep out. They had come out of the mountains in the Western Wilds with the spring thaws. They attacked the few farms and homesteads west of the Foggy River first. The handful of the people who'd managed to escape had come bolting across the bridge into Westham. Tallis had watched them, eyes wide and trembling like rabbits fleeing a fox as they shouted their warnings in the street. The king's soldiers had tried to quiet them and take their report somewhere away from crowds, but Tallis couldn't forget their terror and the way they shouted about the dead rising.

This battalion was meant to push the Shriekers back from the crossing into Westham once and for all. Tallis had heard rumors that battalions were being sent to guard river crossings in other towns along the Foggy River. But even seeing all these soldiers didn't set Tallis' mind at ease. At night, they could sometimes hear the screams that gave the

Shriekers their name. The sound plagued Tallis' nightmares, and her siblings often awoke her with shouts as they slept.

"I'm sure it will all be over soon, Osi," Tallis said with a smile, ruffling his hair.

They followed the soldiers toward the center of town. As they passed the growing encampment, one called out to them.

"You there," he beckoned to them. He was tall, and white curls framed a face that was roughened with age and, Tallis guessed, years at sea. The coat of his uniform bore the three white stripes on the shoulders that marked him as a captain. On one breast of the coat was embroidered the white lion rampant of Okaesa, and on the other the symbol of his own family: three yellow lightning bolts.

Tallis gestured for Aiven and Osind to stay where they were and took a few steps toward the man. She gave a slight bow of her head and then stood tall, unsure of the right way to greet a captain. Her heart raced, wondering what reason this man would have for calling out to them.

"Yes, sir?" Tallis spoke up, drawing the man's attention to herself, and, she hoped, away from her siblings.

The man approached, scanning her face, then turning that same appraising look on Aiven and Osind. There was nothing in his manner that implied a threat, but Tallis moved another step ahead of the group, instinctively putting herself between her siblings and the captain. Finn stood at her shoulder, a position he'd taken often, letting Tallis take the lead, but showing his own protectiveness of Aiven and Osind.

The man chuckled slightly. "Well, now I know you must be Nevra's daughter. I thought so from your face, but you move just like him, so bold and ready for anything."

"How do you know my father?" Tallis asked, caught off guard.

"My name is Vaska Kelison, and I am captain of the Protector's Justice," he said. "Though many years ago, when King Leander was still a prince captaining the *Storm Ghost*, I was his first officer. Your father was under my command in the war with the Kerethi Pirates. I remember him mentioning a daughter, you look about the right age, and Westham is not a large village. It was not a difficult guess. Though, I do not remember what he said his girl's name was."

"Tallis," she said, beginning to relax, but not moving from her spot between Captain Vaska and her siblings.

"Yes," Vaska nodded. "I wish I had the time to pay your father a visit, but this battalion will be crossing the bridge and moving west at dawn, and there's much to prepare before then. However—"

Vaska moved a step closer and turned so that his back faced Aiven and Osind and they could not see his face. He lowered his voice enough that Tallis guessed only she and Finn would hear.

"A word of advice," Vaska said. "We have been encouraging people to stay where they are. It's the harvest season after all, and if the farmlands are abandoned, the dead rising won't be our only problem come winter. But plan a way out. Pack some bags with what you'd need for a journey east, and be ready to run at a moment's notice. You two are the right age to enlist. There is a lieutenant in your town's tavern. His name is Redwan. Speak to him and tell him I sent you. Take the enlistment papers, and keep them with you at all times. You never know when you may need to run, and those papers will get you space on any ship bound for Giant's Isle. If things continue going the way they have been in this fight, that might save your lives."

Tallis shivered, imagining Shriekers pouring over the barricades like the surge of water down the river from the first spring rains and thawing of the snow in the mountains.

"Why are you telling us this?" she asked.

"Consider it a debt repaid," Vaska stepped back, his voice returning to a conversational tone. "Nevra kept me from going overboard in a storm once. I owe it to him to help his family weather *this* storm."

"Thank you, sir," Tallis said hesitantly, though she was unsettled by what Vaska had told her and gratitude was not what she felt.

"Your father is a good man, and was a good soldier," Vaska said. "Had he remained in service, I have no doubt he'd be captaining his own ship by now. If you're anything like him, you could go far serving the fleet."

"May the Protector watch over you in your journey westward, Captain," Tallis was unsure what else to say. She bowed her head and ushered Aiven and Osind toward the town's center.

As they made their way into town, Tallis couldn't get the captain's words out of her head. News had become scarce in recent weeks from beyond the edges of Westham. No one was coming to the villages at the western edges of Okaesa's map anymore except for soldiers, and it seemed their reports were not entirely reliable.

Tallis was so lost in replaying the conversation in her head, she almost didn't notice when Aiven and Osind dashed off in pursuit of some other children their age.

"See you at home!" Aiven called over her shoulder.

"Be back before dark!" Tallis demanded, hearing Mama's tone sneaking into her voice.

When Aiven and Osind were out of earshot, Tallis ducked into a side alley and turned to Finn.

"What do you think of what that captain said?"

"I think that old man is paranoid," Finn shrugged and let out a laugh that sounded forced. "People have always told stories about the Western Wilds to scare children. But nothing has ever come east of the river, why should now be any different?"

"What about the Nightmare Bridge?" Tallis put her hands on her hips and squared off against Finn. "That's even further east than here, and the stories about it aren't much different than those about the Western Wilds."

"The Nightmare Bridge..." the last hint of Finn's wry smile faded, and his voice lost its certainty. "They say it's the currents of the river that drown any who enter the water there, and fumes from the swamp that cause the visions."

"Then why do they all tell the same story?"

Finn didn't answer, and Tallis knew she'd made her point.

"Say we did take Captain Vaska's advice," a contemplative frown creased Finn's brow. "We could get out of here, sail the sea, see Giant's Isle, maybe even see lands other than Okaesa."

"Or we could get eaten by Shriekers, more likely," Tallis grimaced.

"Shriekers don't eat people."

"No, they just turn you into mindless monsters, much better," Tallis teased.

"Tallis," Finn glanced toward the main street, lowering his voice. "Maybe things are worse than we thought. We could at least talk to the officer."

"Whatever we decide," Tallis said, "either we both enlist together, or we stay here together, promise?"

Finn reached out a hand. Tallis took it in her own, clasping it hard.

"Promise."

Together, they hurried across the busy square to the Coat of Arms. At the door, Glynn sat on an overturned barrel and whittled to pass the time. Glynn had served on the same ship as her father in the Kerethi war and they'd been fast friends ever since. He served as the tavern's muscle, keeping the peace as best he could.

"Oy, Tallis, what're you doing here?" Glynn addressed her with a warning tone.

"We're just curious about the soldiers," Tallis assured him.

"And curiosity hooked the fish," Glynn set aside his tools and fixed her with a stern gaze.

"If I promise we won't sign any recruitment papers, will you let us go in, just to talk?" Tallis pleaded.

"Who said anything about recruitment?" Glynn shook his head. Tallis inwardly berated herself for letting him in on more than she should have. "I understand. Westham's a small place and the world is vast. But trust me, now is not the time."

"We just want to talk to them," Finn jumped in. "I've never talked to anyone from outside Westham."

Glynn sighed deeply. "Turn your pockets out when you leave or Nevra will chew my ears off."

"We promise," Tallis rolled her eyes and took Finn's hand to lead him into the tavern.

Inside, Quillon the barkeeper gave them a friendly nod. At this hour, the main room was mostly empty. Quillon's wife, Genicia, paused from cleaning tables and gave them a disapproving look that told Tallis in no uncertain terms that she felt the same as Glynn.

At a corner table, a man sat surrounded by stacks of papers. His uniform bore the single shoulder stripe of a lieutenant, and Tallis guessed this was Redwan, who Captain Vaska had sent them to find. Tallis and Finn made their way to him and he appraised them and sighed. Tallis was beginning to be irritated by everyone's disapproval today.

"Listen, kids," the man began. "What are you, fifteen?"

"Nineteen," Tallis crossed her arms and stared down at the man, refusing to let him deter her. "Captain Vaska sent us."

He raised an eyebrow as though he didn't believe her. "Even so. Boy, you look like hard labor is a foreign concept. And you, girl..."

He seemed to fish for words as he surveyed her.

"I am Nevra Larke's daughter. He served in the fleet under King Leander himself. I know my way around a boat and I'm not squeamish about physical labor."

The man looked even more like a fish as he opened and closed his mouth, searching for a reason to turn her away. Finally, he sighed again and hung his head.

"It's not personal," he shook his head. "But since the Kerethi wars, the fleet has been by application only. Open recruitment feels... wrong."

He drew blank papers from the stack at his side.

"Can either of you read?"

"We both can," Finn said, pride and a bit of annoyance in his voice.

"Then take these. They bear the king's seal and my signature. Sign them, and you'll be admitted into Giant's Isle with no question. But leave them blank, and no one will hold you to it. Take my advice. Keep them as a last resort only if you need them for passage east."

Tallis took the contract, remembering her promise to Glynn, but unsigned it meant nothing.

"Thank you, lieutenant."

"Keep those papers safe," Redwan said with a warning tone. "Better to just keep them at hand. If things go wrong, and you need them, you might not have the time to go digging through drawers for them."

Finn folded and pocketed one and Tallis the other. It would be easy to palm the papers when they turned out their pockets for Glynn. Hiding something from their elders wasn't a new business for them. Though usually what they were hiding was extra sweets, not fleet contracts.

"That... wasn't what I expected," Tallis said when they'd gotten far enough down the street for Glynn to not overheard them.

"Remember what Captain Vaska said?" Finn said. Their feet had carried them out of town and he glanced to the left and right of the road, where ripening crops took up most of the countryside. "If we all panicked and fled east before bringing in the harvest, Giant's Isle could starve. *We* could starve. Imagine the capital overflowing with people too frightened to stay on their farms and no incoming shipments of food? How long would emergency stores last?"

"Okaesa isn't alone," Tallis didn't want to think about what would happen if Finn was right. "The Kerethi may be mostly nomadic, but they have crops on their Isles. And Sabutia is only a two-month sail away. Their growing season lasts later into the fall than ours."

"Gambling on pirates, or close to five months to get to Sabutia and back, doesn't sound like the safest of bets," Finn cast a nervous eye toward the river. Its width and depth, enough that the smaller of the fleet's warships could sail as far upstream as Westham, had once felt a comforting defense against the Western Wilds. Now, it felt like a dam of rotted planks trying to hold back the surge of spring's thaw.

"I should get home, my uncle—" Finn said.

"You could come back with me," Tallis reached out a hand to him. "Mama is always ready to have you join us."

"I need to keep an eye on my uncle tonight," Finn said sheepishly. "He doesn't like soldiers. I want to make sure he doesn't end up going to the inn and getting drunk enough to do something stupid."

Tallis gave Finn a look of concern. Everyone in her family knew Finn's uncle Sefton was a drunk who treated him poorly, but Sefton was his only blood family. His parents had died when he was almost too young to remember, from a sickness that had ravaged Westham and many of the nearby towns and farms.

"I'll be okay," Finn assured her, but Tallis had seen the bruises on Finn's soft olive skin.

"Our door is always open for you, Finn," Tallis said, grasping his shoulder in a friendly farewell before beginning down the road toward home.

CHAPTER TWO

Summer's End

Tallis bolted upright in her bed, certain the cries of Shriekers were cutting the night air for the first time since the soldiers had left Westham. But as she listened, the shrieks of monsters faded from the edges of her sleep into the shrieks of wind whipping through the branches of trees, and through the eaves of the house from windows opened to vent out the late summer heat. Lightning snaked across the sky beyond the open window and thunder chased it soon after, the storm nearly on top of them.

Beside her in the loft they shared, Aiven still slept soundly, undisturbed by the storm. Tallis was about to resettle alongside her sister when she heard her name in her parents' hushed voices from below. As quietly as she could, Tallis slipped out of her bed and slunk along the floor to the edge of the loft to listen from where she couldn't be seen. It wouldn't be the first time she'd eavesdropped on conversations from this loft.

"I won't let my girl be swept off by the soldiers," her mother, Melana, was saying. "Not with everything going on."

"With everything going on, she may not have a choice," Nevra's voice was so low Tallis could barely hear his words.

"Melana, what do you think I've been teaching her sailing and sword fighting for?"

"You know I never liked you doing that," Melana's voice was terse, a tone Tallis knew well and dreaded any time she was caught doing something she shouldn't have.

"You'll be glad I did if the Shriekers breach the river," Nevra sounded worried, unlike the confident and soothing tone Tallis was used to. "There have been rumors the fight across the river hasn't been going well."

From her vantage in the loft, Tallis could see her mama's hands frantically working her knitting needles, attempting to repair a pair of mittens Aiven had torn the past winter. Melana cursed and pulled at the thread, undoing a whole row of stitches that hadn't come out as she'd wanted. Tallis knew from watching Mama work that her agitated hands and slipped stitches meant she was nervous or agitated.

"When I brought the midsummer crop to the market in Lindcombe, I spoke to soldiers stationed there," Nevra continued. "The king sent a battalion to venture as far west as they could to determine the source of the threat. Admiral Grayston, Leander's cousin, led this expedition himself, but he returned alone, pale as a corpse, and spoke to no one. Many feared he'd been bitten, but he passed through and returned to Giant's Isle. None in the battalion knew what the admiral saw, but it was clear he did not return in victory. A few battalions sent west of the river are not going to end this fight."

"All the more reason for Tallis to stay away from the fleet," Melana insisted. "Do you want her sent west of the river?"

"If she enlists, there's a chance we could all flee east, perhaps all the way to Giant's Isle."

"So you'd sacrifice Tallis for the safety of the rest of our family?"

Papa did not respond for several long moments. Tallis again risked a peek over the edge of the loft. The scythe he'd use to reap the late summer wheat laid across his lap, and in one hand, his whetstone rested as though forgotten. His other hand gripped the shaft of the scythe, vice-like. His eyes were glazed over with haunted memories from the war he refused to speak about, even after all the years since he'd come home.

"No," Nevra sighed. "That's not her responsibility. It's mine. Captain Eiran once offered me a permanent position in her crew, and I turned it down for you and Tallis. But perhaps now I could take her up on that offer for the same reason."

Tallis shivered, and before she could stop to think, she was swinging herself over the side of the loft and sliding down the ladder. A cold terror gripped her heart, thinking of every time Papa had halted in his tracks, shaking, some memory of the Kerethi wars seizing his mind, and of every time in recent summers where he paused, hunched over, a hand on his aching back. Tallis had taken over in those moments, picking up his axe, scythe, or the reins of the plow, giving him a moment to rest.

"Papa, you can't!" Tallis wanted to shout, but kept her voice low so as not to wake Aiven or Osind.

"Tallis Larke, you should be asleep," Mama chided.

"I'm not a child," Tallis planted her feet, hands on her hips. "And Papa isn't a young soldier anymore. If either of us is to enlist so we can flee to Giant's Isle, it should be me."

Papa sighed, the tightness evaporating from his shoulders. In place of the rigidity was a resigned exhaustion. The light of the fire flickered off silver streaks in the once all-black ropes of hair that cascaded over his shoulders.

"We don't know yet that either of you need to enlist," Mama put her tangled needlework to the side. "And if it comes to that, I'm not letting it be you, Tallis."

"And I won't let it be Papa," Tallis' hands balled into fists at her sides, determination rising in her throat like bile.

"Oh, my little bird," Papa sighed. "Your mother is right. It's not your job to protect this family."

"Why did you bother with all the things you taught me, then?" Tallis demanded.

"I thought perhaps you could join the fleet one day," Papa said. "But not like this. You've always wanted to fly beyond

Westham, little bird. The fleet could have been a chance for adventure and something more than the life of a farmer, but that was before monsters like this existed as anything more than myths."

"It doesn't matter anyway," Tallis said, "I already have the enlistment papers."

Tallis left out that the papers hadn't yet been signed, so Papa could easily sign his name on them instead of her.

"Where did you get those?" Mama scowled incredulously.

"When the battalion came through Westham," Tallis explained. "I met Captain Vaska. He guessed I was a Larke and warned me to take the papers and be ready to flee at a moment's notice. Said he owed it to Papa."

Papa's hands clenched again on the shaft of his scythe. "If Vaska is still sailing with the fleet, then so could I. He's even older than I am."

"We don't even know that we need to flee," Mama interrupted them. "Need I remind you that the wheat harvest is at hand? What happens if we abandon it and it turns out we've fled for nothing. The whole field could be ruined if we leave it to rot."

"Melana, you didn't see what the battalion in Lindcombe was like. They were—"

A sound split the night, cutting off Papa's words. Tallis froze, a chill running down her spine. First one shriek, then another. They built on top of each other like a chorus of coyotes, until there was no way to guess their number echoing in the fields and woods beyond their farm, closer than Tallis had ever heard them before.

"They're in the fields!" Aiven stood at the edge of the loft, her voice thick with terror. "I can see dark shapes moving from the loft window!"

Papa was on his feet before Tallis could even process what her sister had said. From a chest near the door, he pulled out his old sword, buckling the belt and scabbard around his waist. The bright metal of the blade gleamed orange in the firelight when he drew it.

"Aiven, get your brother," Papa ordered. "Tallis, with me to ready the horse. The three of you will ride to town. Gladiolus is big enough for the three of you. Put out a warning and get help. Melana, barricade yourself inside. I'll hold them off."

"Papa, no!" Tallis begged. "Let me help you."

"Tallis," Papa turned to her and placed a heavy hand on her shoulder. His deep brown eyes bored into hers. "You get your siblings somewhere safe and find some soldiers. That's how you'll help me, understand?"

Tallis wilted under Papa's stern gaze. He was rarely so forceful, so she knew when he was, it was important, and she should do what he said.

"Yes, Papa."

"Good," Papa nodded. "Now stay close to me. I'll protect you."

"Aiven!" Tallis shouted before her sister could come down from the loft, assuming the same commanding tone as her father. "Reach into my pillowcase and bring the papers there."

Trusting her sister would understand the importance, Tallis trotted to follow Papa. He hesitated a moment by the door, holding out an arm as he peered through the window beside it. The shrieks were close, but did not sound like they'd reached the main field between the house and the barn yet. Slowly, Papa eased the door open and stepped outside, glancing in all directions before waving her forward. By now, Aiven and Osind were on their heels, Osind sniffling and stifling whimpers. Aiven stuffed the enlistment papers into Tallis' hand, and she tucked them into the hem of her pants.

"With me, run!" Papa whispered back to his three children.

Tallis ran, heels beating against the hard packed earth. They sprinted directly through to the barn down a row of the wheat field, the sheaves smacking their arms. Tallis knew she'd be covered in little scratches, but didn't care. The shrieks seemed all around them, closer every moment.

They broke out of the rows of wheat and dashed to the barn. Papa wrenched open the doors and ushered them inside.

"Don't bother with the saddle. That will take too long," Papa instructed. "Just bridle him and go. I'll stay here until you've gone, then go back to your mother."

"What if we're not fast enough?" Tallis whispered so her siblings couldn't hear.

Papa didn't answer, just pulled her close in his big arms and held her tight. Tallis choked down a sob of fear and buried her face against his shoulder.

"Fly now, little bird," Papa pushed her away and into the barn.

Tallis grabbed a bridle from a hook and sprinted to Gladiolus' stall. The massive plow horse's eyes were wide, froth at his mouth. The shrieks had spooked him, and he paced within his stall.

"Woah there, big boy," Tallis said soothingly, reaching up to stroke the thick gray hair of his neck. Obediently, he lowered his head for her and she slipped the bridle on.

Aiven was able to mount from a block, but Osind needed to be lifted up behind her. Tallis swung up behind her brother and reached around them both for the reins. She urged Gladiolus into a trot out of the barn.

"We'll be home soon, Papa," Tallis called to him as they passed. He nodded and began to run back toward the house, sword in hand.

Tallis kicked at Gladiolus' sides, clicking her tongue. The horse began to trot, then canter away from the field. At the top of a rise at the edge of the field, Tallis looked back. Dark shapes were moving in the wheat field, visible more by the ripples they made in the wheat, shining like silver water in the moonlight. They swarmed through the field like the murk of floodwaters destroying everything in their path. The light of a flame flickered by the door of the house, and Tallis could almost see Papa's face lit by the glow of the torch in his hand.

Tallis ached to go back, certain if she was at Papa's side, he would be safe, but instead she kicked again at Gladiolus' sides, urging him to carry them away toward the center of Westham, telling herself Mama and Papa could hold out until help arrived.

As they sped away from the farm, shrieks continued to echo from all sides. Tallis gritted her teeth, focusing on steering Gladiolus toward Westham's center. She couldn't wonder now how they'd breached the river. All that mattered was getting help for Papa.

Suddenly, a dark shape loomed ahead of them. Tallis barely had time to register the torn clothes and gaping mouth before Gladiolus reared, his own high whinny of terror matching the figure's shriek. Tallis felt her grip on his sides slip. Behind Aiven and Osind, she was too far back on his haunches for a strong purchase bareback. She tumbled down for what felt like an eternity before the world went as black as the Shrieker's eyes.

CHAPTER THREE

Floodwaters

The temple's bell was tolling. Finn groaned and pulled his pillow over his head to shut out the noise. The sleep it had dragged him from had been deep, and he felt lured to plunge right back into it. There was no way it could be time to begin the day.

The bell tolled on, cutting through the pillow. Finn counted. *Four, five, six,* but it didn't stop. Could he have really slept the entire morning? Impossible. Sefton would have dragged him out of bed by his ears. When the bell passed ten, Finn extracted himself from under the pillow. The room was still dark, with no hint of dawn.

Now uncovered, Finn could hear something else. Someone was screaming. *No,* Finn realized. There were too many to come from just one person, and it wasn't an ordinary scream either. *A fox,* Finn tried to tell himself, *or a fisher perhaps.* But foxes and fishers were solitary creatures, never so loud, and there was a deeper quality to the sound, more guttural, almost human.

Finn froze. A shiver poured over his body, and his heart raced. All exhaustion fled his body, driven out by terror. Another shriek, closer this time, followed by an all too human scream that was abruptly cut off, snapped Finn out of his frozen panic. Leaping out of bed, he shoved his feet into boots which sat beside the door. He'd fallen asleep in loose pants, and didn't bother searching for a shirt. With a hand already on the door handle, he stopped and dashed back to the bed, reaching into the pillowcase to pull out his enlistment papers, realizing he might not get the chance to come back.

Finn sprinted into the hall and flung open the door to Sefton's room. Sefton could be cruel, but he was still family, and Finn thought he could never leave any living person to the fate that now bore down on Westham. Sefton's bed was empty. *Probably still out drinking,* Finn thought with disgust. Finn cared enough to warn Sefton, but not enough to search for him.

He cared enough to search for Tallis and her family though. With luck, their farm would stay safe, but Finn didn't want to take that chance. The telling of the bell would be too faint to wake them, and the rooster they relied on to wake early to tend to the farm would be sleeping too.

With a destination in mind, Finn ran for the front door. He paused for a moment to listen. Screams and shrieks had grown closer and more numerous, but his home was close to the eastern edge of the village center. If the barricade at the bridge had been breached, he might still have time to escape. Glancing out the window, Finn could see only darkness. He took a deep breath and slowly pushed the door open to peer out, tensed to either run or slam and barricade the door behind him.

Finn stared, wide-eyed, down Westham's main street. A torrent of sound hit him like the cold of the first spring dive into the river, sudden and consuming all his senses and his body; shouts, shrieks, the clang of metal on metal, and the roar as a thatched roof went up in flames. In the sudden glow of fire, Finn could see shapes moving. His mind struggled to make sense of what he saw. A mass of lurching, shambling people, some on their feet, still moving with the speed they had in life, others with broken or even missing limbs, dragging themselves along the ground. The horde moved without coordination, individuals drawn one way or another by sounds or movement. Theirs was the destruction of floodwaters, not a strategic invasion. As one stumbled out of the shadows and into a clear space on the road near Finn, the light of the fire illuminated its face.

Though Finn was still too far to see details, he recognized the uniform the monster wore. It had once been a soldier, one of the battalion he'd watched with Tallis and her siblings, he guessed. Its jaw hung open impossibly wide, the skin of its cheeks torn and stretched taught. The monster's eyes met Finn's, and he knew from reports of the creatures that it was not a trick of the shadows that there was no white left in those eyes, only the inky blackness of a moonless night.

Upon seeing Finn, the Shrieker let out the distinctive cry that had given the monsters their name. That sound was enough to snap Finn out of his initial shock at seeing Westham overrun. He turned on his heels and fled faster than he'd ever run before toward the eastern edge of the village center and the road that would lead him to the Larke's farm.

Finn did not look back to see if the Shriekers were pursuing. It didn't matter. He would run as fast as he could and they would catch him, or they wouldn't. There were others running too. He hadn't been the only one to think fleeing east out of the village was the best choice.

"Finn!"

The shout brought him up short. Finn risked a quick glance behind. Some of the soldiers had blocked the road behind him, and he realized he'd managed to put enough distance between himself and the Shriekers that he could afford to pause. His heart raced from the sprint and fear. He looked around, trying to find whoever had called his name.

"Finn—" the voice called again, weaker this time.

A woman named Aralyn sat on the ground with her back up against a merchant's stand. She was only a few years older than him and had occasionally joined the games, usually led by Tallis, that he and others their age would play. She clutched her son to her chest. He'd been born in the spring, before the Shriekers were a threat.

"Please, Finn. Take him, run," Aralyn begged.

"Come on," Finn reached out a hand. "All three of us will get out of here."

"No, we won't," Aralyn held up her arm that didn't hold her son.

Black blood oozed from puncture wounds on her wrist. The veins that ran up her arm were also darkening. It wouldn't be long before Aralyn succumbed to the poison from the Shrieker's bite.

"I was keeping it away from Kian," Aralyn's eyes brimmed with tears. "My husband cut the Shrieker down and told me to take Kian and run. He kept more from following us. I saw the edge of town and thought we'd make it, but then I suddenly felt so weak and my arm it—"

The cry of pain Aralyn let out told Finn what she couldn't with words. Within that cry was a hint of something else. Somewhere, a Shrieker echoed that cry and it sounded almost the same as Aralyn's. *Was that the Shrieker's cry?* Finn wondered. Was it the shriek of pain as what made them human was burned away by the poison?

"Please!" Aralyn sobbed, "take him now. I don't have long. I'll run the other way as long as I can toward the soldiers, and I can hope they'll kill me before I hurt any of them."

"Aralyn, I'm so sorry," Finn could think of nothing else to say. He reached out and took the baby, pinning him tight against his chest. Kian did not cry, only burbled.

Aralyn dragged herself to her feet. Already, there was a lurching quality to her movements.

"If Torin survives, tell him I love him."

Finn nodded. He also hoped her husband had survived, if only for another body to oppose the Shriekers, rather than add to their numbers. Aralyn began to run back the way they'd come, and Finn turned again to the darkness beyond the edge of the village. He ran slower now, encumbered and unable to use his arms, but either he would make it with Kian or not at all.

When he reached the edge of the village, Finn risked a glance behind to see if he was being pursued. In the street behind, Aralyn stood in a flickering pool of firelight. But as he watched, she collapsed to her knees, shrieking with pain, and each new sound out of her mouth sounded less human. At last, she threw her head back and Finn shuddered at the sound of her jaw cracking as her mouth opened so wide that flesh tore and bone broke. Finn turned away from her to flee into the darkness as the Shrieker's cry erupted from Aralyn's corpse.

Only now did Kian begin to cry, his wails echoing those of his mother. Finn didn't slow his pace as he cradled the boy against his shoulder.

"Shh, shh," Fin cooed into Kian's ear, and prayed the baby's cries would not draw Shriekers to pursue them.

As Finn ran further from the village center, the shrieks and screams began to fade into the sounds of any summer night. He'd fallen asleep to the sounds of a storm, but that had now blown away, leaving a clear sky studded with stars. Crickets chirped, a light breeze rustled the grass and leaves on trees, and a barred owl hooted its familiar four note rhythm. Kian finally began to settle as the noise of the Shriekers was replaced by calm that felt so incongruous to Finn. How could such a peaceful night contain the horrors he'd witnessed?

Finn glanced at the road behind them. A nearly full moon lit up the night. If there was anything on the road, Finn would have seen it. But then, anything else would also see him and Kian. Finn slowed to a brisk walk, his chest heaving from the effort of sustained sprinting. The night held the late summer heat and sweat dripped down his skin.

The way from the village center to Tallis' home was so familiar that Finn could have done it on the darkest of nights. He thought of all the times he'd walked there before. Melana would always welcome him in, insisting on feeding him something. Osind would pester him for rides on his back, even though the boy was quickly becoming too big for Finn to easily carry. Tallis would have some scheme to get them in trouble, and some additional convoluted scheme to get them out of it again. They were the family Finn wished he had instead of only his uncle.

Finn froze at the sound of hoofbeats, but no one had ever seen a Shrieker ride a horse. The rider was coming from the direction Finn was going. He needed to stop whoever it was and warn them. The horse crested a rise ahead of Finn and he recognized it as Nevra's massive plow horse, Gladiolus. Aiven had named him when Nevra had purchased him close to her tenth birthday. Astride him, Aiven and Osind looked like young children, not adolescents. Finn pinned Kian to his chest with one arm and raised the other high to wave them down.

"Finn!" Aiven cried, relief and fear mixing in her voice. "Shriekers attacked the farm. Papa told Tallis to take us and run for help. Tallis was riding behind us, but a Shrieker blocked our path. Gladdy spooked, and she fell. He was so frightened, I couldn't get him under control until we were so far away I thought we should keep going for help."

Finn's chest tightened as he thought of Tallis alone somewhere with Shriekers in the countryside as well as in town. He wanted to hand Kian off to Aiven and go searching for Tallis himself, but he knew she'd never forgive him if he left her siblings alone.

"There's no help," Finn told them. "The village center has been attacked too."

"What do we do?" Osind's voice sounded as small as he looked, perched atop the enormous horse.

Finn thought for a moment. If there were Shriekers in the farms as well as in town, where would be safe?

"The abandoned barn," Finn declared, trying to sound confident for Aiven and Osind's sakes. "The Shriekers are bolder at night. The soldiers that came back said they are only active during the day if provoked. We'll wait out the night there, then when the sun rises, it'll be safer and easier to look for Tallis."

She'll know what to do, Finn thought but didn't say aloud. She'd always been the leader, clear-headed in a crisis, and had known what to do to keep others calm and figure out what needed to happen.

Aiven slid down from the horse's back, needing to let herself drop at the end. "Give me the baby. You lead Gladdy. Why do you have a baby anyway?"

The commanding tone in Aiven's voice sounded exactly like her sister. Finn took Gladiolus' reins when Aiven took Kian and began to lead the way to an abandoned farmstead. It had been empty as long as he could remember, its family claimed by the same plague that had taken his parents.

"That's Kian," Finn said, gesturing to the baby. "I— found him and couldn't just leave him."

Finn didn't have the heart to tell Aiven the rest of the story and they continued in silence, straining their ears for any hints of Shriekers. When they finally reached the abandoned barn, Finn handed the reins back to Aiven.

"I'll go first," Finn said. "If it's safe, I'll wave for you to come in."

Finn moved toward the barn before Aiven could protest. He pushed open the door cautiously, but the only sound was the creak of the old hinges. Moonlight streamed through broken windows and a large hole where part of the roof had caved in under a heavy snow a few winters before. After that, Melana had forbidden them from playing here, but that hadn't stopped Tallis, so it hadn't stopped Finn.

Nothing moved within, so Finn beckoned for Aiven and Osind to follow. Finn pushed some of the old hay into a pile for Aiven to set Kian down in, then he helped Osind down from the horse. He found an old table and dragged it to barricade the door.

"Is Tallis going to be alright?" Osind asked, though it wasn't clear whether he expected Aiven or Finn to answer. He'd plopped down in the straw near Kian and stared up at the sky through the hole in the roof. "What about Mama and Papa? It sounded like there were so many Shriekers coming. Papa told us to go for help. He needs help!"

"Papa would want us to stay safe," Aiven sat beside her brother. "Finn was right. We should stay here until morning, then we can see if we can find help once the Shriekers flee the sun."

"The river was supposed to keep us safe," Osind whined, his lip trembling as tears welled in his eyes. "If Westham isn't safe, where can we go?"

"We'll figure that out in the morning, Osi," Finn assured him. "You should both try to sleep. I'll stay up and keep watch."

Aiven and Osind both settled into the hay. Finn found an old bench and brought it to sit by one of the windows where he could see the road. He had no idea how long he would have to wait for dawn, but he knew there was no way he could sleep. The image of Aralyn's body breaking and the sound of her shrieks kept replaying in his mind. He felt guilty for leaving her, but knew there was nothing that could have been done for her. She was already dead the moment the Shrieker's teeth broke her skin. He'd heard stories about what the transformation was like, but no story could have prepared him for seeing it firsthand.

Finn looked over at the three children sleeping in the hay, feeling like barely more than a child himself. When he and Tallis had enlisted, he'd felt so confident. The danger hadn't felt real, but now that it had arrived and destroyed the only life he'd ever known, he wished he could take it back. He couldn't see any other choice though. If he couldn't find Tallis, her parents, or Torin when the sun rose, these three would become his responsibility. Taking them east with him to enlist would at least be a plan, and he could pretend for Aiven and Osind that he felt there was a chance for them all to survive.

The hours until dawn seemed like an eternity. Finn watched the road and the sky, praying for the road to stay empty and for the sky to brighten. Finally, the inky blackness began to fade to the gray blue of pre-dawn. Finn rose from the bench, his legs stiff, protesting how much he'd run and then how long he'd sat in that same position. He woke Aiven, holding a finger to his lips, not wanting to wake Kian or

Osind. He took her by the arm and led her to the other side of the barn.

"Aiven, I'm going to look for Tallis," Finn said. "Take Kian and Osind on Gladdy and go to town. The soldiers were fighting the Shriekers. Now that the sun is rising, maybe the Shriekers will flee or they'll have been beaten back, and there will be help there. If you're at all unsure, though, ride back here. I'll look for you first in town, then here. If there's no help in town, and I don't find you by midday, start riding east. Follow the widest road out of Westham and it will bring you to King's Harbor."

"I don't want to leave," Aiven's lip trembled.

"Please, Aiven," Finn took her hands. "If midday comes and you still haven't found help, and I haven't found you again, promise me you'll flee. You have to get away before night falls. The Shriekers might come back."

Aiven took a deep breath and nodded, squeezing her eyes shut and blinking away tears before they could fall. "I promise."

Finn pulled her into a tight hug, wishing he could do more for her. But if he could find Tallis, he was sure she would be able to do more for her siblings than he ever could. Even better, if he could find Nevra or Melana, they could take care of them all, including him. Finn gave Kian and Osind, still sleeping in the straw, one last glance before slipping out of the barn into the gray light of dawn.

CHAPTER FOUR

Smoke and Ash

Tallis inhaled and smelled earth. It was the rich scent of dirt, worms, and rot. She thought of digging sweet potatoes out of the muddy field with Papa. Shin deep in muck, plunging in until it felt no part of her was clean, they'd come back with golden treasure.

The ground was wet as if with rain, and, dimly, she remembered the storm that had woken her the night before. The idea of opening her eyes hurt almost as much as her head did. Her groping hands explored further, hoping to find some evidence of what had happened. Her fingers met the rough, hard wood of a tree root. Had she reached the forest at the edge of her father's fields?

Tallis rolled onto her back and opened her eyes finally to stare up at the canopy of the trees above her. The sky was the light gray of early dawn above the leaves just beginning to hint with the brilliant reds and oranges of autumn. The morning was quiet in a way it never was at home. There had always been the sound of her mother and father talking. The rooster would be crowing, reminding them there were chores to be done. Aiven and Osind would be chasing each other around the fields. Now there was nothing but the faint rustle of the breeze through the dry autumn leaves.

"Tallis!"

A figure loomed over her, face blurred in the dark.

"Tallis?"

She recognized that voice. Squinting up at the figure, he slowly came into focus, lanky limbs looming over her, and black curls that were mussed and damp.

"Finn?"

"Tallis!"

"Yeah, I know what my name is, Finn," she pushed herself up onto her elbows and immediately sank back down as her head spun.

"Take it easy," Finn said. "It looks like you took a pretty bad hit to the head."

Tallis sat up more slowly this time and leaned up against the trunk of a tree. They were hidden in a hollow among some bushes.

"What happened?" Tallis asked, rubbing the side of her head to find it had already begun to swell. Now that she was sitting, she also noticed Finn had no shirt. "And where are your clothes?"

"The Shriekers attacked in the night, and didn't exactly wait to give me time to dress before I ran," he explained. "Aiven and Osind found me and told me you fell from your horse. By the time Aiven got control of him, they'd lost track of where they were. They went to see if they could find more help, and I came for you. I gave them instructions to find each other again."

Slowly, the details of the night before began to filter back to her through the fog stuffing her head. She glanced around, and saw a body lying nearby. Her heart leapt to her throat and she began to draw away when she realized its head had been crushed. This must be the Shrieker that had spooked the horse. It looked as though Gladiolus' hoof had flatted its skull, which she supposed must be just as good for killing the monsters as removing the head.

"And my parents?" Tallis asked when her heart began to slow again.

Finn shook his head. "I went to your farm first. There's no one there."

"Maybe if we go back we'll find something—"

"Tallis..."

"A clue, a track, something, maybe they got away."

"Tallis, I don't think—"

"Finn, shut up, shut up!" Tallis shouted. "You don't get it. You never even knew your parents, just your stinking uncle, you don't get it!"

Finn recoiled as if she'd slapped him.

"I'm sorry, Finn... I didn't mean..."

"No, you're right," he shrugged. "I don't know. Come on, we'll go see the farm. I just thought it might be better if you didn't see."

"I have to."

Finn took her hand and together they threaded their way through underbrush and over gnarled tree roots. As they walked, the sky slowly lightened from gray, to blue, to purple. Finn led, and Tallis followed behind, afraid of what they would find. It felt wrong. Usually she was the one running ahead, dragging him reluctantly along. She gripped his hand so tightly her own fingers ached, but he didn't say a word of complaint.

They saw the smoke first; thin gray tendrils that crawled upward toward the pink dawn sky. Tallis broke into a run once she sighted the forest's edge, releasing Finn's hand and ignoring his protests. The muddy field sucked at her boots and did its best to send her sprawling. But she kept running. The fields had all been trampled. The crops yet to be harvested ground into the mud, ruined beyond recovery.

Tallis skidded to a halt beside the barn. Little remained of her family's house but blackened timbers, smoldering on the ground. The image of the last she'd seen of Papa, sword in one hand and a torch in the other, flashed through her head. Had he dropped the torch? Tallis choked on the ash-filled air. It seemed the only color left in the world was the lightening sky.

Someone moved near the edge of the trees and into the ruin of the field.

"Papa!" Tallis shouted, her voice cracking with relief.

"Tallis, no!" Finn's voice barely registered as Tallis began to run, tears blurring her vision.

"Tallis, stop!"

This time, the terror in Finn's voice made her pause. She'd heard him scared before. He'd warned her to run when he'd accidentally disturbed a wasp's nest. He'd called for her to help when his leg had broken through a thin patch of ice on the river, cracks splintering around him. When her knife had slipped while gutting fish and sliced open her palm from thumb to forefinger, barely missing tendon, he'd gone running for Glynn, pleading for him to send for Westham's healer. But she'd never heard him scream for her with such wild desperation.

Nevra raised his head slowly, as though weary, and lifted his eyes to meet hers. His eyes had been a rich brown, like the coffee he'd once bought her as a treat on a visit to the Serpent's Mouth. A rare import from far to the south, it had been so dark it was almost black and so bitter it made her cough. Then he laughed and splashed in milk until it nearly matched the tan of Finn's skin. Her papa now opened his mouth, and for a moment, Tallis thought she was about to hear that laugh again, one that came from deep in his chest and never failed to lift her spirits. But the dark of Nevra's eyes was no longer like the warm comfort that coffee had been once he'd sweetened it with milk and honey. They were cold, and the whites of his eyes were bloodshot black.

Tallis screamed, anger and terror mixed in one wordless shout and her papa answered, a shriek ripping from his lungs that chilled the blood in her veins. The thing that had once been her father began to move, slowed by an injured leg, but still too fast. Tallis looked down at her empty hands. Take off the head. Tallis remembered, but with what?

By the side of the barn door, a pitchfork lay in the ash and mud. Tallis dashed for it and scooped it up, wheeling to face the monster that was no longer her father. It wouldn't take the head, but it would hold him off. She braced herself, one foot forward, one back, just like Papa had shown her when he'd begun teaching her to use his sword.

Nevra raised his sword, teeth bared in a snarl that dripped black poison. Tallis caught the blade between the tines of the pitchfork. Papa was bigger than her, and the force of his run pushed her back, feet sliding in the mud. She pushed back, throwing all her weight against him.

"You said you'd protect me," Tallis sobbed. "You promised!"

The creature gave no sign it understood, merely pulled back to raise his sword for another swing. He had been injured, gashes in both his sword arm and a leg. The blood on his clothes around the wounds was red, so they'd been dealt before he turned. Injuries didn't stop the Shriekers, but could slow them down. His movements were clumsy and Tallis moved before she could think, driving the pitchfork into his chest and bearing down on him with all the strength years of aiding him around the farm had given her. The injured leg buckled, and he collapsed to the ground. Tallis bore down, pitchfork tines slid through flesh and into the soft earth below, pinning him to the ground.

A scream tore its way from Tallis' stomach up through her throat and Nevra screamed back at her, for a moment sounding almost human. Tallis shuddered and tears blurred her vision. She wanted to run and never stop running, but she knew the moment she lifted her weight from the pitchfork, the monster who'd stolen Papa from her would rise, slowed only somewhat by the blow she'd dealt.

"Finn," her voice was weak. She didn't know where Finn was anymore or if he'd even heard. "Finn!"

This time, he was at her side in a moment.

"I'm so sorry, Tallis," was all he could manage to say.

"Hold him here," she demanded

"What do you—?"

"Just do it!" she cut him off, voice cracking.

Finn didn't say another word, but came to her side and placed his hands by hers, pushing his weight into the pitchfork as requested. Tallis stumbled away, still fighting the urge to flee. Papa's sword lay discarded a few feet away. He must have lost his grip on it when she'd knocked him down. Tallis wrapped a hand that didn't feel like hers around the hilt and hefted it above Papa's face.

"Tallis, you don't have to," Finn said, realizing what she meant to do. "I could."

"No," Tallis shook her head. "I have to. He was my papa."

Not my papa anymore, Tallis forced herself to admit. The thing that lay at her feet should be a corpse, and if she left it as it was, it would drag others with it into this cursed undeath. Tallis raised the sword above her head and brought it down. The head rolled to the side and Tallis squeezed her eyes shut, unable to bear looking at him.

Tallis shrugged off the hand he tried to put on her shoulder and moved toward what remained of the house. She walked as though her feet were not her own. She didn't want to see, but she couldn't turn away. Her home was gone. She didn't have a home anymore.

Where the doorway once stood lay a handful of burnt corpses. Tallis felt her stomach churn and tried not to look. Burnt, they didn't look any different than she supposed any regular person would. The bodies would have been her father's work, his military training unforgotten.

Tallis was about to turn and leave when a glint caught her eye. From underneath a fallen timber, a blackened thing reached. It was hardly even recognizable as a hand anymore, save for the glint of gold around one stub. The scorched bones were buried into the dirt, as though the hand had been trying to claw its way out of the burning house.

"Mama."

Tallis dropped to her knees and pulled the ring from the dust and crumbling bones. It was the only gold her family owned. Mama had told her the story, how a charming and foolish young Papa had sold his best cow for that ring. It felt so small and insignificant in her palm. How could such a little thing be worth a whole cow?

Finn was at Tallis' side again. He knelt in the ash beside her and wrapped his arms around her. Tallis buried her face in his chest and felt his ragged breathing as he tried to mask his own grief. He'd loved her mama too. Melana had been as much of a mother to him as she could, with three children of her own to care for.

"She's dead," Tallis' voice was strangely calm. "Gods be thanked, she's only dead."

"Let's go find Aiven and Osind," Finn pulled away and took her by the arm. He gently helped Tallis to her feet and began to lead her away from the house. "They'll want to know you're okay. I don't know what state the village center is in, but maybe there are other survivors."

Thinking of her siblings made the pain in her stomach worse. They were still children, born after Papa came home from years serving in the fleet. Tallis had always helped Mama and Papa with them, but now she would have to take care of them by herself.

Tallis closed her hand around her mother's ring and held on so tight her fingernails dug painfully into her skin. She felt as though she should do something, scream, cry, fall on the ground and refuse to go on. But her body kept on moving without her willing it to. Her feet carried her back to Papa's body. She squeezed her eyes shut, as though blocking him from her vision could make him disappear. She fumbled until her hands found the buckle of the sword belt. Rising, she did not open her eyes again until her back was turned to Papa. Finn began to lead away from the farm, and Tallis resheathed Papa's sword, buckling it around her own waist, having to cinch it all the way to the narrowest hole. Even then, it still felt loose and sat low on her hips.

"What now?" Tallis asked as she followed Finn down the road toward the village.

"Nothing's changed," he said. "We have our recruitment papers. We can use them for passage to the capital and join the army to fight back against these monsters."

"Everything's changed," Tallis shook the memories from her mind and looked up at her old friend. "We don't have a home to return to when it's over anymore."

"We've still got each other," Finley said. "We're both orphans now. But we'll stick together. We'll survive. We have to."

"Great, I'm stuck with you," Tallis rolled her eyes and forced a smile.

"Could be worse, my uncle's too old to enlist."

Tallis could not help but smile for real this time.

As they got closer to the village center, the damage became more apparent. Where once were golden and green fields, and little homesteads like Tallis' own, only the gray of smoke and ash remained. In the distance, Westham rose, black and smoking, out of black earth. But there were no signs of active Shriekers, so they kept going.

Tallis kept her eyes fixed ahead as they entered what remained of the town, determined not to look at the carnage. There were bodies in the street where there were once peddlers selling goods. There were fallen timbers and crumbled stone in place of carts in the market. The cobbler's shop was still standing and had been repurposed as a makeshift shelter. From within, Tallis could hear children crying and injured moaning in pain.

"Tallis!"

The shout was quickly followed by two small figures barreling into her. Aiven was almost as tall as her now, but thin as a scythe, growing faster than their mother could feed her. Osind was still much smaller than both his sisters. Tallis easily wrapped her arms around both and pressed her face against their black locks, identical to her own. The two smelled of ash and mud.

Aiven wriggled her way out of Tallis' arms, but Osind stayed pressed against her, his face pressed against her stomach.

"Did you find Mama and Papa too?" Aiven asked.

Tallis opened her mouth, but the words stuck in her throat. She felt as though she'd swallowed a stone that weighed in her stomach and stuck her voice in its tracks.

"I'm sorry, Aivs, they didn't make it," Finn answered for her. "You'll be okay, though. Me and Tallis will keep you safe, promise."

Tallis inwardly thanked Finn but still could not find her voice. She gave him a look she hoped he'd be able to read. He nodded at her. Tallis could feel Osind trembling against her. Aiven's eyes were glossy, and her fists were balled at her sides. Tallis wrapped an arm around Aiven's shoulder again, and this time her sister didn't pull away.

"Where do we go?" Osind had managed to press himself closer to Tallis. She could hear tears in his voice.

"Let's find out, okay?" Tallis finally managed to say, trying not to look at Aiven's face. In an instant, it seemed to grow much older than her twelve years.

A crowd had gathered in the main square. A captain stood on top of a pile of rubble where all could see them. Tallis recognized him as Vaska, the man Papa had served with and who'd encouraged them to enlist. An ember of rage burned in her throat that Papa was gone and this captain was still standing. It was supposed to have been his job to keep them safe.

"We have received orders to move out," Vaska announced. "All the bridges south of King's Harbor are to be destroyed. The king has ordered a full retreat to Giant's Isle. You have until midday to prepare. Take only what you absolutely require. We go on foot and must move quickly. If the barricades fell here, it is only a matter of time before they fall in every village along the Foggy River, so speed may mean your lives. Those who fall behind will be left behind. Understood?"

The villagers were silent. Tallis looked around to see faces made of stone. They were all survivors now, all refugees, all homeless, but not one of them looked prepared to give up yet.

"May the Protector shield us all," Vaska said as he stepped down from the rubble.

The crowd was slow to disperse. There was a tension among the few survivors, like they all felt there was more the soldiers could do to help them. Tallis knew that no one wanted to leave Westham behind. It was their home.

"Where's Kian?" Finn asked, and Tallis frowned at him in confusion.

"We found his father," Aiven said. "They're in the chapel."

Finn exhaled deeply and some tension seemed to leave his shoulders.

"I found Torin and Aralyn's son alone," Finn explained, but refused to meet Tallis' questioning gaze. She knew this meant he was lying, but she didn't want to push him on it in front of her siblings. "We kept him safe through the night. I was afraid we wouldn't find either of his parents. I should go talk to Torin, though maybe I should go find some real clothes first. We can meet back here before we move out."

Tallis nodded, still not trusting herself to speak through the anger, fear, and grief that blended and simmered inside her. She watched Finn go, unsure of what she should do. There was nothing to make ready. Everything they'd had was gone except for what they were already carrying.

"Thank the Protector and the Lady!" a man pushed his way through the crowd toward them. It was Glynn, and Tallis' heart leapt to see him. He pulled Tallis into a quick embrace before pushing her back to examine her for any injuries. His gaze lingered long on her eyes, making certain she hadn't been infected by the Shriekers' poison. "When Aiven and Osind showed up alone…"

"I'm okay, Glynn," Tallis assured him. The relief that someone older who she trusted had survived was almost overwhelming. "Thank you."

"Let's get your head cleaned up," Glynn led them away from the square with a hand on Tallis' shoulder. "It wouldn't do to survive a Shrieker attack just to get sick from a dirty cut. And let's find you three something hot to eat. We might not have much chance for a good hot meal before we get to the Serpent's Mouth."

Tallis took Aiven and Osind's hands and followed Glynn, glad to have someone else taking charge for the moment.

CHAPTER FIVE

Driftwood

Finn stood on the threshold of the chapel, unable to bring himself to enter and face Torin. He closed his eyes and placed his hand over his heart, hiding his hesitation beneath respect for the Protector of the Skies and the Lady of the Waters, who together watched over Okaesa. He took a deep breath and pushed open the door.

Inside, morning light streamed through stained glass windows that depicted scenes of the ocean and sky in various seasons and weather. When the door swung shut behind him, muffling the noises of survivors preparing to leave, Finn could almost pretend nothing had changed. The chapel was quiet and still, with only a few people seated in the pews, heads bowed in silent prayers. Finn's footsteps echoed heavily as he made his way down the aisle to where two statues, both carved from white driftwood, stood side by side.

Finn knelt before the altar that stood before the two statues and gazed up at their faces. On his left was the Protector, a tall man with clouds for hair, and a mantle of feathers around his shoulders. His face was grim, his gaze fixed downward so he looked as though he was staring at

Finn where he knelt. One hand was down by his side, palm open in a welcoming gesture, the other was raised, a sword in the shape of a lightning bolt in his fist. To his right stood the Lady of the Waters, her hair of seaweed falling around her shoulders. Her mantle was made of fish scales, and her long skirt was crashing waves and sea foam. In white hands clasped by her belly, she held a chalice made of silver. During services, a priest would sprinkle water from the chalice on the foreheads of the attendees before they left, but Finn saw no priests present. In their absence, he dipped a finger into the water and pressed it to his forehead.

Lady, we seek your grace, Finn prayed. *May your waters stand between us and the Shriekers, and may your waves take their bones.*

Finn stood and scanned the faces in the pews, finding Torin seated toward the middle. His head was lowered, but Finn could see his shoulders shaking. Kian was cradled in his arms, his sleep as peaceful as the chapel's quiet despite the chaos outside. Finn felt as though he were wading through river muck as he dragged his feet toward the two.

Torin started and looked up when Finn slid into the pew beside him. The movement jostled Kian, who whined and scrunched his tiny face. Torin bounced him, making shushing noises. Finn sat beside them in silence, waiting for Kian to settle. He didn't know what he should say to Torin, only that if he said nothing, he knew he'd regret it.

"Aiven told me you found Kian," Torin broke the silence first, voice barely more than a whisper. Anything louder always felt wrong in this place. Only the priests spoke for all to hear during a service. Otherwise, the chapel was a place of stillness.

Finn nodded, gazing down at Kian's slowly calming face rather than meeting Torin's eyes. There was nothing he could have done for Aralyn by the time he found her, but there was still a pang of guilt that he ran and survived. He'd turned his back on her while everything that made her who she was got eaten away by the Shriekers' poison.

"You just found him?" Torin asked, a hint of accusation in his voice that stung, but Finn couldn't help but think he deserved it. "By himself? Aralyn would never have left him alone."

"She didn't," Finn admitted. "She gave him to me."

"No one's found her."

The words hit Finn like he'd been punched in the gut. If no one had found her dead in the streets, that meant she could still be out there somewhere. He'd hoped one of the soldiers had found her and ended her suffering.

"She was bitten," the truth he'd been holding back from Tallis and her family rushed out. "I wanted to help her, but it was too late. She bought us time, while she could, but I watched her. She—"

Finn couldn't bring himself to say more, his breaths came faster than he could control, his heart racing as the moment replayed itself in his mind. Her body convulsing, and the shrieks becoming less human with each one out of her mouth.

"Don't tell me anything else, please," Torin said, his voice wavering. Finn gulped down air and counted to five with each inhale and exhale to slow his heart.

"I'm sorry," Finn said. "She told me to tell you she loves you."

Torin nodded. This time he was the one avoiding Finn's eyes by looking down at his son. Finn didn't know whether he should stay or let Torin have some space with his loss.

"Thank you," Torin finally choked out. "You did what you could, and because of that I still have Kian. If you hadn't taken him, I'd have lost them both."

"I couldn't leave him, and I didn't want to leave her either."

"These monsters take what we love and turn them against us," Torin looked up at the driftwood statues of the Lady and Protector. "How can such a thing exist? When explorers came back from the Western Wilds, blabbering about the dead rising, I thought, 'send anyone so far away from the sea for long enough and they'll start getting crazed ideas.' The

Lady of the Waters can't guide a man out there. Watch enough companions die from hunger and cold, and anyone could go mad. I didn't believe any of it."

Finn also turned his gaze to the statues, wondering how the Lady and the Protector could allow such creatures to exist. Or, what could possibly be more powerful than the skies and the seas to defy their will? The Western Wilds might be beyond the Lady's reach, but the Shriekers advance east seemed relentless, no matter how close it drew to her waters. The river hadn't stopped them, but no bridges crossed the sea. There was hope the Lady's grace would keep them safe if they managed to reach Giant's Isle.

"We know they're real now," Finn said.

"We should have left when we had the chance," Torin's eyes filled with tears suddenly and he choked out his words. "It's my fault she's gone. Aralyn has a brother in King's Harbor, and she wanted to run to stay with him as soon as the rumors became reports of attacks. I convinced her to stay. We grew up together here, and we were building a life here with Kian. I was afraid to leave, but I should have been more afraid to stay."

"You still have a chance," Finn tried to sound encouraging. "The remaining soldiers are escorting us east. You and Kian can still survive this."

"I know," Torin wiped his tears on his sleeve. "We'll be ready to go. I just need a few more moments alone here to pray for Aralyn now that I know what happened to her. I came here to pray I'd find her, but you've given me the answer to that prayer."

"Waves take her bones," Finn whispered.

"Yes, I hope they do."

Finn stood to make his way back to his home to see if anything useful could be salvaged. When he'd returned for more proper clothes, he'd dressed hurriedly and rushed to the chapel, anxious to find Torin before they began their journey east. He'd seen no sign of Sefton while he'd been there, and Finn wondered if he'd ever find his uncle, or if he even wanted to. Sefton was family, something which was in short supply. But he couldn't help the feeling that losing Nevra and Melana would be a greater hurt than if he'd lost Sefton.

The streets were busier now. Wagons and people crowded the street as all the survivors prepared to flee. Finn threaded his way through the chaos, dodging stamping horses and ox-carts until he made it to his home, where Sefton was sitting on the threshold, a bag already packed at his side.

"So, you survived," Sefton grunted, not quite sounding disappointed, but definitely not pleased or relieved to see him still alive.

"So did you," Finn replied with the same neutrality, though he had to fight to keep the bitterness from his voice. He couldn't help but wish the Shriekers had gotten to Sefton instead of Nevra or Melana. What had his uncle done to deserve being spared where they had perished?

"Everyone's always telling me, 'Sefton, you should spend more time at home and less at the tavern,'" Sefton laughed humorlessly. "But being at the tavern might have been what saved me. When the Shriekers reached the bridge, the soldiers warned us and we all sprinted across to the chapel and barricaded ourselves in there. Shriekers can't break through stone, or those big chapel doors. But not many who were home in bed survived. So, how did you?"

"I ran," Finn admitted.

"Coward," Sefton sneered. "And you think you can play soldier with those papers you've been keeping with you day and night."

The accusation stung, but Finn couldn't deny it. The first sight of Shriekers and he'd turned tail and fled. But what else could he have done? He wasn't a soldier yet and had no weapon. Tallis had needed to fight with a pitchfork, and there was nothing so useful against monsters in his household.

"Go get your things," Sefton growled, gesturing at the house. "Don't expect me to wait for you when the soldiers move us out."

"Wouldn't dream of it," Finn muttered as he pushed past his uncle and into the house.

In his hurry before, he hadn't noticed the scuff marks on the floors and walls. He imagined Shriekers dragging themselves down the hall, sniffing out any people hiding within. He shuddered and rushed upstairs.

There was little for him to pack. Finn shoved a couple spare changes of clothes into a bag. He then carefully opened a drawer in his nightstand and slid back the false bottom Tallis had helped him craft years ago. Sefton had been at an especially low point, and sold all the silverware that had been passed down from Finn's father in order to fund his drinking. All Finn had left of his parents was a locket with their faces painted on either side, something Melana had made for him with her memories of what they looked like, memories that Finn didn't have. Finn had found Sefton digging through his drawers one night and feared the locket would be found and sold, so he'd asked Tallis to help him hide it.

Now, Finn pulled the locket out of the drawer and clasped it around his neck, tucking it under his shirt. He owned nothing else worth the extra weight in his pack. If he needed to run, he didn't want to be weighed down. Finn turned his back on the room, feeling a certainty that it would be the last time he'd ever see this place, and hurried outside to find Tallis.

Finn found Tallis in the town square. Glynn had loaded an ox-cart with food and other supplies. Aiven and Osind were tucked between crates and bags in the bed of the cart, leaning on each other and dozing. Tallis sat on a crate that hadn't yet been loaded. She sat rigid, with glazed eyes rimmed red as though she'd been crying, but now were dry and staring at nothing.

She didn't move as Finn approached, and didn't respond when he called her name. Finn reached out a hand tentatively and gently touched her arm. She startled as though he'd struck her.

"I'm sorry," Finn jerked his hand back.

"No," Tallis sighed. "I'm sorry, I didn't notice you. I was…"

"It's alright," Finn said, scooting onto the edge of the crate beside her. She shifted to give him space and he draped an arm around her shoulder.

"I was working so hard to keep it together in front of Aiven and Osind," Tallis said, sniffling. Finn felt her draw a shuddering breath and saw her eyes glistening with new tears. "Once they fell asleep, I couldn't hold it in anymore."

"You don't have to," Finn drew her closer and she leaned her head against his chest, her shuddering breaths growing toward sobs like an incoming tide.

Finn held Tallis as she let out the torrent she'd been holding back. He squeezed his eyes shut, his own eyes burning and a few stray tears leaked out. Against the blackness of his eyelids, he could see Nevra, shambling through his field for the last time, and Tallis running to him, not realizing what he'd become. Finn imagined something similar must be going through her mind too.

A shout carried through the crowd that it was time to start moving. Finn gave Tallis' shoulders a final squeeze and stood, reaching out his hand.

"Come on," Finn said. "I'll help you load this last crate and we'll be ready."

Tallis nodded, but her still trembling lip told him she wasn't ready yet to speak. They hoisted the final crate into the cart, the weight of it causing it to bounce on its springs. Aiven and Osind stirred, looking around groggy-eyed. Finn fought to stifle a yawn in response to theirs. He tried not to think of how little sleep he'd gotten the night before. That exhaustion would catch up to him eventually.

Glynn appeared, a sword Finn had never seen before strapped at his hip. He guessed it was a relic of Glynn's time serving with the fleet, the same as Nevra's sword that Tallis now carried.

"Hop on," Glynn gestured to the bed of the ox-cart. "These oxen are strong enough for all of us to get a bit of rest. We can't ride the whole way to King's Harbor or they'll tire out, but I'm sure none of us got a good night's sleep last night."

Gratefully, Finn pulled himself up onto the cart. He reached a hand down to help Tallis up as well. They tucked themselves up against some sacks of dried corn kernels, which were the softest things in the cart.

The line of refugees began to make their way slowly out of Westham. The cart jostled and bumped, but Finn was still relieved to be off his feet finally. His limbs felt suddenly heavy with fatigue, his legs feeling the hard sprinting of the night before. Despite his weariness, Finn couldn't bring himself to close his eyes as the cart drew away from town. He swept his gaze over every building, trying to burn the place into his memory in case he never saw it again. Finn put a hand to the locket under his shirt, wondering if, like his parents, paintings would soon be the only memory left of Westham.

CHAPTER SIX

The Nightmare Bridge

They'd been on the run for almost two days. The previous morning, the lucky survivors from the barricades who'd managed to find horses had caught up with them. The Foggy River was breached. Unless they crossed the Serpent and reached the ships, they were doomed.

The sound of a distant scream, not nearly far enough behind for comfort, did nothing to slow the frenzied rush. Oxen and horses were being spurred as fast as they could manage, and some had already abandoned carts and begun to run at the sound. That would have been the sick girl. There hadn't been the time or supplies to help her, so she was one of the ones they'd left behind. Now she'd become one of their pursuers.

They're catching up, Tallis thought.

Tallis finally saw the river through the trees, the water sparkling gold in the afternoon light. The front of the line of refugees had already reached the forest's edge. A tumult of incoherent shouting broke out, and those who'd reached the riverbank halted. Tallis held out an arm to hold Aiven and Osind back before jogging ahead.

"We're human, you daft sons of dogfish!" a refugee was shouting.

Arrows scattered the riverbank, and Tallis realized the soldiers guarding the bridge had fired on the refugees. From what she could see, none had found a mark, but she shuddered at the thought that it had reached a point of shoot first, ask questions later.

Captain Vaska pushed through to the front.

"Stand down!" his voice boomed across the river, quelling the shouts. The soldiers guarding the gates lowered their bows as soon as they spotted the captain's stripes on his uniform.

"We've lit the fuses already! Start running and we'll all get out of here before the bridge blows!"

Vaska swore loudly and began ushering people across. Before she could think, Tallis turned to sprint back to where she'd left her siblings. Fighting her way through the sudden rush of people felt like trying to swim upstream. She spotted Glynn first, towering above the crowd. He had thrown Osind over his shoulder like a sack of flour, pushing his way through the crowd with Finn and Aiven close at his heels. Relieved, Tallis fell in beside them.

Villagers from Westham and other neighboring villages crowded across the narrow bridge in a terrified frenzy before the fuses burnt down. Tallis pushed her way across with the stragglers, her heart in her throat, keeping Aiven and Osind in sight ahead of her. Her boots hit wood just as the first explosive began to fizz. Finn struggled across behind her, limping from an ankle he'd twisted on the uneven road.

"He's not going to make it!" someone shouted.

"He's on the bridge, he'll make it!" Tallis responded, hoping Finn would hear her voice above the crowd and try to run faster.

"Too far, he's in the blast range. It'll take the bridge and him with it before he can cross."

The things I do for him.

"Aiven, watch your brother!"

Tallis sprinted across the bridge, in the wrong direction. Finn had been her first friend. They'd grown up together. Now, he was keeping her strong as she looked after her siblings the way their parents would have if they'd escaped.

"Come on, slowpoke, get moving," Tallis grumbled as she slipped his arm over her shoulder.

"Tallis, wait!" Finn pulled her back.

The hiss of fire crackled behind them. Tallis turned to see the fuses burning down to their ends. There was no way they'd reach the other side before the bridge exploded. They were closer to the western bank.

"Come on!" Tallis began to sprint toward the western bank, back the way they had come, bearing as much of Finn's weight as she could.

Their feet had barely touched the dirt of the road when the air exploded. The blast hit them in the back, sending them hurtling up the riverbank. Wood snapped and shards whipped past. Tallis threw a protective arm over both of their heads and pressed her face into the damp dirt of the riverbank.

When it was over, Tallis slowly pushed herself up, ears ringing and skin tingling from the heat and splinters. Debris settled onto the bank and rushed downriver. The bridge was in flames. Their traveling companions watched from the safety of the far bank, huddled together. Some looked on with pity, the rest with no expression at all. Tallis spotted Sefton in the group, staring across the river at Finn with a cold, pitiless gaze. Tallis wondered if Finn getting left behind would be a relief for Sefton.

"Tallis!" Aiven and Osind were screaming. Glynn was holding them back from the river's edge.

"We'll find another way across, I promise," Tallis called across the river. She had never meant anything so sincerely in her life. "I'll find you in Giant's Isle. Don't wait for me."

Osind was still crying out her name as Glynn pulled them to follow the group. But Aiven had fallen silent and her face was grim. Tallis wondered if Aiven was feeling what Tallis had felt when she'd realized she'd have to take care of the two of them. Now Aiven was the eldest and the responsible one.

The rest of the refugees from Westham left without a word or a second glance. Two fewer to crowd space on their boats. Two fewer mouths to use up their provisions. Two orphans were not worth their tears. They turned and continued down the road without them. Even the soldiers from the city didn't care. So long as they returned with new recruits, a few casualties along the way didn't matter.

"Tallis?"

Tallis didn't answer. She dragged herself to her feet and walked away from him, toward the water. The Serpent was wider than the Foggy, with strong currents that could suck someone foolish enough to try swimming it into deceptively deep waters. Those that drowned in the Serpent were almost never found. With the bridges destroyed, Tallis wondered if the Serpent could succeed where the Foggy had failed in halting the Shrieker's advance eastward. It would be a comfort, if it wasn't also halting their own journey east.

"Tallis, what do we do?"

"I'm thinking," Tallis snapped back more harshly than she'd meant to. She closed her eyes and bowed her head.

"Are you mad at me, Tallis?"

Tallis didn't answer. She couldn't be mad at him, not when it had been her choice not to leave him behind. But that didn't stop her wishing they were both on the other side of the river, making their way to the harbor with Aiven and Osind.

Another shriek echoed out of the woods, and a shiver ran down Tallis' spine. Finn still lay where he'd fallen from the explosion, eyes wide at the sound.

"Finn, get up, we have to go."

"Where?"

Tallis looked up and down river. Going upriver would bring them to the main bridge closest to King's Harbor. That bridge was better built, easier to protect, and could be drawn up to close the passage. The safe route was tempting, but on foot, the journey would take at least three days if they walked dawn til dusk with no rest. The fastest of the monsters following them would catch up soon and they didn't have any hope of fighting them off with only one sword between the two of them. It would be better to go south. They could get to the Serpent's Mouth within a day if they hurried.

"That way," Tallis pointed downriver.

"That way?" Finn turned pale and shivered.

"Yes, that way," Tallis rolled her eyes. "You got a better idea?"

"They'll keep the bridge to King's Harbor open," Finn cast a longing look upriver. "We don't have to go to... that one."

"We have no time," Tallis explained. "They'll catch up to us well before we reach King Harbor's bridge. I think I'd rather take my chances with the Nightmare Bridge than with them."

"You've heard the stories though," Finn's dark eyes were wide. "People change when they cross that bridge. They find people wandering the woods, shriveled and muttering. That bridge drives people mad."

"Would you rather possibly go mad," Tallis asked, "or become a Shrieker? I trust my own eyes more than stories. My father always said never to trust those who spread tales. I've never seen anyone go mad. I *have* seen what happens to you when the Shriekers catch you."

"Your father didn't believe in the Shriekers either," Finn mumbled.

"None of us did," Tallis snapped. "Not until they started attacking. Now what's it gonna be, Finn, Shrieker fodder or the Nightmare Bridge?"

"They could have at least waited for the last of the soldiers to come back. We could have been safe across that bridge by now if they hadn't set it on a fuse and run."

"Would you have wanted to stick around to find out what was coming from the west?" Tallis pointed out. "The Shriekers are right on our tails. If they'd waited, it would have been risking a massacre, or a breach of the Serpent. It's bad enough Shriekers have made it across the Foggy."

Finn sighed and his shoulders slumped. Tallis could see the fight going out of him and feared he'd give up even on running. There was no way she'd be able to keep going alone, especially if it meant facing the Nightmare Bridge alone. Finn couldn't give up, because neither could she.

"We're wasting time," Tallis grabbed Finn under the armpit and hoisted him up off the ground. "The ships won't wait for us."

With one last look at the ruined remains of the bridge, Tallis began marching southward, trusting Finn would follow. They kept to the woods, but still in sight of the river. Here, so close to the ocean, the trees were still green though they had hardly traveled south from their home at all.

As they walked, the trees began to thin, almost imperceptibly, and the ground became softer underfoot. Tallis knew this meant they were approaching the marshes around where the Foggy River and the Serpent joined. They set up a camp where the trees were still thick to wait for dawn to make the rest of their journey to the bridge. From here, they would be forced to cross the marshes in the open.

Tallis sat up, taking the first watch and trying not to nod off while Finn quickly fell asleep beside her. The fire they'd built burned down to little more than embers, but at least it gave some extra heat. Clouds covered the stars and moon above, so the red glow was the only light she had in the darkness.

"The Shriekers are just a fairytale, Tallis," her father's *voice soothed her. "They can't hurt you. Go to sleep."*

Tallis jolted awake as her head fell forward on her chest. She shivered and shook herself. After so much walking all she wanted was to be back home in her own bed. Her shoulders ached from the pack she carried, and the rest of her ached from sleeping on the ground night after night.

"We can take the boat, go south. They say the harbors are secure enough to keep them out," Tallis had heard her mother whispering to her father, one night after they thought she was asleep.

"The river will hold," Papa had assured her. "Here we have a life, a livelihood. What would we have if we left? There's nothing for us if we leave here."

They couldn't have known, Tallis told herself. Her father thought he was doing the right thing. She couldn't blame him. *I had the papers. I could have made them leave.* Tallis tried to silence that voice, the one that nagged in the back of her head that it was her fault they were dead. Papa had sent her to find help, and she'd fallen from their horse and failed at the last task he'd ever give her.

"Don't you worry, Tallis," Papa had soothed her what felt like years ago, when the rumors had begun to spread like wildfire. "Papa's here. Papa will protect you."

This time a noise woke her. Tallis looked up as her heart leapt to her throat. *Just a dream, it was just a dream.* But somewhere, out in the night, she heard a shriek.

"Finn!" Tallis whispered, shaking him.

He opened his eyes and Tallis clapped a hand over his mouth before he could make a sound. His eyes widened and Tallis could feel him tremble when he heard the noise. A distant, guttural muttering and bestial cries broke the unnatural silence of the night.

"Tallis?" Finley's voice sounded like a frightened child's. "What do we do?"

Tallis looked around, trying to make it seem like she had a plan. She gripped the hilt of Papa's sword to keep her hands from shaking. Not that she believed the blade would do any good against what lurked in the shadows. She'd managed to stop the Shrieker that had once been Papa, but it had already been injured, and it was impossible to tell how many were out there. Like coyotes, they shrieked back and forth to each other in an endless chorus that made guessing at their numbers a fool's game.

"The underbrush," Tallis suggested. "We can't outrun them now, they'll hear us. If we keep quiet enough, perhaps they'll pass us by."

Finley nodded. They packed their blankets as quickly as they could without making too much of a racket. They slid into the shadows beneath the thick branches of the underbrush that surrounded the clearing. Tallis pulled Papa's sword from the hilt at her waist and crouched, ready to fight or flee.

The monsters drifted like shadows into the little clearing. Papa had been newly turned, and had still looked like a man, other than the eyes and mouth. But these Shriekers were far older. Pale flesh hung limply from bones. In places the skin was so torn she could see the muscle and even bone underneath. They were shriveled and dry, like autumn leaves baked in the sun. They moved with jolting, shuffling steps, as though pulled by some external force. It looked as though a strong wind could scatter them like ash, but Tallis knew better.

It was the eyes that sent shivers down Tallis' spine. She'd tried so hard not to look at Papa's eyes, but could not turn away now. Bloodshot and sunken, but their blood was cold and black, leaving the sockets like empty voids in their skulls. Still, she could tell they'd once been human. She could recognize features. One had been an old woman, one a young boy. Another looked to have once been a soldier, with short, cropped hair and the blue of its uniform still showing through the grime. The last was the little girl they'd left behind, young enough that baby fat still clung to her cheeks.

Tallis' stomach churned and she felt bile in her throat as the stench of death and decay drifted to them on the breeze. But she swallowed it down and breathed through her mouth, covering her nose with the hand that didn't hold the sword. The Shriekers continued their shambling march through the clearing, compelled onward by some instinct or edict. Though Tallis did not dare imagine what sort of greater horror could be commanding these creatures.

"Tallis, let's go," Finn whispered in her ear. "We have to get away from them."

Together, they pushed away from the clearing at barely more than a crawl, inch by inch. Tallis' heart pounded so hard she was sure the sound of it would alert the Shriekers, even if they managed to move with the silence of owl's wings through the branches around them.

When the Shriekers—and the glow of the embers that had drawn them out of the night like moths—were both out of sight, they finally stood to walk. When no sounds of pursuit came, they quickened their walk to a jog, then a run, desperate to leave the woods behind and reach the final bridge that might take them to safety on the western bank of the Serpent.

"We must have lost them by now," Finn panted when they began to see the faintest suggestion of light above them.

Tallis sank down into the grass. The Shriekers avoided daylight for the most part, and were slower and clumsier in the sun. They were as safe now as they were likely to get before crossing the Serpent.

The forest had given way to vast expanses of yellow fields and marshes between clusters of trees. They were getting close. Tallis remembered the rank, salty smell of the mud flats that surrounded the place where the Foggy River merged with the Serpent to flow into the sea at the Serpent's Mouth. The Nightmare Bridge was not far upriver from the meeting place.

Tallis took the lead. She didn't really know the way beyond following the general path of the river, but at least she'd been this far south. Finn had never ventured far from Westham. Tallis had sailed far enough with her father to have seen the ocean and to have explored this sort of terrain. They followed a path little more than an animal track of trodden grass. Around them, the dry grass rose to their knees and, in some places, as high as their chests. The wind sent waves and ripples across the rattling stalks that stretched on and on, an ocean of reeds a pale reflection of their salvation.

Small black flies that were common here swarmed around them and no amount of swatting kept them away. They seemed to multiply the more they killed them, and Tallis remembered from previous encounters they'd leave red itching swells on the skin. Tallis' thoughts drifted to the Shriekers, whose numbers also swelled with each death, but whose bites left a mark that could never heal. Did the transformation hurt, she wondered, or was the loss of self so quick that one was spared from suffering? Had Papa suffered?

Tallis grit her teeth against tears that blurred the sea of reeds around her. There would be time to grieve, but not yet. If she failed to find a safe harbor for herself and Finn, then Papa's sacrifice to give her and her siblings time to escape the farm would have been for nothing. She knew Glynn would keep Aiven and Osind safe. She had no one but Finn, who had always looked to her to lead, ever since they were children.

As the sun arched past midday and began to sink toward the horizon, clouds rolled in and fog rose up over the marshes. It swirled around them so thick they could hardly see the path before them. The ground grew softer until their boots squelched and stuck in the wet mud. Twisted, dead trees loomed suddenly out of the damp gray surrounding them to quickly disappear again when they passed.

Tallis heard a crack as her boot landed on something harder than mud in a pool of water. She looked down and jumped back with a cry, drawing her sword. The face of a Shrieker stared up at her from beneath the water. Its black eyes bulged from its swollen white skin. Tallis poked at it with the tip of her sword.

"Is it dead?" Finley croaked from behind.

"I think so," Tallis breathed a sigh of relief. For good measure she swung her sword down and severed the head from the bloated body. The water turned black with blood. It seemed the monsters could drown, all the more reason to reach Okaesa's island capital.

"What killed it?" Finley asked, coming forward to stand at her side.

Tallis looked up at the path ahead and shook her head. She wasn't sure if she wanted to know. "We must be almost there."

"I don't like it here," Finn shivered and stepped closer to her. "Do you think the Guardian of the bridge killed it?"

"Let's just be grateful it's dead," Tallis said and forced her feet to keep moving, but kept her sword in hand. Finn followed so close on her heels she could hear his fast, nervous breaths.

Now she was looking down as much as forward, Tallis noticed more Shriekers dead in the water. None of them jumped out of the water to attack so she didn't bother straying from the path to behead each one. Tallis hoped the swamp would hold them. Perhaps the Lady of Waters herself had reached her hands up the river from the ocean to stop the monsters. Her father had always said the goddess watched over those who stayed near her waters. The monsters had come from the west where she had no power.

There were other bones in the water as well. Old bones. At first, Tallis thought they were stones, but upon seeing a skull she realized these must be victims of the bridge and its Guardian; others like them who were either desperate or foolish enough to try to cross here. Finn clung to her arm and whimpered as he trod on an unseen skeleton that cracked and echoed across the otherwise silent swamp. Tallis gritted her teeth and kept walking, determined not to look down except to keep her footing.

The bridge materialized ahead of them as though made of fog itself. The old dark wood looked as though it had grown up over the sluggish river rather than been built. The water was deceptively shallow as it flowed through choking reeds beneath the gnarled bridge. Its soft trickle was the only sound and Tallis shivered as she imagined it as the last sound she'd hear as the water sucked her down to join the other bones.

"You sure we couldn't swim across?" Finn whispered so softly Tallis could barely hear him.

"If it was midsummer? Maybe," Tallis said. "But the Serpent is too deep to ever get very warm. By now, it's probably already snowing in the mountains where its source is. The cold will drag us down as much as the current."

"Even the Shriekers couldn't cross here," Finn pointed out. "How are we supposed to get past when they can't?"

Tallis had no answer for that but to continue toward the bridge.

"Tallis, don't leave me," Finn cowered behind.

"Well then, you go first if you're so afraid of being left behind on your own," Tallis turned back to him and motioned for him to go ahead.

"Couldn't we try going together?"

"You know the stories," Tallis reminded him. "You have to go alone. That's how it works. The Guardian only lets one across at a time."

"I also know the stories say that no one gets across," Finn cast a nervous eye up at the bridge.

"If no one ever got across, how would we know about the bridge and the Guardian at all?" Tallis pondered.

Finn shrugged. "Fair enough."

"Now do you want to go first or wait for me to try it?" Tallis asked. She was getting sick of waiting. The longer they waited the more likely it would be they'd never even try at all.

"I can't even see the other side," Finn peered through the fog. "I'd never even know if you'd made it."

"I think that's probably the point," Tallis grimaced, wondering if the fog was natural, or if the Guardian had summoned it to obscure his domain.

"I'll go," Finn took a deep breath. "You're more likely to make it across than me. If you get across and I'm not there... well you know just to keep going then."

"We're both going to make it," Tallis assured him, though she wasn't so sure herself. She took his hand. "Good luck."

Finley smiled and squeezed her hand before making his way toward the bridge. Tallis paced while she waited to keep from losing a boot to the muck. She watched Finn approach the bridge with a growing feeling of dread gnawing at her stomach. What would she do if she made it across and he wasn't waiting for her? Without him, she'd be forced to continue on to Giant's Isle alone. She couldn't stand the thought of joining Okaesa's army without him.

Tallis held her breath as Finn stepped up onto the bridge. Even at this distance, she could hear the soft thud of his boots upon the wood. He walked slowly up and over the river. At the peak of the span a dark shadow formed out of the fog beside him. Tallis gripped her sword tighter and resisted the urge to run to his side. Finn kept walking, but glanced behind and down over the side of the bridge.

The shadow reached what could be an arm around Finn and he stopped at the edge of the bridge, leaning out over the water.

"No, Finn, don't!" Tallis screamed.

The shadow turned to her and Tallis could feel its gaze from unseen eyes upon her. Finn jumped back from the edge and bolted out of her sight into the fog. The shadow followed, disappearing further across the bridge. Tallis could only hope Finn would be waiting for her if she made it to the other side.

"Your turn."

The voice was carried to her on the wind. The shadow had not returned, but Tallis knew both the voice and the shadow must belong to the Guardian of the Nightmare Bridge. She found herself rooted to the spot, unable to work up the nerve to answer the summons.

"Your turn," it repeated, this time more of a command than an invitation.

Tallis knew she'd come too far. There would be no turning back now. Even if she had a choice, there was likely worse behind than there was ahead.

Finn is waiting, Tallis told herself. If she was to see the other side, she had to believe it was true.

Tallis raised her sword to defend herself and stalked forward, ready. She didn't believe the sword would do any good against what waited for her on the bridge, but holding it made her feel braver. With it, she'd given her father the mercy he deserved, and if she survived, she could do the same for other souls the Shriekers had claimed.

The wood was hard beneath her feet, a strange feeling after hours of dragging through the mud flats. Her wet boots slid on the grain of the bridge as she climbed the rough carved steps upward. The fog above her seemed darker than that behind. *Just a trick of the light,* Tallis told herself.

She reached the span of the bridge and paused. The shadow that had confronted Finn was still nowhere to be seen. The end of the bridge was still somewhere out of sight in the thick fog. Tallis drew a deep breath and tiptoed forward as silently as she could.

"Don't you worry, Tallis. Papa's here. Papa will protect you."

Tallis froze as she felt the same eyes that had turned on her when she'd screamed for Finn bore into her back. All of a sudden she felt naked and defenseless despite the sword in her hand. She turned.

Even without a head, her father stood taller than her. His head rested in the cradle of his elbow and wore the same old smile she remembered, but his eyes were black and cold.

"You could have saved me, Tallis," it said. "I sent you for help. Every Shrieker I cut down, I thought, this must be the last one. My little bird will find help and the Shriekers will stop coming. But they never did. My little bird flew away and left me behind. What are you now?"

"I'm a soldier," Tallis stood tall as she spoke, the way the soldiers she'd seen stood when on duty.

"Are you now?"

The head laughed, blood dripping from its mouth. The thing started toward her, holding the head up as though it was a weapon. Tallis braced herself, and raised her sword. *It's just an illusion. An illusion can't hurt me.*

Tallis dodged the charge and threw her whole weight at the monster as it bowled past her. The sword sank deep to its hilt into flesh. It felt very solid for an illusion. The Shrieker screamed as she drove it toward the edge. Tallis wrenched her sword free as it toppled down toward the water. It crashed down with a splash then dissolved into black fog. As the fog cleared, Tallis could see another body in the water, tangled up in the reeds. Dark hair swirled around his face.

"He believed me."

Tallis jumped and looked around, but could not find the owner of the voice.

"Weak little boy. Watched the Shriekers come up behind and kill you. Poor fool. Should have run along and left you behind."

Tallis looked down again and saw the body was Finn's. *No, Finn's waiting for me on the other side.*

"Loved you too much to bear the thought of fighting on without you."

Tallis laughed.

"You think that's going to work?" she called out to the fog. "I guess you don't know either of us as well as you think. Finn's not that much of an idiot."

Tallis continued on down the bridge. It seemed like she walked for miles, but still the end remained out of sight in the fog. On either side appeared visions of ships burning and Shriekers overrunning the capital. She saw soldiers barring the harbor and preventing people from boarding the ships as hordes of the monsters descended upon them. Tallis kept her eyes fixed on the bridge ahead of her and kept walking.

"Tallis! Supper's ready, Tallis, come inside!"

The fog faded like memories of a dream. Tallis sat up. She must have fallen asleep in the barn again. Her mother was calling from outside the doors. Tallis stood and brushed straw from her worn out work clothes. She pushed open the door of the barn. Outside, the farm was green. The dog bounded toward her, barking and tail wagging. She smiled as he danced around her feet. She inhaled the fresh smell of the autumn air and wood-fire smoke that wound up out of the chimney of her home. The smell of smoke brought back a half-remembered fragment of her dream. Something had been burning.

Mama stood on the threshold of their house. Papa was coming in from the fields, wiping mud from his hands with the cloth that hung from his belt. The dog dashed toward his master and jumped up, nearly knocking him over. Papa's laughter boomed over the farm as he wrestled the dog down.

"You leave that dog alone," Mama scolded. "He's even filthier than the field. I won't have you at my dinner table looking like that. Go wash up."

"Yes, ma'am," Papa grinned and went around the back of the house to the well.

"Come along, Tallis," Mama called, waving to her. Tallis took a step toward her mother.

But something was wrong. Tallis stopped with one hand still on the door of the barn and squinted at Mama's hand. Her wedding ring was missing. She only took it off to do the washing. Tallis remembered burnt fingers reaching out from under charred timbers. Something cold chilled the skin on her neck. She reached up and pulled the chain out from under her shirt. Her mother's golden ring shone with the sunlight where it rested in her palm.

"What are you waiting for?" Mama's voice was so sweetly familiar. "Supper will be cold if you don't stop dilly-dallying."

Tallis put a hand to her belt and found an empty scabbard, but she'd never had a sword. Papa had a sword, and he kept it locked safely within a chest.

"It's not real."

Tallis stumbled and fell back from the edge of the bridge. She grimaced as she landed with a thud on the hard wood. Flames rose up out of the water and licked at the wood of her home. The dog was barking somewhere. Papa screamed. Mama's smile faded and she dashed into the house, slamming the door behind her as the fire consumed her home entirely. The black smoke faded into the fog and soon nothing was left.

Papa's sword lay forgotten on the bridge beside her. Tallis took up the sword again and wiped away the tears that had begun to sting her eyes. She pushed herself back to her feet and kept walking. The end of the bridge descended into the fog just ahead of her. Tallis picked up her pace and rushed toward salvation before the Guardian could think of something else to tempt her off the bridge.

On both sides of the bridge, illusions swirled out of the mist: ships leaving docks filled with screaming people while

Shriekers assaulted the gates of the Serpent's Mouth, the fleet burning on the open sea, and on some distant beach, Tallis watched herself beheading a bitten woman.

"You think the worst of it is behind you now?"

Tallis paused at the top of the stairs that would take her out of this nightmare. She turned to see nothing but shadow behind her.

"Better you had stayed with me. It would have been easier than what's to come."

"Not going to happen," Tallis spat and dashed down the stairs, leaving the shadow alone with its bridge of illusions.

CHAPTER SEVEN

Whims of the Waves

Finn shivered in the shelter of a twisted copse of nearly dead trees. Dirty and bramble-torn, his shirt clung to his clammy skin, and he felt chilled despite the end of summer warmth. The fog had cleared almost as soon as he'd stepped off the bridge. Before the bridge, the afternoon had felt nearly dark as night through the fog and the bridge's shadows, but now though the sun shone brightly overhead, its light couldn't pierce the shadows that still lingered in Finn's mind.

Any time his eyes closed, flashes of fire streaked across his vision. But even with them open, drinking in the coastal landscape that was entirely new to him, sounds echoed to him as though he'd never left the bridge behind: the boom of cannon fire and cracks of stone crumbling, Aralyn's shrieking, and someone laughing as a Shrieker bore down on him, jaw wide and so near his face he could feel its poison dripping onto his skin.

But the last vision had somehow been the worst. Beyond the fog and the shadow at the apex of the bridge had loomed the mountains of the Western Wilds. They towered high above, standing out dark and black against the white fog and a red sky beyond. Atop the highest peak stood a lone figure, face shrouded in darkness, yet Finn had felt the heat of eyes staring at him. The sight had filled Finn with a dread worse than anything he'd ever felt.

Every minute he waited stretched impossibly long. It seemed as though the sun had been halted in its tracks. Finn was certain it should have been low to the horizon by now, sinking into twilight, but it stayed stubbornly high, beating down on him with light too bright for the horrors he'd passed through.

Finn got up and began to pace, staying within the confines of the copse, unable to bring himself to either continue on alone, or go back to the Nightmare Bridge to look for Tallis. Doubt crept into the edges of his mind, like the fog of the bridge was seeping into his thoughts. What would he say to Aiven and Osind if he met them in Giant's Isle alone and had to tell them he'd left their sister behind?

A sudden wail, so full of despair that Finn knew immediately it wasn't a Shrieker, broke the silence. Finn sprinted toward it, praying the sound had come from Tallis.

Tallis was crumpled at the foot of a decaying stump. Nevra's sword lay on the ground beside her, and she was curled into a tight ball, barely breathing between sobs. Finn felt torn between relief and concern, and he knelt at her side, reaching his hand out to touch her shoulder tentatively. She shied away from him and stared up with red-rimmed eyes swimming with tears.

"Finn?" Tallis gripped both his arms tight in her hands. Finn nearly winced at the intensity of her grip.

"I'm here."

"Where were you?" she demanded. "You were supposed to be waiting for me. I thought you were dead, you ass."

"It's good to see you too," Finn raised a hand to her face hesitantly, fearing she might fade into mist at his touch. "I'm sorry, I couldn't stand being in sight of the bridge and I didn't know you'd gotten across until I heard you screaming."

Tallis surprised him by beginning to laugh. She wrapped her arms around him and clung on hard. For a moment, he stood in shocked confusion before returning the embrace.

"Don't you dare let me think you're dead again," Tallis said as she pulled away.

"Only if you make the same promise," Finn forced a smile. "Let's get out of here. I could die happy never coming within miles of this place again."

Tallis nodded and retrieved her sword from where she'd dropped it. She resumed the lead, and Finn followed obediently, comforted to be back in his usual place in her wake. The riverbank was more solid on this side, so they were able to make faster progress as they continued to follow the river toward the ocean, hoping there were still boats that would take them.

They smelled the sea before they could see it. The wind rushed up to meet them as the road began its descent toward the harbor, bringing the sharp smell of salt and fish with it. Despite everything they'd endured, Finn's heart leapt as they crested a hill and the harbor appeared, the ocean beyond glittering gold and blue in the late afternoon sunlight. It stretched as far as the eye could see, and Finn thought he'd never seen anything more glorious in his life.

"It's so big," he exclaimed, unable to find words that could contain his wonder.

"That's one way to describe it."

Tallis smiled and closed her eyes, taking a huge breath of the salt air before they continued walking. They walked side by side now, the road clear before them.

"I loved it when Papa would bring me here," Tallis said as they walked. "So many people and things to see. Traders from distant lands, Kerethi pirates with ropy locks of hair bound in gold, olive-skinned Sabutians with ships built to look like sea serpents carving through the water. Ships of all shapes and sizes packed the harbor. Papa always kept me close, but let me decide where we'd explore."

At this, the joy drained from Tallis' face, and she didn't say another word. As they drew nearer to the harbor, Finn could see it was almost nothing like what she'd described. It looked almost empty. No foreign traders or merchants packed the harbor or the streets. The only ships left were a handful of great, hulking war galleys with the silver lion rampant of the king rearing upon a bright blue field flying on the highest masts. The banners of the captains flew below. Finn could make out a scarlet rose upon purple, a golden snake eating its own tail, and a seated white lion on dark blue that marked a lesser branch of the king's house. They were still too far for him to make out the other three.

"Who goes there?" a soldier shouted down from the top of the stone wall that surrounded the harbor.

"Two refugees from Westham," Tallis called up and pulled out the paper the soldiers had given her and waved it over her head. "We were recruited but got separated from the others."

The soldier disappeared and soon the wooden gates creaked open. A different soldier came out to them. The woman took their papers and surveyed them with a doubtful eye.

"The recruits from Westham were meant to make for King's Harbor," she told them.

"We got separated from the other refugees, so we took my father's boat down the Foggy to get here," Tallis had always been quick with a lie, and Finn was grateful she was the one doing the talking.

"Not sure I believe you," the woman raised a brow, glancing in the direction of the river, where it was clear there were no boats. "But you're here so I suppose the how doesn't really matter. Let me see your eyes."

The woman first grabbed Tallis roughly under the chin and tilted her head to closely examine her eyes. She finally released Tallis' face and moved to give Finn the same treatment. She regarded him with pale blue eyes that held no trace of feeling. If she found any hint of black in his eyes, Finn knew her sword would end his life in a blink.

"They're clean!" she shouted up to the wall, where Finn expected bows had been drawn to strike them down if this woman had given the word.

The soldier surveyed the papers again, closely inspecting the king's seal and the signature of the officer who'd given them the orders. She seemed to find nothing wrong and ushered them inside. The gates slammed shut behind them and the soldier pointed in the direction of the harbor.

"You'd better go fast if you want to get on one of the ships," she said. "The orders just came. We're to move out today. Shriekers have been sighted east of the Serpent."

The news felt like a kick in the gut. The whole time they'd been on the run, their concern had been the western bank of the Foggy. When they'd reached the Serpent's eastern bank, they had let down their guard, sure they were safe. Tallis took Finn's arm, gripping harder than he thought necessary, and led the way toward the sounds of a crowd down by the harbor.

"With a welcome that warm, you'd think we had black eyes and poison pouring out our mouths already," Finn shuddered and glanced behind. "Didn't think my eyes were that dark brown."

"They're leaving today," Tallis said. "If they're so picky about letting people in, it must mean there's not enough space on the ships."

"We'll make it, won't we?" Finn asked as they passed by empty inns and boarded-up shop fronts. The streets were empty, as though the harbor had been abandoned already.

"They let us in, didn't they?" Tallis pointed out. "If they weren't going to let us on a ship, why bother?"

"I hope you're right," Finn's eyes widened as they stepped out onto the wharf.

A mob had formed around the docks where three of the warships were docked. The other three waited out in the harbor. Smaller ships were carting supplies and soldiers out to those three. Other soldiers formed a line that barred the gathered refugees from the docks. Tallis and Finn pushed their way forward, clinging tightly to the papers that might be their only salvation.

"Any able-bodied recruits or volunteers, and women with children, board the ships first," an officer was shouting.

"And what about the rest of us?" an old woman gave voice to what they all were thinking.

"You will wait, and what space is left will be offered to any who can still lift a sword," the captain told them. "The ships will come back for the rest of you."

"Return for us? By the time you come back we'll all be dead or worse. You're just leaving us behind!"

"These orders come from Lord Admiral Grayston Adamaris," the officer drew his sword as the crowd pushed against the soldiers that held them back from the docks. "The king's own blood speaks with the king's voice. To question his orders is treason. Now, recruits, mothers, and children first. No exceptions!"

The crowd boiled with angry shouts. Finn looked around only to find every gaze he met was hostile. They knew he'd have a place on the ships, and they hated him for it. He couldn't blame them.

"Finn, let's go," Tallis whispered. "Before it gets any worse."

"They're leaving people behind," Finn shook his head, horrified.

"Let's not get left behind with them."

Tallis grabbed Finn by the hand and dragged him toward the docks. It seemed to take forever. They had to force their way through people the soldiers were refusing to let pass. Finally, they reached the edge of the crowd. Tallis held up the paper with the king's seal on it that labeled her as a recruit as though it was a shield. She was pulled toward the docks, and Finn was dragged along behind her.

"Why do these farm brats get to go before us?" someone shouted just as they passed through the line of soldiers.

The words snapped the mob like taught rigging suddenly broken by a storm. Suddenly, protests turned into fighting. Soldiers pulled out swords and cudgels, and pushed back against the throng with their shields. Finn saw a spray of red and someone dropped, trampled underfoot, their scream drowned out by the angry roar of their fellows. Then he was being dragged toward the ships.

Finn lost Tallis' hand in the confusion. He shouted her name as she was pulled away from him across the docks, but she couldn't hear above the riots breaking out on the wharves. Strong hands pushed him toward a ramp and he couldn't resist them. Over the heads of the crowd, Finn spotted Tallis boarding another ship and he relented. She was safe and that was all that mattered.

"You might need this, boy," a sailor said gruffly, pressing a sheathed sword into his hands. Finn held it as though it were a snake. Nevra had included him in some of his lessons with Tallis, and she'd dueled him with sticks plenty of times, but she had always won, and he'd come away with bruises on both his ego and his skin.

Above, the ship's banner bore a seated lion on a field of blue. He'd never learned much of the nobility's heraldry. But even he knew this was the coat of arms born by the king's family who were not in his direct line. Since the Kerethi wars had claimed the lives of all the king's brothers, only one ship sailed under that banner now: the flagship of the fleet, the *Lady's Kiss*.

Craning his neck over the crates, Finn sought the helm of the ship, and there at the wheel stood the ship's commanding officer. Lord Admiral Grayston was a tall man, with milky skin. Thick auburn curls crowned his head, and a sharply shaped beard covered his chin. A pair of silver lions reared against each other on his coat, marking him as part of the king's family, and the four stripes on his shoulder marked his rank as the fleet's highest-ranking officer. Finn was near enough to hear his conversation with his first officer.

"Admiral, we've lost control of the situation at the docks. Our soldiers won't be able to hold them back forever. If the mob swarms the ships, who knows what damage they could cause."

Grayston's face was grim as he surveyed the surging mass of people desperate to flee the mainland. "Order the ships out. We'll moor a safe distance from shore. They can't riot forever. When they settle, we'll send rowboats back for more. We can't risk the integrity of any of our ships."

"Yes, sir."

Before the first officer had a chance to relay the order, something changed in the crowd. First, there was only a nearly imperceptible moment of stillness, then an inhuman scream Finn had grown to recognize far too well.

"One of the refugees!" a soldier shouted up to the deck of the *Lady's Kiss* just before the riot became a massacre. Someone had been bitten and not noticed, or thought somehow they wouldn't meet the same fate as everyone else who'd met with the monsters' poison. For some, the change was immediate. Others could last for hours, but no one escaped it once it was in the blood.

"Signal the other ships to get out of here!" the admiral shouted and did not wait for the flag signalers to send his message but waved his arms at the ship moored opposite the *Lady's Kiss*. "Go! Go!"

"What about us, Admiral?" the first officer asked.

"Keep our ramp down as long as we can, let any human on board, I don't care who they are," Grayston commanded. "Hoist the sails and be ready to cast off the moment there is any danger of Shriekers boarding."

Finn forced himself to look toward the docks. Visions that had formed from the fog around the Nightmare Bridge materialized again before him, but these were no phantoms meant to weaken his resolve. Real people scrambled toward the ships as the soldiers fought now to destroy the Shriekers rather than hold back the crowd. In the mad dash, some fell and were trampled underfoot. He heard a woman howl in agony, not from a blade or monster's jaw, but from the boot of a fellow refugee crushing her hand. The Guardian had shown him near identical illusions that had faded away into the mist as he'd fled for the river's far bank, but what he saw now kept happening. Countless faces contorted in panic and pain, so desperate to escape the fray that many fell from the pier before ever reaching the dock.

The ship moored beside the *Lady's Kiss* pulled away from the dock. Refugees flung themselves toward it, a few catching hold of the ropes and scrambling aboard, some falling short and crashing into the water. Still more poured aboard the *Lady's Kiss*, more than Finn guessed the admiral had meant to take.

"You, boy!" a voice at his side startled Finn. He looked up to see the ship's first officer. "You want to put that sword to use? Round up the refugees coming aboard. No one goes below deck until we can inspect them. If anyone tries, use force if you must. If you see a bite, kill them."

"I—" Finn meant to stammer out a protest. How could this man expect him to fight innocent people?

"Those are the Lord Admiral's orders," the man said with a finality that forced Finn to yield.

"Yes, sir."

All Finn could do was pray he wouldn't need to use the sword in his hands. But who to pray to, Finn wondered. The Protector to shield these people from himself? The Lady to embrace any who he might have no choice but to cull? He knew what a bite would mean. The ship could face the same fate as the docks if even one refugee had been compromised.

"To the fore, the lot of you," a lower ranking officer was barking at the arriving refugees. Finn took his place in a line of soldiers corralling them into a corner at the bow. He tried not to look them in the eyes lest they see he was just as terrified as they were.

"Lay aloft! Loose all sails!"

The admiral's voice echoed across the ship. As though the man commanded each sailor with puppet strings, the five sails on each of the ship's four masts all descended one by one in perfect unison.

"There's still people on the docks!" a refugee protested.

"We can't leave yet!" another wailed. "My wife is still back there!"

A few refugees broke from the clump they'd been herded into, screaming names of loved ones still unaccounted for. Finn blanched as some of them careened toward him, heedless of his upraised sword.

"Stay where you are!" the officer's voice bellowed. "Unless you want to be left behind."

The words halted most of the scattered refugees in their tracks. Some still made for the ramp, shouting incoherently. Finn steeled his nerves and stopped one, pushing the flat of his blade against a woman's chest.

"My brother!"

"Going back won't save him," Finn pleaded with the woman, willing her to stay.

The woman's gray eyes bored into his. They glistened with tears of rage. She pushed against his blade with a force that surprised him, her hands raking across the blade, staining it red.

"Look!" Finn dropped his sword and grabbed her by the wrists instead, refusing to cause her further injury. He turned her to see the chaos behind them, though he was himself loath to witness the slaughter. "You can't help any of them."

The fire of fury in her eyes snuffed out, as swift as a torch dropped into the sea. She leaned against the rail of the ship, bloody hands leaving glistening stains upon the wood. The *Lady's Kiss* was already pulling away from the harbor. With each moment, the Shrieker numbers swelled, overwhelming the few soldiers that had been left behind. People began throwing themselves into the water, but the ships were leaving faster than they could swim.

"Lady save us," the woman gasped as she beheld the catastrophe with glassy eyes.

"She already has," Finn stepped toward her, hoping to comfort himself as much as her. "Look, in the water. There are Shriekers drowning. We're in the Lady's hands now, out of their reach."

"Waves take their bones."

The prayer felt hollow in the woman's voice. As they watched the harbor fall to the Shriekers, Finn wondered how she'd meant it. For one already passed, it was a prayer for their rest in the hands of the Lady of the Waters. Yet when spoken for an enemy that still drew breath, it was a battle cry that promised death. So whom had she spoken for, the monsters or their doomed victims? Perhaps both, Finn decided.

"Regroup the fleet," the admiral's voice once again sliced the deck. "Us, the Star Bird, the Morning Star, and Bloody Lady will double back to the Serpent's Mouth. Distribute the refugees among the *Storm Ghost*, the Ouroboros, and the Elk Horn. I won't risk civilians retaking the harbor."

"Sir, the harbor is overrun," a scout reported, passing his scope to Grayston. "We should save our ships and send them to defend King's Harbor."

Grayston raised the scope to his eye. His face was a mask of unreadable stone. Finn returned his gaze to the harbor, but already they'd sailed a considerable distance from shore. All he could see without a scope was an amorphous clamor at the docks and smoke beginning to rise. Buildings had been set ablaze by careless attempts to fight back the Shriekers. All aboard the *Lady's Kiss* was suspended in silent anticipation. There was nothing to drown out the sickening cries of those who'd been left behind.

The admiral's shoulders sagged and the noble bearing seemed for a moment to slip. Dark lines creased his brow, betraying a weariness as deep as the waters beneath the ship. Finn tried not to imagine what the man had seen, but the Guardian's visions still played in his mind, and he knew all too well what Grayston must have witnessed. One Shrieker within the walls was all it took for a city to fall, just as one false step upon a crumbling bank could bring a whole bluff crashing into the waves below.

As though it had never wavered, Grayston's demeanor of calm authority settled about his body like armor. His back straightened, the lines of his face smoothed and when he spoke not a hint of hesitation could be heard.

"Turn the cannons upon the city," Grayston ordered. "Bombard the piers. Make those monsters pay for what they've taken."

"What of any survivors?" one of his officers protested.

"There will be no survivors," Grayston's hands clenched, knuckles near as white as a Shrieker's skin, around the rail of the ship. "Let them taste the Lady's mercy, for they are out of reach of the Protector's hands now. Standby the cannons."

The admiral's orders were carried across the upper deck and down to the lower gun deck.

"Cannons ready!" came the reply from the crew.

"Fire."

Finn turned away from the harbor, unable to bear watching. Blasts of cannon fire and the splintering of wood and stone as the iron balls found their marks echoed in his ears.

Waves take their bones, Finn prayed, both for mercy and for justice, and for the first time, his prayers were genuine. All his life, he had sung praises to the Lady of the Waters and prayed for her guidance and her mercy, but how could he worship something he had never seen? His prayers to the Protector of the Skies had felt more real. Spending as much time as he had working on Nevra's farm, he'd known what it was to be subject to the whims of weather. He'd prayed for rain, and he'd prayed for it to please just stop raining. He'd prayed for the sun in the depths of winter when it felt he'd never feel warm again, and for even the smallest breath of wind while wiping sweat from his brow as he tilled a field.

But as the span of open water between him and the Shriekers grew, and the harbor shrank almost out of sight, Finn felt a faith he'd never found in days spent sailing upon the Foggy River. Endless water stretched as far as the eye could see. To find its end would be a journey that would take him from equinox to solstice. It was her whims that held his life in her hands.

Finn leaned against the rail that stood between him and a grave in unimaginable depths. Around him, refugees were being ushered below deck one by one after being thoroughly inspected for signs of infection. The ship's crew were busy at their tasks, and for the moment it seemed he'd been forgotten. The blade in his hands had cut him away from the rest of the refugees, but he was not yet a part of the crew.

With shaking hands, Finn retrieved his sword from where he'd let it fall to the deck. The red drops on the bright shining steel made his stomach churn. Quickly, he wiped the blood away with a rag from his coat pocket then tossed it out to the sea. He returned his sword to its sheath and sagged against the rail of the ship.

"You a new recruit?" a voice, light, almost as a child's, came from behind him and Finn wheeled, startled.

Finn was surprised to see a boy his own age. His hair was golden as the late summer wheat in the sun and eyes were as blue as the sky breaking through clouds after a storm. Finn found himself too tongue-tied to answer so only nodded.

"Me too!" he nearly bounced with excitement. "They picked me up in King's Harbor. When the *Lady's Kiss* went to reinforce the Serpent's Mouth, they packed me off with it, rather than send me to Giant's Isle with the refugees. Trial by fire for both of us, too literally."

His voice was hurried and nervous, flying through his words with the speed of a gull in a high wind.

"I'm Finley Tyne. Finn."

"They call—well, called me Cormorant. Or Cori."

"Cormorant?"

"It's how the King's Harbor street kids name each other," Cori explained. "Most of us never got names from our mothers, or we don't remember them. There's the Daughters of the Sea; they take in stray girls. I was given to the Sons of the Sky. We all get animal names until we grow up and move on: Daughters take the names of creatures from the sea, and Sons from those of the sky."

"A cormorant is both," Finn pointed out.

A look passed over the boy's face that was difficult to read. For a moment it seemed like fear, but it faded to a light in his eyes like Finn had told a particularly witty joke.

"Yes, I suppose it is," he shrugged. "But it's time for me to pick my own name now that I've left the Sons. I liked when my brothers called me Cori. I think I'll keep that."

"It's good to meet you, Cori."

"Are you on your own?" Cori asked.

Finn's throat constricted. Even though he'd seen Tallis board another ship, it seemed like this journey was determined to separate him from everyone he'd known. He couldn't help but imagine how a Shrieker had managed to get inside the walls of the Serpent's Mouth. He dreaded what would happen if the same thing happened aboard one of the ships. In that cramped space, a single Shrieker could wreak havoc.

"I am now," Finn admitted. "I was with a friend. I saw her get on a ship but..."

"You're still worried."

"Yes."

"Come on," Cori gestured toward the stairs that led below deck. "The crew will be too busy to pay you any mind. You look exhausted, and filthy, no offense. There's some fresh water you can at least splash your face with, and you should grab a hammock before you keel over. When we get to Giant's Isle, we'll find your friend, I promise."

"Thank you," Finn stammered and let Cori lead him away from the rail and the dwindling sight of the burning harbor behind them.

CHAPTER EIGHT

The Lion Gate

Burning buildings and screaming people filled Tallis' vision. In the midst of it all, stood Finn. He alone was motionless among the leaping fire and seething masses of people clamoring to escape. He seemed far away, but Tallis could see his eyes, flames reflected red against his irises. In the darkness, his eyes looked black as deep waters at midnight, though whether from a trick of the light or from a monster's bite, she couldn't tell.

Finn's mouth opened as if to speak, but all Tallis could hear was the harrowing howling of the Shriekers.

Tallis jolted from her nightmares to find light finally streaming into the ship's hold. Night had fallen quickly as they'd pulled away from the Serpent's Mouth. Soldiers had shepherded them below deck, but that hadn't shut out the sounds of screams and cannon fire. Now, the ship jolted and swayed in the waves. The ship creaked as it moved through the water, and she could hear the sound of boots on the deck above.

Tallis sat up and leaned her head back against the wall of the ship. The image of Finn in her nightmares refused to leave her mind. She felt his hand slipping from hers and drew a shuddering breath. She could only rely on faith that Finn had gotten aboard one of the ships as well. But all she could hear were the screams that became shrieks, and she felt cold despite the heat of the cramped hold of the ship, as though the damp chill of the fog around the Nightmare Bridge had lodged itself in her lungs.

One of a pair of freckled twins stirred. They had flame orange hair and skin so white it was almost blue and had settled beside her in the hold. She sat up, rubbing her eyes. The twins seemed to be a few years younger than herself, barely older than Aiven and still gaunt from growing faster than they could eat. Tallis wondered how they'd managed to get themselves recruitment papers, because they were clearly too old to have been let on with the children. The capital must have been truly desperate for soldiers.

"Seems like we'll be neighbors for a while," the girl turned to her, reaching out a hand. "Hemma Guihelm. My sleepy lump of a brother is Harrin."

"Tallis Larke."

Tallis nodded and shook her hand. She had longer hair than her brother, but Tallis knew that soldiers kept their hair shorn, so soon there would be little to tell the two apart.

"Where are you from?" Hemma asked.

"Westham."

"Westham?" Hemma frowned. "Isn't that a bit far for you to have come to Serpent's Mouth?"

Tallis shrugged. "The bridges were burnt and the road north was crawling with Shriekers, so my friend and I came south. Where'd you two come from?"

"Born and raised in Serpent's Mouth," Harrin answered. "Our father was a fisherman and traded with farmers from away up north."

"Might have met my father then. He'd bring his boat filled with our crops down here. I went with him a few times," Tallis' throat felt tight speaking about Papa, and she turned the subject away from family. "Are you enlisting too?"

"Father guessed it'd be the surest way for us to get a spot on the ships," Hemma shrugged, face grim. "Seems he was right. Took a bit of convincing for them to let us in, seeing as we're so young. But father has a friend on the *Storm Ghost*, she's the one with the rose banner. Her captain agreed to take us on as lookouts, seeing as we're small enough to get way up high easy."

Tallis nodded. She didn't want to ask about the rest of their family, fearing the answer had been left behind them in the ruins of the Serpent's Mouth. From the sound of cannons, Tallis guessed there would be little left of the town, and if Shriekers had gotten within the walls, there was little chance any survivors would remain.

"Come on," Hemma stood up, stretching. "I'm tired of being crammed down here in the dark. Let's see which ship we're on."

With nothing else to do, Tallis followed Hemma toward the stairs that led to the deck. As they emerged from the hold, they found it bustling with activity. They kept to the side of the ship, staying out of the way of anyone in uniform as much as they could. Above, a black flag with a white lion's paw flapped from the mast.

"The Howin coat of arms," Hemma explained, gesturing to the flag. "My father taught us as much heraldry and history as he could, testing us whenever a ship entered the harbor. The Howin family branched off from the royal family a long time ago, so distant they're not even remotely in line for the throne. But they kept the lion in their coat of arms and that means this ship is the Lion's Pride."

Hemma scanned the deck and pointed to a man at the helm, tall with black hair. "There, that's Captain Erment Howin."

Tallis was drawn to the rail of the ship. She had little interest in the politics and lineage of captains and nobles. Who sat on the throne had made little difference to life in Westham until another family's bid for power had led to the Kerethi wars and taken her father away when she'd been too young to remember. It seemed to her that events in the king's court only had the power to disrupt her life.

Leaning at the rail, Tallis gazed across the water. The waves sparkled with gold in the morning sunlight. It stretched as far as the eye could see in all directions, and Tallis felt a strange pull toward the horizon, wondering what lay beyond the borders of Okaesa. If it weren't for the Shriekers, joining the fleet might mean she'd get to find out, and she longed for that to be what she was sailing for, not fleeing for her life.

Hemma was still chatting about the ships around them. Directly to starboard, where they leaned against the rail and looked out, the largest ship Tallis had ever seen cut through the water as though it were a knife through butter. While the smaller ship they stood on rocked in the waves, this one sailed straight and steady.

"That's the flagship, the *Lady's Kiss*," Hemma sounded dismissive. "She's huge and powerful but not the best for exploration and can't maneuver nearly as well as a smaller ship. Not like the *Storm Ghost*."

Hemma pointed to the next ship over, only its mast visible above the hulk of the *Lady's Kiss*. From it flew a red rose upon a field of purple. Tallis longed to be able to see more of it, to be able to envision Papa walking its deck again like he had long ago.

"My father said the *Storm Ghost* is one of the oldest ships in the fleet," Hemma explained. "But that means it's gone the longest without sinking. If there's any ship to hope you're assigned to, it's that one."

Tallis imagined standing where Papa had once stood, and the thought brought some comfort. As she gazed across the unending water, she felt her body relax for the first time since Westham had fallen. Tallis closed her eyes and thanked the Lady of the Waters for deliverance from the Shriekers, and prayed that she had Finn in her hands on another ship.

* * *

Tallis lost count of the days as they continued their journey eastward, cramped below deck like livestock. The sailors kept them below deck for the most part to keep them out of the way, and the stench of seasickness and waste became nearly unbearable. Each day blurred into the next and Tallis never saw anything on the horizon, just endless water. When one morning the sound of excited commotion and footsteps bounding back and forth across the deck above her, Tallis perked up at the unusual excitement.

"Come on, Tallis!" Hemma knelt above her. "We're here! They say you can see Giant's Isle now. Let's go!"

Tallis leapt out of her blankets and slid her feet into boots. She didn't bother to lace them before she was running after Hemma above-deck, slipping her arms into the sleeves of her jacket as she went. After days at sea, the prospect of finally reaching land was a welcome relief. For a moment, Tallis was blinded by the morning sun. In the confusion of people crowding the rails to catch their first glimpse of the city, it took a moment for Tallis to properly see what the fuss was about.

When at last Tallis looked up, she couldn't contain her gasp.

"It's just as beautiful as they say," Hemma elbowed her as she gaped up at the towering gates before them. Tallis couldn't help but agree. They spotted Harrin leaning up against the rail and pushed their way to his side.

In reality, Giant's Isle was three islands joined together: the Hands and the Head. Legend said a great giant had once drowned in the ocean here, and the three islands were what was left of his body, sticking up above the water. The Head was the largest of the three, and held the main city and King Leander's keep. The Great Hand now stood to their left as they approached. Though larger than the Little Hand on their right, neither was much more than an outcrop of gray stone jutting up from the white foam of the sea.

A great wall wrapped around the high cliff faces of the Head and stretched around to connect to the Hands. The Lion Gate stood between the two Hands, large enough for the greatest of the king's warships to pass with ease. The portcullis stood open before them, a great fanged mouth ready to swallow the ship whole. Two giant lions reared on hind legs, roaring at each other over the peak of the gate, carved in intricate detail in the white stone. Their eyes were dark holes that opened into passages within the wall.

Tallis knew from the stories that the wall stretched all the way to the sea floor, built up from smaller islets and underwater shoals, with only a handful of smaller iron-barred gates to allow for lesser traffic in and out of the bay within. It was said no army had ever managed to breach the wall, even if they managed to get past the fleet to land on the white-sand beaches of the Head. Tallis could understand why as the ship passed under the gaping Lion Gate. She could hardly stretch her neck far enough to see the top from right under the wall.

Once within, the bay sprawled with ships, both smaller trading vessels and Okaesa's famed fleet. A myriad of flags flew from the masts, dancing in all the colors of the rainbow in the wind. All flew the white lion above their own standards.

A second wall encircled the Head, separating the upper city and keep from the bay as a last line of defense. Below the inner wall was the port town, a mess of wood and stone buildings jumbled around the docks. Above it rose spires and towers taller than Tallis could have imagined possible. She could not understand how they managed to rise so high above the ground without toppling. Their roofs glittered gold, silver, and white in the morning sun. One silver tower rose high above the rest: the Tower of the King. The city formed a shining crown for the giant's head.

"Who knew a city could be so big?" Harrin said as he gawked up at the capital.

"And I thought the Serpent's Mouth was big," Tallis laughed in disbelief, her terror and worry momentarily forgotten in the shadow of her wonder.

For the first time since rumors of the Shriekers had become reports, Tallis felt safe. Looking back at the wall that encircled the harbor, she couldn't believe anything could possibly get past it, especially not with the fleet guarding all the gates. Tallis prayed Aiven, Osind, and Finn had seen what she'd just seen and she would find them somewhere in this city.

The docks were too crowded for the newly arrived ships to moor. Instead, smaller dinghies were sent out to cart people and goods ashore. Tallis waited her turn on the deck, drinking in all the sights and sounds of what would be her new home.

"I wish my papa was here," Tallis said to the twins. "He always talked about Giant's Isle. He came here not long after I was born to fight in the Kerethi war. It's as amazing as his stories. I think he wished he could see it again."

Tallis trailed off, trying to imagine her father on a ship like this, seeing the city for the first time. The thought of him standing on the deck of a ship and bound for enlistment in the fleet brought a lump to her throat. He'd left behind a wife and a daughter and knew that when the war was done, he could return to the life he had with them. Tallis was like him, young and about to be lost in a city grander than anything she'd ever seen, with the prospect of a war looming over her head. But she had nothing to return to, not even a home. That had burned along with Mama, and Papa's corpse was rotting in the mud. If she ever went back, there would be nothing left but charred timbers and the collapsed frame of what had once been a home full of laughter and love.

"At least you got here," Hemma said. "I'm sure he'd be glad of that at least."

Tallis nodded and did her best to shake thoughts of her parents out of her head as soldiers beckoned them forward to the next dinghy. They crowded tight onto the benches and the boat sat deep in the water as it bobbed its way toward shore, oars pumping against the clear blue water.

The dock was bustling with soldiers and workers unloading and checking supplies. Refugees and recruits were shuffled into separate lines to be processed by bored-looking soldiers. Children clung to mothers' skirts with wide eyes. A handful of older ones were pulled over to the line of recruits while the mothers protested. Tallis shivered. Aiven and

Osind might be old enough to have received the same treatment.

"Official orders," a soldier said, as he pulled one child by the wrist away from a sobbing mother. "We need runners to cart supplies and messages to the wall. No child under fifteen will be put on battle lines, you have our word."

Tallis tried not to look as children filed into line behind her. She was thankful her siblings were too young to have been put with the soldiers, but fifteen still hardly seemed grown enough to be handed a weapon and told to defend the city. She tried to tell herself that desperate times called for desperate measures, but she couldn't help but cringe when she glanced at the small number of frightened refugees compared to the growing line of recruits.

"I wonder how good their word will be if the city is attacked," Harrin muttered.

"Don't," Tallis shook her head. "Don't even think it."

"Tallis!"

Someone was running to her from a boat that had just unloaded. Tallis hardly dared to breathe or believe what her senses told her for fear he would fade away into mist like another illusion from the Nightmare Bridge.

"Finn?" Tallis gasped when he finally careened to a halt before her. She reached out a shaking hand and brushed her fingers against his cheek. When his solid skin beneath her hand did not immediately dissolve into fog, she grabbed him by the shoulders and pulled him into a tight embrace. "I thought—"

"I'm alright," he assured her.

"Keep moving," a soldier commanded. "Recruits come forward to receive your assignments."

They were ushered to a line forming by a man with a book of notes and sheaves of recruitment papers. Finn reached back and took Tallis' hand. His was cold but sweaty. The relief from just moments ago was gone. He was afraid. Tallis squeezed back and swallowed a rising feeling of nausea as they slowly approached the front.

"You, boy, come."

The soldier called Finn forward first as they reached the front of the line. Tallis waited, hands clenched at her sides, doing her best to stand still.

"Name. Birthplace. Age."

"Finley Tyne, sir," he stuttered, "of Westham. I'm eighteen."

The man scanned his notes, repeating Finn's name under his breath as he went, "Tyne, yes. Admiral Grayston has requested you return to the *Lady's Kiss* after completion of your training. Report to crew training under Commander Sydas. You'll follow that group there."

The soldier pointed. The recruits were being sorted into two bunches waiting for further directions. With a glance back at Tallis, Finn went to join his new companions.

"Girl, come."

Tallis took a deep breath and approached the soldier. He looked her over with what appeared to be scorn. Tallis shivered and wondered if she'd get turned away now, after she'd gotten so far, just for being a farm girl they wouldn't want among their ranks.

He sighed and repeated the same instructions he'd given Finn, sounding exhausted.

"Tallis Larke. Westham. Nineteen." She answered in the same rote tone.

"Ever sailed a boat, Tallis?"

"Yes, sir, but—"

"Good, you'll be on the ships," the soldier said and scribbled more in his book without looking at her. "You'll be assigned to Lady Eiran Garray, Captain of the *Storm Ghost*. Follow that last boy."

Tallis' heart sank, dreading the now inevitable moment of separation from Finn. In all their efforts to get here, she'd never imagined they might be assigned to different ships. But despite this disappointment, she couldn't help but feel a twinge of excitement at the assignment, though one that was stained by bitterness. To be assigned to the same ship as Papa and Glynn, even if the crew and captain would be different, seemed almost like fate. Papa had loved to tell her how he had sailed under the command of the man who later became king, even though Leander had been third in line at the time. Maybe Papa was still watching over her after all. Besides, he'd survived his time serving on the *Storm Ghost*. Maybe she would too.

"Is there a problem, girl?" the soldier asked.

"No, sir, sorry, sir," Tallis stammered and went to rejoin Finn. She caught his eye and saw in them the same fear she felt.

"Which ship did you get?" an excited voice asked her.

Tallis turned to see the twins had joined them.

"The *Storm Ghost*."

"You'll be with us!" Hemma beamed. "Captain Eiran is famous, ever heard of her?"

"My father mentioned her," Tallis left it at that. Thinking of Papa's stories returned the painful lump to her throat and she almost couldn't breathe. His face, twisted and paler than it had ever been in life, even in the depths of winter, surfaced in her mind. Tallis shivered.

"Captain Eiran was the first woman to ever join the king's forces," Hemma continued in breathless excitement. "Broke all the rules and proved everyone wrong and became a captain for it. Story is, she was a highborn lady all set to marry into the royal family before some scandal broke off the engagement. She disguised herself as a boy and snuck onto one of the ships and was such a good soldier that, when she was found out, they didn't even try to kick her out. Now there's lots more women in the fleet and even in command positions, but she made that possible."

"Sounds like a great story," Tallis wondered how much of it was true. From Papa's stories, she'd heard the part of Eiran disguising herself to join the fleet, but he'd never mentioned anything about her past before they'd served together. No matter what the whole truth was, this captain's choice had opened the door that Tallis herself had just stepped through. If it hadn't been for her, Tallis might have been left on the mainland to die.

"I'll be on the flagship with the admiral," Finn said, a hint of pride in his voice, but it quickly turned somber. "Though I'd rather be with you, Tallis."

"So would I."

Tallis reached out and took Finn's hand, squeezing in what she hoped felt more like comfort than clinging.

"Alright, soldiers, we move out," a soldier called. "You'll get your uniforms and your quarters and then it's straight to training. Let's go."

Tallis gave the dock a final scan, longing to see her sister and brother, but the crowd was full of strangers and the group was beginning to move. The soldiers shepherded them away from the docks and toward the streets.

They were led through the city toward the inner castle wall that loomed high above the harbor town. People in the streets parted for the soldiers. Men and women crowded into corners and doorways to watch them pass from a respectful distance. The street they took ran straight and wide up from the harbor to the castle gates, lined with large inns, taverns, armorers, and carts shouting prices for goods.

It was like how Tallis remembered the Serpent's Mouth before the invasion, but larger than she'd thought possible. More side streets branched off from the main one than she could count. Tallis couldn't picture this city as her new home. She was certain there was no way she could ever find her way around on her own.

Two figures separated themselves from the strangers filling the edges of the street and bolted for Tallis. She had only a moment to process black curls before she was nearly knocked off her feet.

"Aiven? Osi?"

Tallis peeled the two off of her and held them at arm's length. She scanned them head to toe. Aside from a few more patches in their clothes than she remembered, they looked unchanged.

"Keep moving, soldier."

It took a moment for Tallis to realize she was being spoken to. The group had continued their way up the street and she had lagged behind.

"But my family…"

"You'll have time to visit them later. For now, keep up."

"Don't go again," Aiven begged.

"I'm sorry, I can't—" Tallis glanced from the soldier to her siblings. "How do I find you when I can?"

"They got us running errands," Aiven explained. "They're putting up any children on their own in inns around the city. We're in the Crow's Nest. Ask for Maija."

"I promised I'd find another way across the river, and I did," Tallis said. "Now I promise I'll find a way to take care of you here."

"We missed you, Tallis," Osind said.

"I know, I missed you too. I'll see you soon"

Tallis kissed them both on the forehead before sprinting after the group of sailors. Finn had lagged behind to wait for her. He took her hand again when she reached them and squeezed it.

"I'm glad they're okay," Finn said.

Tallis nodded, sure that if she said anything then all of her feelings would tear their way out of her throat and strangle her. Aiven and Osind were safe, but still beyond her reach. Some woman she'd never met was watching them, and they were being forced to work for their place on Giant's Isle. Tallis wondered why they were alone, and the thought nagged, leading her mind down dark paths. Glynn would have taken care of them if he could. She thought of the Serpent's Mouth and the massacre at the docks, fearing King's Harbor might have suffered the same fate.

As they approached the castle gates, the street grew cleaner and the cobbles beneath their feet less cracked and uneven. The walls were built of the same white stone as the outer wall that surrounded the island. A wooden gate stood open, guarded by blue-uniformed soldiers.

Tallis had little time to take in the bright colors and shining spires of the inner city before they were herded into barracks. The doors slammed behind them and she was no longer a recruit, but a soldier.

Inside, it sounded like the day she'd gone with Papa to help Glynn shear his sheep. Clippers snipped and hair fell in clumps to the floor. By regulation, all soldiers had to wear their hair short. Long hair was considered a danger in battle and an inconvenience while sailing.

Tallis had always loved her hair. She would spend lazy afternoons with Mama and Aiven and the three would weave each others' hair into long braids with bright flowers they found along the river. Once, her mama had cut Tallis' hair short because lice had made their home there. It had taken years to regrow and had made a halo of black fluff for a long time before its weight let it fall down her back.

The soldiers had put the refugees to work and an older woman with a knife and razor sat her down to cut her hair to soldier regulation.

"It's a pity," the woman said as she grabbed Tallis' long black curls with one hand. "Such lovely hair on these girls and I have to cut it all off so they can be sent off to fight."

The woman lifted her knife and Tallis closed her eyes and grimaced as she made short work of the bulk of her hair in one slice. It fell on the floor to rest on the growing pile of hair. The woman cut the rest close to her scalp, but since her ringlets stuck close to her head, did not shave it off as completely as she had with others who had straight hair. Tallis fought the tears that burned beneath her eyelids. She could see her Mama's laughing face as they enjoyed the first warm days of spring. Mama with a big lily Aiven had found drooping out of her long braid. Aiven with bluebells that rang with her giggles. Tallis had chosen buttercups because yellow was her favorite color.

A uniform was shoved into her hands, and she was directed behind a screen to change. She used her tattered and dirty old shirt to brush wisps of hair from her shoulders before pulling on the sailor's uniform.

When she was given a brief glimpse in a cloudy mirror, Tallis could hardly recognize herself. The face that stared at her from the mirror reminded her of Papa in a portrait of her parents when they were young that hung above the fireplace. The portrait had been done right after Papa had returned from the last war, before his hair had grown out again to the long ropes Tallis remembered and was often scolded for grabbing. He'd even worn the same uniform: a crisp white shirt, a blue jacket, and a doublet with a small white lion of the king embroidered upon the breast. The one difference was Papa's jacket had born two lions facing each other, as he'd been under the command of one of the royal family. Tallis' jacket had a single red rose in place of one of the lions: Captain Eiran's sigil.

Finn found his way across the room to Tallis. Never as tightly curled as hers, his hair had once fallen in waves around his face near to his shoulders. Now, it sat nearly straight above his ears, with only the hint of a curl at the ends. His uniform looked like her Papa's, having been assigned to the admiral, who was son to an elder cousin of Leander.

"You don't look awful," Tallis said, flicking a stray chunk of clipped hair off his shoulder.

"Gee, thanks, neither do you."

Tallis allowed herself a laugh and together they joined those waiting for the next orders. They were taken from the main room and men and women were separated into different chambers filled tight with bunks. Tallis was reluctant to leave Finn so soon after finding him again, but the flow of people took him and Harrin away. Hemma shouted in dismay and tried to fight the current to reach her brother.

"We'll find them later," Tallis said, wrapping an arm around the girl's shoulders and guiding her toward the women's quarters. Her heart ached, thinking how close Aiven and Osind were to being old enough to be in Hemma and Harrin's place.

Inside, the quarters were cramped and messy. Tallis dumped her things on an empty bunk. Hemma settled down next to her.

"I've always shared a room with my brother," Hemma whispered to Tallis, a hint of nervousness in her voice.

Tallis nodded, thinking of the loft she'd shared with Aiven in the home that was now nothing but ash and char. "And I always shared a room with my little sister. But we've got each other now."

Hemma gave a half-hearted smile, "Thank you, Tallis."

A pale girl with a light brown fuzz of hair gestured at the bed on the other side of Tallis.

"May I?"

"Of course." Tallis shrugged.

The girl reached out a lithe hand. Tallis couldn't imagine that hand holding a sword as she took it in her own. But despite the girl's light frame, her hands were rough and her grip was firm. Maybe she wouldn't be as soft as Tallis had first thought.

"I'm Fadren," the girl said. "I'm on the *Storm Ghost*."

"Tallis."

"Hemma," the other girl reached over as well. "We're all for the *Storm Ghost*!"

"Your accents," Fadren noted. "You're from the mainland?"

"I grew up on a farm just outside of Westham," Tallis explained.

"My brother and I were from the Serpent's Mouth," Hemma said. "You're from Giant's Isle?"

Fadren nodded. "I was a barmaid at the Crow's Nest. My mother is the owner."

Tallis perked up at this. "My siblings came here separately from me, they said they've been staying at the Crow's Nest."

Fadren gave Tallis an appraising look. "Aiven and Osind? You look like them."

Tallis nodded.

"Yes, my mother agreed to take in a few children who came here without adults to look after them," Fadren said. "She's a caring woman. Couldn't stand the thought of refugee children left on their own when she had open rooms and plenty of food. It will hurt her profits, sure, but what are profits when the world is ending, she said."

"How do I get there?" Tallis was desperate to see her siblings.

"Follow the main road you took to get here," Fadren directed. "Turn off to the right when you see a blacksmith with a dog painted above the door. That road will take you straight to the Crow's Nest, but you shouldn't take too long. Training starts at dawn."

"Thank you."

Tallis said her farewells to Hemma and their new friend and hurried out of the barracks toward the gates. They were opened for her without question. She supposed the uniform she wore might come in handy after all. She followed the soldier's directions, trying her best not to run and risk missing the turn she was supposed to make.

When she came at last to the turn, she found the road off the main street much different than what she'd seen before. The first thing she noticed was the smell. The main street was kept mostly clean, but here, she could smell chamber pots that had been dumped out of windows, and filth had permanently stained the cobblestones a dark brown. Tallis wondered if they had once been the same white stone that made much of the rest of the city.

Tallis' heart leapt to her throat when she saw a sign carved with the silhouette of a man gazing through a scope at the top of a mast, with "The Crow's Nest" painted above it. She pushed the door open to find a surprisingly pleasant main room. A bright fire crackled in one corner, and the place smelled of some sort of meat stewing, a welcome relief from the smell of the street. At this hour, many of the tables were filled with a jumble of citizens from the city, soldiers, and refugees.

"How can I help you, dear?" an elderly woman with shining green eyes welcomed her in. Her gray hair was pulled into a tight bun. "Fresh from the docks? I can tell by the way your hair hasn't had time to settle into its new length yet."

"I'm looking for my brother and sister," Tallis stuttered. "Their names are Aiven and Osind. They told me to come here. And another recruit, Fadren, said they were here."

The woman's smile brightened. "I'm Maija, and yes, I know the ones you're talking about. Sweet children. And Fadren, that's my own girl. I'm so glad you've come. They'd talk my ear off about you. Said you were coming. I was convinced they'd be like every other orphan I've taken in, claiming family was coming for them that never showed. It's nice to be wrong for once."

"Thank you for taking care of them," Tallis had no idea how to properly thank this woman. "I'm afraid they may have to stay here for now. I can't exactly bring them to the barracks."

"Don't you worry," Maija wrapped an arm around her shoulders and led her to a spot near the fire. The way she spoke it was clear this woman was used to talking and being listened to. Tallis didn't mind. She was content to let the woman worry over her. "You met my eldest daughter. My second was a surprise many years later. She's only four, so I'm used to having children around. Plus, I took in a baby your siblings brought with them. I won't ever turn away a child who needs a bed and food. You stay here, I'll bring you some stew and tell your siblings you've come. They're helping out in the kitchen right now. Food will be on the house, don't you worry. I'm sure you've had quite the ordeal getting here and a good hearty meal will be just the thing."

Maija left Tallis at a small table near the fire and hurried off to the kitchens. Tallis closed her eyes and inhaled deep breaths, feeling as though she'd run for miles, not simply walked from the upper city to the lower. It felt like all the time since before the Shriekers had attacked Westham had passed in a rushed blur, like a hurricane's rough winds had picked her up and blown her away from her old life.

After days on the road, followed by being packed into the damp underdecks of a ship, sitting by a fire inside was a great comfort. The sounds of laughter and the smell of beer and fresh bread and meaty stew were all so familiar. She could almost be back in Westham, at the Coat of Arms, the tavern that was the heart of the village. She would go there with her father sometimes, after they'd spent the day selling their crops at the market. When she was young, she would just get water, or if she was lucky, a hot apple cider. As she grew older, Papa would sometimes let her sample his beer, a bitter ale that made her grimace as it burned her throat. When he finally let her choose her own drinks, she'd found the sweet mead to be much more to her taste.

Tallis was exhausted, and in the warmth of the fire had almost nodded off by the time two happy voices called her name. She opened her eyes to find Aiven and Osind had joined her. They perched atop the table's other chairs and leaned on the table with their elbows in a way Mama would have scolded them for.

"You cut your hair!" Osind rubbed a hand on Tallis' scalp, and she laughed more genuinely than she had since before the attack on Westham. "You look like a soldier now!"

He tugged at the sleeves of her uniform.

"I *am* a soldier now," Tallis said, ruffling Osind's curls that were now longer than hers for the first time in their lives.

"How'd you get here? We waited for you every day at the docks when new ships would come in. We were starting to get worried you wouldn't..." Aiven trailed off, a dark look in her eyes that broke Tallis' heart.

In just the short time they'd been apart, Aiven had lost a certain brightness about her, and light in her eyes. Tallis cursed the fact she hadn't been with them. If she'd just stayed with her siblings, maybe she could have spared them whatever troubles they'd seen. But then Finn would be dead, and Tallis couldn't bear the thought of losing any more than she already had.

"Finn and I made it to the Serpent's Mouth," Tallis said, deciding not to go into more detail. "We got a ship from there. What about you two? Where's Glynn? Why isn't he with you?"

Aiven exchanged a look with Osind. They both looked older than she'd last seen them. They were being forced to grow up too fast.

"We were attacked on the road," Aiven shivered and Osind pushed his chair closer to Tallis, clinging to her arm. "Glynn was on watch, so he woke us up first, while shouting to the others. The soldiers tried to fight back, but Glynn gave Kian to me and told us to go. I—we didn't want to. We didn't want to be alone, but Glynn grabbed us and ran. He took a mace from a dead soldier and smashed through Shriekers to get us away. We ran and ran, but the Shriekers were after us. Glynn told us to keep running and he stood his ground. He told us not to look back, but I did and... and..."

Aiven trailed off, tears welling in her eyes. Osind buried his face in Tallis' shoulder. Tallis pulled Aiven closer to her as well, and felt her little sister's shoulders shaking.

"They killed him, Tallis," Aiven sobbed. "They didn't turn him. They—they tore him to pieces. Captain Vaska and a few other soldiers managed to break away from the fight. He grabbed my hand, and we ran until we saw the walls of King's Harbor. I don't think anyone else from Westham made it. Things in the harbor were so crazy. Captain Vaska rushed us to the docks and got us on a ship before we could look around or ask if anyone else from Westham was there."

Tallis wrapped Aiven and Osind in her arms and held them close, planting a kiss on both of their heads. It took all her effort not to cry as well. Her whole village was gone, except for them and Finn. It was more than she felt she could take, but she couldn't let herself cry now. She wanted to be strong for her siblings.

"I should have helped him," Aiven mumbled into Tallis' shirt. "I should have made him keep running with us. Glynn was Papa's friend. He could have taken care of us."

"Shh, Aiven, shh," Tallis comforted her. "Glynn was taking care of you. That's why he did what he did. You did the right thing getting yourself and Osi away from those monsters."

"Are we safe here, Tallis?" Osi looked up at her with glistening eyes. "If they could get across the rivers, couldn't they get across the ocean too?"

Tallis' stomach clenched at the idea. "No, of course not," she told him with a confidence in her voice that she didn't truly feel. "Even if they could sail, there's no way they're getting past the fleet and those tall walls. We're safe here, Osi, I promise."

Tallis hoped more than anything that her words were true. But the Shriekers had already spread faster than anyone had thought they could. At first, they'd all thought they'd be safe east of the rivers, then when the rivers had been breached, they thought they could retreat to the harbors. Now, even the harbors were lost. What if they weren't safe in Giant's Isle either?

"Will you stay here with us?" Aiven asked.

"I can't," Tallis sighed. "I have to live up in the barracks with the other soldiers, so I can train."

"Will you come to visit us?" Osind asked.

"Of course I will," Tallis promised. "As often as I can."

"Maybe we'll see you in the keep sometimes!" Osind said. "Sometimes we bring messages or deliveries up there."

"Yes, maybe you will."

Maija returned with three steaming bowls of stew and soft warm bread and butter to go with it. It was nothing fancy, but it was filling and better than anything Tallis had eaten in what seemed like ages. The taste made her ache for her mama's cooking. A hand went to the ring that hung from her throat. Even if her parents had survived the attack, they might have been left behind at the harbor, or killed along with the rest of the survivors from Westham.

Tallis shook the thought from her mind and did her best to put on a brave face for Aiven and Osind. Their tears slowly dried, and soon, they were laughing together as though they were sharing a meal back home. When she finally left, promising again that she would be back soon, it took all her strength to drag her exhausted body back up the road to the keep and the barracks where the rest of her fellow soldiers were all already snoring.

She thought she would fall asleep immediately, but when she collapsed into her small bed, all she could see was Westham. There had only been one main road, flanked by a few shops with tradesmen's homes above them. At the center of the village was the small chapel, its wooden pillars in the entrance carved with waves, and the roof carved with stars and birds. The chapel of the Protector and the Lady and the tavern, the Coat of Arms, across the street from it were the heart and soul of Westham. Everyone knew everybody by name, and now each and every one of them were gone. Martha the baker, Quillon the barman, Embette the seamstress, Grahaim the cobbler, Glynn, Mama, Papa... Tallis couldn't help all the names running through her head.

Tears burned Tallis' eyes as she tried to remember Westham as it was, but the image of it burned, buildings broken, and bodies in the street kept breaking into her mind. She tossed and turned late into the night, the line between waking and sleeping blurring as the images of her destroyed home melded with the nightmares of her escape.

CHAPTER NINE

Moving Targets

The morning dawned, and with it, a horn blew to wake them. Tallis rubbed at her eyes. It seemed she had just laid down, and it couldn't possibly be time to get up yet. She doubted she'd slept more than a handful of hours, and her sleep was almost as exhausting as waking. It seemed like in all her dreams, she was running.

"Can't be time yet," Hemma groaned, rubbing at her freckled face with her hands.

A middle-aged woman stomped down the rows of barracks, barking for the girls to get up. The single stripe on her uniform marked her as a low-ranking officer. Her strawberry blond hair had grown out enough from its initial shear for her to trim it neatly and comb it back from her face in a way that was actually attractive.

"I am Cara, bosun of the *Storm Ghost*," the woman said once she'd gotten their attention. She stood at attention in stark contrast to Tallis and her fellow recruits, who were mostly still in various states of undress and tired confusion. "Until you separate to your ships and your captains, you will listen to me, and you will listen to Commander Avedis of the Elk Horn. He is currently waking the boys. I suggest you all begin to dress while I speak, though I expect your silence and your attention. Most of you wouldn't last a minute against a Shrieker in your current state. What little time we have to train you must be used to change that."

Tallis' first thought was that she had lasted more than a minute against a Shrieker. But there was an air to this woman's attitude that encouraged no argument, so Tallis and the others hurriedly began pulling on their uniforms. The basin of water beside Tallis' bed was icy cold, but she splashed it in her face and its briskness helped wash away her weariness.

"Commander Avedis and I will be responsible for combat training," Cara continued. "This will make up the bulk of your time. You will also receive lessons in rigging and navigation, as well as basic ship maintenance. Few of you will be responsible for these jobs unless you show unexpected proficiency, at which point the existing crew members may tutor you personally. Most of you will be merely soldiers and deckhands. Your main responsibility is to remain alive, and if you die, take as many of those monsters down with you as you can and stay dead yourself."

A few frightened murmurs echoed Cara's last words and she silenced them with an icy stare. "I will not coddle you. The reality is that many of you will die. These monsters do not take captives. To die is a better fate than to become one of them. Heed your training, work hard, and get up and ready when that horn blows *the first time*. The second time means to come out. Do as you're told, and you may increase your chances of seeing the other side of this war."

As if on cue, the horn blew a second time. Tallis was still in the middle of scrubbing at her teeth. Some girls hadn't even pulled on their jackets yet. Cara raised an eyebrow at them and sighed. She pointed a hand toward the door.

"Let's go."

Cara stomped out as sternly as she'd come in. Tallis exchanged a glance at Hemma, who was still only halfway into her uniform. Together, they joined the line of girls leaving the barracks. Tallis gritted her teeth as she shoved her arms into the sleeves of her coat. Well, at least it couldn't be that different from home, where she'd have to be up at dawn to help her father on the farm.

They entered the training yard that filled the space between the girls' and the boys' barracks. Once outside, recruits gravitated toward those they'd come with, and the separation between the boys and girls quickly vanished, to be replaced by a hard line of status. The children of noble families stood apart, looking on at the rest with an air of scorn, but Tallis knew there were no farmers or lords among the Shriekers. Once turned, a monster was a monster, no matter who they'd once been.

Finn and Harrin found their way to Tallis and Hemma's side. They looked just about as well rested as Tallis felt. They barely exchanged mumbled greetings before a tall man in an officer's uniform began to speak.

"Boys, you've already met me. Girls, I am Commander Avedis, second in command to Captain Markence of the Elk Horn," the man paced before him. "Today, we will be starting you off with wooden swords and shields. You will not be given a proper sword until you have convinced me you won't slice your own fingers off with it. Practice swords and shields may be found on the edge of the training grounds to your right. I want each one of you to pair off, and Bosun Cara and I will demonstrate some basic sword fighting exercises. Now, get your swords."

There was a bustle of movement as everyone went for the swords at once. Tallis pulled a sword out of the barrel when it was finally her turn. It was heavier than she'd expected. It must have been weighted to feel like a real sword.

"Partners, my lady?" Finn gave her a mock bow with a sweep of his own practice sword.

"I thought you'd never ask," Tallis grinned.

They took their place on the training ground, each pair of recruits facing Cara and Avedis.

"I remember Melana used to scold us if she caught us doing this with sticks in the woods," Finn said as he squared off against Tallis. Avedis showed them how to stand, with one foot forward, and one back, and Finn presented her with his side to make himself a smaller target.

"And I remember I always used to beat you," Tallis steered the conversation away from her mother and raised her own sword.

"It didn't used to be a fair fight, you grew faster than me," Finn struck as Avedis had, and Tallis blocked as Cara had. "Now I'm the taller one."

"Excuses, excuses," Tallis shook her head and launched an attack of her own, but holding back so Finn could learn to block. "Let's see if your skill has grown as well as your legs."

The training yard was soon filled with the clack of wood on wood, as well as occasional thwacks followed by grunts of wood on flesh. Despite the early autumn chill, Tallis was soon wiping sweat from her eyes between bouts.

Tallis twisted around Finn, turning his attack against him and knocking the sword from his hand into the dirt at their feet.

"I only used to win because I was taller, eh?" Tallis teased as Finn retrieved his sword.

"Alright, alright, you're just better than me," Finn rolled his eyes. "Happy now?"

"Switch partners!" Avedis called over the noise. "You need to learn how to face different fighting styles."

"Don't have too much fun without me," Finn said as he moved to their left to fight Harrin.

Tallis found herself facing a small, golden-haired boy she'd never met.

"Tallis," she said, holding out a hand.

"Cori," the boy mumbled and shook it.

They didn't have time for more of an introduction before Avedis called for them to start. The boy rarely struck out offensively unless he was told by Cara or Avedis as they made their way around the yard, commenting and correcting forms. He mostly hid behind a shield that was too large for him in a way that reminded Tallis of a turtle. Tallis went easy on the boy, who seemed like he'd rather be anywhere else. She couldn't exactly blame him for that.

Tallis found herself opposite Fadren next. The girl was young. Tallis remembered Maija mentioning Fadren's younger sister, and wondered how much older Fadren could be, and how a girl so young had ended up enlisting.

Fadren's short-cropped hair was a deep brown. A constellation of freckles was strewn across her face. She fixed Tallis with determined eyes, her wooden practice sword raised defensively. The two circled each other, each looking for a break in the other's focus to strike. Tallis pretended to stumble, and when Fadren took the moment to strike, Tallis ducked under the blow, momentum carrying her past the younger girl. Tallis tapped on Fadren's back with her wooden sword.

"I hope the Shriekers aren't so cunning," Fadren laughed.

"But you could be," Tallis winked. "Find advantages where you can."

"Maybe being a barmaid won't be so useless after all," Fadren raised her sword again. "At least I've got good practice dodging others in a crowded room."

"Use what you have," Tallis shrugged.

For a moment, while Fadren collected herself, Tallis caught the gaze of a woman she hadn't seen before, leaning against the walls of one of the barracks, watching the recruits. A twisted scar that looked fairly new took up most of the left side of her face and gave her a permanent scowl. Unlike some other women, she'd taken no effort to neaten up the scruff of her regulation-short black hair. Strands of white in her hair and creases at the corners of her eyes suggested she was older than her strong physique implied.

The woman's uniform showed her to be one of the fleet's captains. But since she stood in the shadows, Tallis couldn't make out the insignia that would have told her which ship this captain belonged to. It seemed the woman had been watching her, and before Tallis turned back to her fight with Fadren, the woman gave her a quick nod.

Tallis tried her best to ignore the woman, and the confusion over why a captain would be watching her directly. Fadren had already raised her sword again and Tallis mirrored her. The two went back and forth, striking and parrying. Fadren was smaller than Tallis, but she hadn't been lying about having practice dodging. She was quick, and now that she knew to look out for tricks, she matched Tallis fairly well. By the time Avedis called out for a quick break, they were both sweating and breathing heavily.

Tallis and Fadren sat side by side on the edge of the yard, taking long swigs from skins of water. The captain who had been watching Tallis had disappeared from the yard, and Tallis did her best to put thoughts of the woman out of her mind. It could have been merely coincidence that their gazes had met. This certainly wasn't the first captain Tallis had seen come to appraise the new recruits. Instead, she turned to Fadren.

"Your mother asked me about you last night," Tallis said, hoping she wouldn't sound rude. "She's worried about you. You seem a little young to enlist."

"I'm seventeen," Fadren said, crossing her arms defiantly. "The twins are younger than me."

"What have you got to gain from being here?" Tallis asked. "It seems you did it willingly, not out of necessity. There must be safer jobs you could do."

Fadren stared at the wooden sword leaning on the bench next to them. "My sister. I've done so much to help raise her. I couldn't bear the idea of her growing up in a world where she has to fear the dead. I want her to be safe."

"What about your father?" Tallis asked before she could think to stop herself. She hoped it wouldn't offend Fadren.

"We don't know where he is," Fadren's shoulders slumped. "He was stationed aboard the Star Bird, which hasn't been seen since the fall of King's Harbor."

"I'm sorry."

"That's the other reason I joined," Fadren straightened, determination erasing the despair that had weighed her down. "I want to find the Star Bird, and my father."

Their conversation was interrupted by Avedis calling them back out to the training yard. They switched partners and continued the drills he gave them, eventually switching from wooden swords to real swords to get used to their different weight, but careful not to actually strike each other.

By the time they were done, Tallis' sword arm ached and her back and hips were stiff from constantly moving to both defend herself, and attack her opponent. The soldiers said a moving target was harder to hit, but being a moving target for hours day after day was exhausting.

They trained from morning until night with only brief pauses for unexciting meals between work and sleep. Separated by barracks assignments, Tallis only saw Finn at meals and on the training yard. At meals, they often focused more on shoveling food into their mouths than talking, and in training, the older soldiers would chide them for side conversations.

They continued to be separated into pairs to train dueling, moving on from the fundamentals of sword-fighting to more complicated maneuvers. Tallis wondered at the point of learning one-on-one dueling, as it was unlikely they'd ever face just one Shrieker. But few of the recruits had ever even touched a sword. Many were from occupations that hadn't even given them the upper body strength Tallis had taken for granted growing up on the farm. There were children of healers, scribes, merchants, and other such jobs that required more of the mind than the body. Not to mention children of nobility who had enlisted, dreaming of glory, or orphans raised by priests and priestesses and who had lived lives of relative comfort compared to some of their peers.

There were more rules, instructions, and skills than Tallis thought she could ever absorb, but slowly she began to adjust. Blisters turned to callouses, sore muscles strengthened, and she quickly learned that the fact she'd sailed a boat at all already put her ahead of many of her peers. While the others were struggling with the basics of rigging, Tallis was able to move on to more of the specifics of a tall ship.

Tallis continued to see the black-haired captain watching the training yard. While other captains came and went, Tallis never noticed any of them paying attention to her, but she kept catching the eye of this woman. Tallis wondered who she was and what she wanted, but was left with little time or energy to spare for conjecture.

Days passed in a haze of the training yard and nights collapsed onto her hard bunk too tired to care. In rare spare time, she would return to the Crow's Nest to see Aiven and Osind. Sometimes, Fadren would accompany her to visit her mother and sister. It seemed fitting. Maija could take care of her siblings, and in return, Tallis promised herself she would look after Fadren when the fighting started.

Like the streambeds that filled each year with snowmelt and spring rain, but with summer dried to sand, the steady flow of ships from the mainland ran dry. Tallis refused to imagine what this meant and instead poured all her energy into her training, drowning out the rip tide of thoughts of everything she'd left behind that threatened any moment she paused too long to drag her beyond a point of return.

CHAPTER TEN

Sons of the Sky

Finn sat up, restless, in the yard of the barracks. The sun had sunk below the horizon hours ago. Now, the sky was dark and starless, foreboding an upcoming day of training soaked to the skin with rain. He should have taken advantage of the chance to rest, but a thought had been nagging at the back of his mind since they'd landed in Giant's Isle and tonight it wouldn't let him sleep.

Tallis hadn't said a word about what she'd seen while crossing the Nightmare Bridge. There hadn't been much chance since they'd begun training, and Finn's own mouth felt dry and words stuck in his throat when he thought of his crossing. Still, he ached to know what she'd seen, what she'd heard, and whether it was anything like what he'd experienced.

What kept a knife in Finn's gut was not that he'd felt the urge to jump as he crossed, but that he'd felt a desire, almost a need, to go back once he'd reached the shore. At first he'd attributed the feeling to his concern for Tallis, doubt creeping in that she would make it, and that somehow he could save her if he turned back. But that aching longing still lingered at the back of his mind. There was an unshakable feeling that he'd made a mistake, and that the Guardian had been right. It would have been easier to stay.

When he did manage to sleep, Finn awoke with screams echoing in his ears, and fire at the edges of his vision. How many people had been left at the Serpent's Mouth? Who might have boarded this ship in his place had he and Tallis not pushed to the front, brandishing their recruitment papers? Finn felt he could almost put a face to this person. They were young, too young to have enlisted but too old to have been boarded first with the children. They would have lied, said they were older than they looked and begged the soldiers to take them. Desperate for help against the Shriekers, they would have taken this nameless child aboard. In saving his own life, Finn wondered if he had inadvertently doomed another.

"How many people have you outlived, Finley?" the Guardian had asked him. *"Your parents, even Tallis' parents who all but took you in. How many fell in Westham? How many more will continue to fall and how many will have your blade at their throat? Tallis is here because of you. If she never joins you on the far shore, her blood will be on your hands. Your hands will be dripping ere this war ends. Spare yourself the guilt, and spare those whose place you seek to take in finding refuge on the Giant's Isle."*

Finn looked down at his hands, remembering his blade cutting into the palms of the refugee woman. She had relented and stayed on board the *Lady's Kiss* because he'd dropped his sword and gotten her to understand the situation they were in. Would a different soldier have done the same? Giant's Isle was not an end to the journey, only the start of a far more dangerous one wearing the colors of the king's infantry. But the Guardian had been wrong. He and Tallis had made it this far, and fighting the Shriekers would mean saving lives. The blood on his hands would be the black blood of monsters, not the red blood of people.

"Brooding again?"

Cori plopped down onto a bench near Finn.

"Following me again?" Finn almost laughed.

The boy he'd met aboard the *Lady's Kiss* had taken the bunk beside Finn's. As days of training wore on, Finn felt he saw more of Cori than he did of Tallis. This was not the first night Finn had left the barracks to escape his nightmares. The first, he had tripped over his own boots and Cori had woken and followed him out, claiming he needed the air.

"I can go," Cori looked almost hurt.

"No," Finn protested. His heart yearned for company, but it was Tallis he wanted to see.

Tallis had begun to grow distant. She excelled in training in a way that astounded him and earned herself a reputation. Everyone, save for the noble born who felt too good for her, wanted to pair with her. Finn felt left behind as she flourished in their new home, while he still floundered. Cori had become a comforting presence on the training yard, taking his focus away from Tallis and the grace with which she moved through their exercises.

"Tell me about King's Harbor," Finn said, hoping to take his mind off his own thoughts, "and about the groups you grew up with."

"King's Harbor is almost as big as Giant's Isle, if you take away the keep," Cori began, seeming to sense Finn's need for a distraction. "I knew every street. The Sons of the Sky and the Daughters of the Sea have the run of the place. Sure, the priests at the chapels would help us with food and shelter when we needed it, but mostly we took care of our own."

"How old were you when you joined the Sons?"

"Only an infant," Cori explained. "I never knew my parents. The groups got their names from the reasoning that those of us with no family were the children of the gods. Our duty was to protect each other, and others on the streets, because we were brothers and sisters, and families should look out for one another. Too bad you weren't in King's Harbor, perhaps you could have joined us, instead of living with your uncle."

"I wish I could have," Finn admitted. Though he'd told Cori little about Sefton, it was enough for his new friend to guess at how it had been. Westham had been home, but this brotherhood sounded better than his uncle. Without thinking, Finn blurted out more than he had ever said to anyone but Tallis. "I don't imagine the children of the gods had uncles who came home drunk and beat them."

Cori sat in stunned silence for a moment. When he responded, his voice was soft and solemn. "No, we didn't. Sure, there were hardships, but we looked out for each other."

"So they raised you then?" Finn asked and Cori nodded. "You haven't mentioned any adults in the Sons. What happened when you grew up?"

"Various things," Cori shrugged. "Some found apprenticeships in trades. Others joined up with the fleet. The name of the Sons of the Sky holds a weight in King's Harbor. It helps the older boys find things to do with their lives."

"It sounds like a good system."

"It certainly didn't work for everyone, and it had flaws, but for those it did work for, it sure beat being alone," Cori said.

"So what happened to them?"

Even in the darkness, Finn could see Cori's pained expression. "I had eleven brothers. Three of them went West with the first wave of attacks and never came back. When King's Harbor was assaulted, four of the older boys stood their ground so I could escape with the three youngest, along with a few other children in our charge. I was ready to do the same if I had to. We managed to force our way to the ships because of the children. Another boy and I were the only ones old enough to enlist, so we did or else we'd have been left behind. Tern was stationed on the Star Bird, which hasn't been heard from since King's Harbor was lost. My younger brothers, Piper and Wren, stayed with the kids to take care of them. I had eleven brothers. Now I have only two."

"I'm sorry."

"Everyone's lost someone."

"Doesn't make it any easier," Finn tried to imagine the loss of nine brothers. He'd never even had one. Aiven and Osind were the closest he had to siblings. If they hadn't made it to Giant's Isle, he'd have felt even more certain the Guardian had been right.

"Neither does sitting up feeling sorry for yourself when a storm is coming and we have training in the morning," Cori bounced up from his bench. "Come back inside."

"Yes, sir," Finn rolled his eyes and got up to follow Cori back to the barracks.

When they got inside, Finn undressed as quietly as he could so as not to disturb the others. Cori slipped into his bunk almost fully dressed. Finn realized he'd never seen his friend changing, though most of the boys had gotten comfortable enough and tired enough to be beyond caring about propriety. Briefly, Finn wondered how a boy who grew up with eleven brothers could be shy about such things, but he put it out of his mind when rain began a sudden percussive fanfare on the roof over their heads. He fell asleep dreaming of muddy fields and sodden grass, a welcome relief from his dreams of fire.

Captain of the Rose

Tallis gulped down water as she caught her breath in the corner of the training yard. As she rested, she watched the other recruits bashing at each other, their wooden swords clattering. A brief smile touched her face as she remembered herself and Finn, running through the fields outside of Westham with other children of the village. Mock tourneys would be arranged, often with the prize being a kiss from a pretty girl sitting out as the "princess", or some treat bought at the market. Tallis had excelled at these competitions, beating down the other children with her stick sword to claim the title of Golden Knight, though she'd never cared for a kiss as a prize whether it was a prince or princess sitting to the side. She'd done this often enough that some of the other children had begun complaining and she started losing on purpose to give others a chance.

But here, Tallis found herself straining with everything she had to perform her best. Occasionally, she would go easy on Hemma or Fadren, but only to help them learn their weaknesses and find their strengths. This was no game, and when they sailed, their swords would not be wood, nor would the swords of their enemies. A false move or slip would have far greater consequences than a bruise or a skinned knee. They would not go home to their mothers at the end of the day to have cuts bandaged and torn clothes mended. When they were children, failure meant a damaged ego. Now, failure could mean death.

A commotion nearby drew Tallis' attention. Cori had had the misfortune of being paired in dueling with Vilmos, a lord's son who looked nearly twice his size. Tallis had done her best to avoid Vilmos and his friends, and for the most part, they'd done the same. The children of nobles did not mix well with the refugee recruits. These lord's sons did not understand the stakes like the refugees did. To them, this was still a game, a way to win glory and the favor of the king, perhaps set themselves on the path to command.

Vilmos struck a heavy blow that knocked Cori's sword from his hand. The boy raised his shield just in time for Vilmos to tackle him, then went sprawling into the mud of the yard. Rather than letting up, as was expected when one's opponent went down, Vilmos kept up the attack. He launched blow after blow with his sword. Cori caught some with his shield, knocking him further back and down any time he tried to get up. Some landed on his arms or legs with a thwack that made Tallis shudder.

"Yield!" he cried. "I yield!"

"Should have stayed on the mainland, whoreson," Vilmos sneered, not relenting in his attacks. "Scum like you befoul our fleet. Crawl back to the docks with the rest of your filth, bastard."

"Please, I yield," the boy pleaded again.

Tallis glanced around. Their instructors were too busy tutoring others to have noticed this scuffle. Without thinking, Tallis grabbed her practice sword she'd set down and stormed in the direction of the fight, standing straight and using her full height. She was tall for a girl, possibly taller even than Vilmos, and hoped she could intimidate him into backing off.

Vilmos raised his sword to deal the boy another blow, but Tallis stepped in and parried.

"Pardon me, my *lord,*" Tallis put as much malice into the word as she could muster. "Mind if I cut in? Or are you afraid of an actual challenge?"

Vilmos stared at her a moment in silent shock, before recovering his composure. He laughed, and his friends who stood nearby joined in the laughter. "What, you think a skinny village girl like you can do better than that boy? What were you, a farmer? Go back to your fields and let real soldiers do the work of decimating these monsters."

"Those monsters burned my fields," Tallis snarled. "I've seen them. I've fought them, and I'm still alive. Can you say the same, little lordling?"

Vilmos seemed to stutter a moment, unsure what to make of Tallis' words, but a hot anger soon replaced his confusion. "You should show your betters some respect, *girl.* That you're here at all shows how far standards have dropped. You should show us some gratitude."

"Forgive me, sir, I wasn't aware you were the one in charge of recruitment guidelines," Tallis replied sarcastically. "I was under the impression that the king made those."

By now, Tallis could see that this scuffle was no longer going unnoticed. Other recruits had paused to see what the argument was about.

"I see you have a sharp tongue," Vilmos replied coolly. "But is your sword as sharp?"

Vilmos gestured to one of his friends, who grabbed one of the metal training swords and tossed it to him. Vilmos hefted it into a defensive position and stood off against Tallis. The sword was not combat sharpened, but would still do far more damage than a wooden sword. Tallis considered backing off, reluctant to bite off more than she could chew, but she could feel the eyes of other recruits on her, and her pride kept her feet where they were.

"Tallis! Here!"

Tallis turned to see Harrin had grabbed another sword like the one Vilmos had held. He tossed it and it landed with a thump in the hard packed sand at her feet, hilt toward her.

"Stop this, both of you," one of the soldiers training them stepped forward.

"Remember which captain you're sworn to, sir," Vilmos eyed the soldier. "By my father's authority, I will see this insult answered."

The soldier threw up his hands. "Just don't give her an injury that will impede her fighting. Even your father wouldn't protect you if the king lost a soldier for a petty squabble."

The soldier's casual indifference and confidence that she would lose fueled Tallis' fire to win even more than Vilmos misusing his status. Tallis knew that there would always be people above her using that power against her. But if she let Vilmos win, as she'd let boys who complained loudly enough to annoy her when she was a child, then he would just continue to walk over people like her and Cori with no chance of retribution.

Go easy on him at first, Tallis thought. *Let him underestimate me. Get cocky. I'll show him what a farmer's daughter can do.*

Without taking her eyes off Vilmos, Tallis snatched the metal training sword Harrin had thrown to her. The last time she'd had a proper fight, her opponent had been trying to kill her. Last time, her opponent hadn't been human. She could manipulate a person. Against a Shrieker, she had nothing but her brute force and skill with a blade. Now, she had all of Vilmos' prejudices to use against him. He'd made it clear he thought she was weak and unworthy of her place.

Before Tallis had the chance to settle herself, Vilmos rushed at her, striking hard. Tallis lifted her sword in an intentionally weak parry, barely turning the blow away from her body. She stumbled away from the boy, putting on a show of catching her balance.

"Pathetic," Vilmos shook his head. "I almost pity you."

Tallis squared off against Vilmos without a word. Her determination to knock this lord's son off his high horse grew with every word out of his mouth.

Vilmos struck again and again, never relenting the offensive, and Tallis made no effort to push past his attacks. She remained on the defensive, watching his movements and waiting for him to make a mistake. But he was not another farmer's boy for her to beat in a field. There was skill and deliberation behind his movements to almost match his ego. These past few days had not been the beginning of his training. Even turning the blows away began to take a strain on Tallis and she wondered if she had made a grave mistake.

With a yell, Vilmos brought down a blow harder than the others. Tallis felt the force of it through her aching hands. For a brief moment, their eyes met and Tallis could see rage in the boy's cold eyes. He hooked his blade's crossguard with hers so she couldn't pull away fast enough when he rammed his shoulder into hers with surprising strength. Having been focused on his eyes, Tallis had failed to notice his feet until one had already swept her legs out from under her.

Tallis felt the air fly from her lungs as she hit the ground hard. But the pain of the blow was nothing compared to the wound it dealt to her pride. If she gave up now, Vilmos would never let it go and after watching her get taken down, no recruit would stand up to his torments.

"Had enough yet, farm girl?"

Farm girl. From his mouth it was an insult, but she was sure she'd endured more in a day working for her father than this lordling had ever experienced in his life.

Use it against him, her papa's voice came suddenly in her mind.

Tallis tightened her grip around her sword and rolled over into a crouch to put some distance between herself and Vilmos, feigning more pain than she felt. For a moment, her eyes met Finn's across the yard. He stood at Cori's side, an arm protectively around the boy's shoulders. Finn shook his head, his eyes pleading. Tallis gave him a wink that Vilmos couldn't see and she saw Finn deflate and roll his eyes, exasperated with her stubbornness.

"Just give up already, or are you really as dumb as you look?" Vilmos braced himself, preparing for a charge.

If a bull charges, Papa's voice spoke again, *use his momentum against him. Side step so he charges past you. Only if you can't get away, hit him with something, hard as you can. A branch, an axe handle, a rock. Anything that makes him realize you're not an easy target. Make him not want to mess with you.*

What was Vilmos now if not a charging bull? Even the set of his shoulders and the way he planted his feet reminded her of a bull squaring off. She could see Vilmos was ready to charge, and he was big enough he'd knock her right back off her feet if she tried to stand her ground. But if she could just be faster than him and throw him off balance, she might just gain the upper hand.

Tallis raised herself to her knees, seeming ready to stand, but instead readying herself to spring to the side. The sound of Vilmos and his friends' laughter sent daggers of rage piercing through her heart. She wanted to stand, hold her ground, and face him. But Tallis knew to have any chance of taking him down, she would have to play her own game.

Vilmos charged, exactly as she'd anticipated he would, throwing his weight into it to build momentum. If she rose to block, his force could send her flying, and this time, she wasn't sure getting up on her own would be so easy.

Tallis waited, and the moments seemed to stretch as her eyes met his, blue and cold as ice. Despite all Papa's lessons and warnings, Tallis had never actually faced a charging bull. She'd known which fields to skirt and which were safe to cross, but she'd seen others less wise nearly pay with their lives for crossing the wrong pasture. Vilmos was not even twice her size. She risked her pride, not her life in this field, yet the stakes felt just as high.

Vilmos did not break his charge, but lowered his shoulders to throw his weight behind the impact he anticipated between his shield and her body. Tallis lunged, not up at him as he'd expected but pirouetting to his side. She threw the force of her spin into the swing of her sword. Suddenly faced with air where she had been just a moment before, Vilmos stumbled, his weight and momentum turned against him. Tallis slammed the broad side of her sword down across his shoulders with all her strength. His balance already compromised, the force of the blow sent Vilmos sprawling into the dirt.

Tallis could not help a moment of smug satisfaction as Vilmos struggled to pick himself up. She imagined the bruise that would blossom across his shoulders and thought she could have done more and called it a just reward for his treatment of Cori.

"You'll pay!" Vilmos' voice trembled with rage as he dragged himself up. He raised his sword again to lunge, but a bright flash of metal broke through the space between Tallis and Vilmos. As quick as it had appeared, the other sword vanished into a sheath and Vilmos' went flying from his hand.

"Had you been fighting in earnest," the intruder said, "you would be dead, Vilmos Howin. Take this as a lesson, if you are capable. Brute force is rarely the surest path to victory."

The stranger's voice dripped with scorn. Tallis could only see their back, but noted the captain's stripes upon their uniform with alarm. Her fight with Vilmos had escalated far beyond training. What would a captain have to say about a brawl? No matter what Tallis said, she was sure any captain would take the word of a lord's son over that of a farmer's daughter.

"Go clean yourself up, boy," the captain spat, venom in their voice. Tallis blinked in shock, and she saw Vilmos do the same. She'd only ever heard Vilmos addressed with respect, even by most officers. The shock was enough that Vilmos turned on his heel and limped away with only a backward glance that stabbed as sharp as daggers into Tallis.

The captain turned and Tallis' amazement doubled to see it was the same woman she'd noticed watching her many times before. Who was she that Vilmos, who constantly spouted against women in the fleet, would obey her without question? Most captains ranked below a lord's son off the battlefield, but clearly not this woman. She raised a hand to point at Tallis, and the intensity of her storm-gray eyes almost stopped Tallis' heart. "I want a word with you. The rest of you go back to your training. This show is over."

Like sheep before a shepherd's dog, the recruits who'd accumulated to watch the fight began to scramble out of the yard. Tallis remained rooted where she stood, transfixed by this captain whose words carried command with an ease that demanded obedience. As the training yard emptied, Tallis examined the woman more closely. Her stormy eyes and fine-boned face suggested that in her youth, she could have commanded men with her beauty alone. But now, lines of age and wear creased her brow, and the new scar gave her an aura of power that transcended youthful beauty.

"So, you are Tallis, then?" the captain asked, though her tone implied she already knew. There was a hardness to her voice, but none of the venom it had held when she'd addressed Vilmos. Still, Tallis wasn't sure she wanted to know why a captain already knew who she was.

"Yes," Tallis replied, but quickly remembered who she was addressing and pulled a hasty salute, fist over heart, "Captain."

"Come, walk with me, Tallis," the woman beckoned then began to leave the yard at a brisk pace that forced Tallis into a jog to not be left behind. "I am *your* Captain. I saw the name on my roster. Tell me, who is your father?"

Understanding dawned on Tallis in a flash as quick as Eiran had disarmed Vilmos. Captain Eiran Garray had been a high-ranking noble before she'd been a captain, and was high in the king's council. Only those of the king's own blood might dare defy her. Papa had told stories of her with unconcealed reverence.

"His name was Nevra, Captain."

Eiran stopped suddenly and turned to face her, a look of concern evident in her eyes. "Was?"

"The Shriekers got him," Tallis hesitated, her changed papa's face haunting her memory. "He's dead now."

"May waves take his bones," Eiran's voice held unexpected, yet genuine sadness. "I knew your father. When I saw the name Larke, I thought you might be his child, and when I saw you in the training yard, I was almost certain. You look so much like he did when I knew him. He spoke of you often. I am Eiran, we served together in the Kerethi war. Your father was a good man."

"Captain Eiran, I am honored to meet you," Tallis stuttered, awe mixing with nerves to compromise her voice. "My father always spoke highly of you."

"It seems someone taught you your manners well." Eiran turned away and continued down the path out of the yard and toward the inner wall. "So, Tallis, tell me, how is it you got all the competence and left none for your fellow recruits?"

Tallis was glad Eiran had turned away so couldn't see the flush of confusion and embarrassment that crept onto her face. "I don't understand, Captain. I'm no blademaster. In a fair duel, Vilmos would have won."

"The Shriekers won't give you a fair duel," Eiran glanced over at her. "Nor will most enemies you face in a real fight. Duels are for children. You gave Vilmos a mild taste of what he'll face when the fleet sails. Personally, I'd say you did him a favor back there. That charge was foolish. Vilmos could make a good soldier, with some discipline, but today he let his pride get the better of him."

"So did I," Tallis admitted. "I shouldn't have done that."

"Vilmos will never learn to be a good soldier, or a good man for that matter, if no one ever teaches him humility," Eiran said. "You stood up for a fellow recruit and held your ground against petty insults. Such pride is to be commended. It is not always a vice. Take mine, for example. I am proud to be the captain of the *Storm Ghost*, and the first woman to join the fleet. The *Storm Ghost* is a good ship, and I'm glad to welcome you to her crew."

Tallis was lost for words. She'd expected a reprimand or even strict punishment for having dueled with Vilmos. Eiran was nothing like Tallis had grown to expect from senior officers.

"I... thank you."

"I should be the one thankful for you," Eiran raised an eyebrow. "At least I've got one good fighter on my crew. I was afraid I was to be stuck with green children and sea-worn elders. The *Storm Ghost* isn't one of those pretty flagships that get their first pick of the crop. She's small and fast, so gets sent out scouting or in the first wave of attacks when the fleet sails. Fancy words for a pawn to test the enemy's strength before sending in the big guns."

"Thought you said she was a good ship," Tallis muttered under her breath.

Eiran laughed. "Why do you think she's still sailing and I'm still captain? She's fast enough to turn tail and get out of the way when things get too dirty, or get places the big ships can't."

"Sorry, ma'am."

"First lesson, kid," Eiran leaned toward her, all traces of her smile gone. "The sea's a rough place. The fleet's not like the King's army. Out there, there's no time for pretty manners. Preened and proper soldiers soon learn a boat's too small for perfectly timed marching and the wind's too strong for posturing. If I'm to make a proper sailor out of you, you have to lose that sweet face of yours and your well-learned 'ma'ams'. You call me by name, or you call me 'Captain' if you must."

"Why are you telling me this... Captain?" Tallis asked hesitantly.

For a moment, Tallis thought something softened in Eiran's eyes and she saw underneath the hardened captain's mask, but it disappeared after only a moment.

"I've reviewed my crew," Eiran began. "I'm in need of a new first officer. The last one, well, the last one is going to be one of those we're fighting. I want you to take his place."

Tallis gaped at the captain, unable to comprehend.

"Put away that fish face," Eiran rolled her eyes. "You get sick of fish fast out there. You may think you're just a little farmer's girl with no place amongst pampered high-borns who never had to do a proper day's hard work growing up, but I say command could use a few more like you. Won't take the position for granted and won't complain about the ship's ropes ripping up soft hands."

Tallis looked down at her hands, tanned a deep brown and rough from working the farm, now calloused from weeks with a sword in them.

"I know you've seen me watching before today," Eiran continued. "Sure, you're not the only competent fighter, and I'm sure there's more than Vilmos who could put you in the dirt, but you've done more than train your own skills. I've watched you helping your friends, leading by example, and today, put yourself at risk to defend another."

"No one else was paying any attention," Tallis began to protest.

"You didn't have to do a thing," Eiran said. "There are so many people who looked the other way. You really think you're the only one who noticed? You could be out there for no one but yourself, just trying to survive, and I wouldn't fault you for it in the slightest. But you're not, and that's why we're talking right now. Vilmos has been 'training' far longer than you have, but has always boasted more than he's learned. You took him down and showed far more than skill with a blade. You showed a willingness to stand up for those weaker than you, against those who would abuse their strength and power. And you showed poise and cool under pressure. You did more than fight well, you fought *cleverly*. I saw every slip you made was calculated to your advantage. These are traits I need in my first officer."

"But, I've never sailed a ship on the sea in my life," Tallis pointed out. She could feel the flush in her face growing with each word of praise out of the captain's mouth.

"Thing is, I've got crew on my ship who have," Eiran pressed on, unaffected by Tallis' protests. "And I've got a bunch of fresh faces who've got no idea what they're doing. I need those with experience at their posts so my boat goes where I want it to. You'll learn your way around soon enough. But what I need is someone who's got the strength of will in them to do what needs to be done."

"And standing up to a bully makes you think that's me," Tallis said, raising an eyebrow, certain there was more to this than the captain was letting on.

Eiran regarded her a moment before continuing, brow wrinkled. "The soldiers asked how you survived being left behind on the wrong side of the Serpent. I don't buy the tale you gave them. I was there at Serpent's Mouth. I saw the riots. I saw the Foggy running red with blood and bodies. There's no way you could have sailed that river from Westham and survived."

Tallis tensed, afraid the captain would report her for a liar.

"It's fine," Eiran shook her head. "The army doesn't need to know your secrets. But if I'm to trust you and make you my second in command, I need to know the truth. How did you and that other boy survive?"

Tallis squirmed under the captain's questioning gaze. She'd tried to block what she'd seen and done to get here out of her mind, but in her sleep her father's twisted face would still attack her and the morphing mist of the bridge would swirl through nightmares. But Tallis felt she could trust this woman. Papa had known her, and had only ever had praise. For that at least, Tallis felt she owed her something.

"Tallis?"

"We—my friend Finley and I—went south by foot along the Serpent, and kept to the woods to hide," Tallis explained, voice shaky.

"And the river? How did you cross?"

"The Nightmare Bridge."

Eiran blinked and shook her head, stunned. "But no one..."

"We did," Tallis said. "It was that or worse."

Eiran sat back on her bench and examined her with a more appreciative eye. "Now I am impressed. This Finley, he's not on the *Storm Ghost*."

"He was assigned to the *Lady's Kiss*."

Eiran made a disapproving grunt. "A shame."

"Why's that?"

Eiran shrugged. "Admiral Grayston—the captain of the *Lady's Kiss*—and I don't quite see eye to eye. But that's not important now. I can understand why you'd lie about how you got here. That's not a tale to tell to just anyone."

"And not a tale I care to tell more of," Tallis admitted. "Captain."

Eiran nodded. "Then you needn't say more. I've heard enough to know you can handle whatever we'll face out there. If you accept, I'll propose your appointment to the king."

"I don't know if I'm ready," Tallis said.

"You survived the Nightmare Bridge yet now you're afraid of a promotion?" Eiran laughed.

"It's one thing to run and survive, another to be responsible for others."

"You're already a leader," Eiran said. "I've seen you in the yard. Younger recruits look up to you, and even those your age or older respect you. You learn quickly and you help others who learn slower. If I can see potential in you now, then my crew will see it too if you show them. As my second, your training would transfer directly to me, and I won't throw you to the wolves on day one."

Tallis thought for a moment. Command would mean hard work, but it would also mean security. She could rest easier knowing that they wouldn't decide at any moment that she was unneeded and would be thrown out to the refugees. Or worse, sent back to the mainland if they decided there were too many mouths to feed. The riots and the fact no more refugees had come since she'd landed in Giant's Isle had convinced her the capital meant to survive, and would do what it had to, no matter the cost. Now, she was close to the bottom of the order. Rising in rank would mean raising her chances of staying alive. It also meant she'd be in a better position to protect Aiven and Osind.

"I'll do it," Tallis considered for a moment, wondering if she was in a position to do what she was contemplating.

"I sense a 'but'," Eiran raised an eyebrow.

"I have a sister and brother," Tallis explained. "They're too young to fight. Right now, they're working as errand runners. But I'm worried about them. I want to know they'll be safe and cared for when I leave Giant's Isle."

"I have the ear of the king, perhaps more so than many captains," Eiran said. "Tell me their names and where to find them and I'll see what I can do about getting them somewhere safer than where they are now."

"Aiven and Osind, they're with Maija at the Crow's Nest."

"That name... Osind."

"My papa named him after a friend of his. He died in the war with the Kerethi."

Eiran nodded. It seemed she would say more about it, but instead she said "I'll take the matter to the king then. For now, you'll stay here and continue your training, but you'll hear from me again soon. Until then, it's best this matter stays quiet. You're not a commander yet. You'll still take what orders you're given by senior officers."

"I understand."

"Good," Eiran stood and made to leave. She paused in the doorway and turned back. "Understand I'm putting a fair deal of faith in you, Tallis. Don't disappoint me."

"I'll do my best, Captain," Tallis promised.

"I'm sure you will," Eiran smiled and left Tallis to her work.

CHAPTER TWELVE

The Silver Fish

Finn lay awake, staring at the woodwork of the ceiling. It was quiet, save for Cori's light snoring from the cot beside him and the breathing of his fellow soldiers. He hadn't seen Tallis return after being led away by a captain, and his mind raced with worry over what kind of reprimand she might receive for fighting a lord's son. Giving up on sleep, Finn slipped out of his bunk as quietly as he could and pulled on his boots and jacket. He left the barracks and made for the inner wall. Only a handful of people were up at this hour, manning the gate and patrolling the wall. None of them paid him much mind. He found an isolated corner he'd come to before and curled up with his back against a rampant facing out over the harbor.

The sound of the ocean crashing against the outer wall and the wind whipping through the city were all that broke the silence of the night. Finn looked up at the stars to see the Silver Fish constellation shining bright above him. Its eye pointed west no matter how far from Okaesa one sailed. Now, it pointed toward the mainland, toward home.

"Finn? Is that you?"

Finn jumped and turned to find Tallis standing behind him. Between training and the separation of men and women's barracks, they hadn't had a moment to themselves since they'd reached the Serpent's Mouth what seemed like an eternity ago.

"What are you doing here?" Tallis asked.

"I could ask the same," he said with a grin and patted the ground next to him. "I come here often. It's a good spot to escape when I can't sleep."

"You have a snorer in your barracks too?" Tallis joked.

"It's not home," Finn said, glancing over at her. "I miss you."

Tallis rested her head on his shoulder, but didn't answer. Finn stroked the fuzz of her shorn hair with a rough calloused hand.

"You okay? That was some nasty fight you got yourself into," Finn's voice wavered between teasing and concern.

"I bet my body is less bruised than Vilmos' ego," Tallis smirked. Finn sighed, remembering every scuffle Tallis had gotten herself into and always dusted herself off after, ready for more.

"That captain who broke up the fight. What did she want? I hope you didn't get too harsh a reprimand."

"Quite the opposite," Tallis sat up straight again and her knees began to bounce, something Finn knew meant she was nervous. "She asked me to be her first officer."

"What?" Finn pulled away and stared at her in disbelief. The divide between barracks had already felt like a rift opening between them. Tallis moving to the officer's quarters would be an impassable chasm.

"That captain was Eiran Garray, the same captain I'm to serve under," Tallis explained. "She's been watching us, and it seems I've impressed her. She offered me the promotion, and I accepted."

"Tallis, just being on the ships is bad enough, now you'll have a big target embroidered on your uniform saying you're important."

"You think the Shriekers care who they target?" Tallis asked. "You think it makes any difference what uniform I'm wearing? If Shriekers get on the ship it'll be kill or be killed and maybe being in command will actually give me a better chance. I won't be just another sailor that can be sacrificed. They'll want me to survive."

"Will they?" Finley shook his head. "You think those highborn asses like Vilmos will like this assignment? Haven't you noticed the way they look at us?"

"I don't care what those other officers think," Tallis asserted. "Eiran offered the position to me, and hers is the opinion that matters. And in exchange, she's offered to find more secure positions for my brother and sister."

Finn sighed and his shoulders sagged, knowing nothing he could say to dissuade Tallis would matter more than Aiven and Osind. In her position, he'd have made the exact same decision if it meant they'd be safe.

"Please just promise you'll be careful."

"No, I was thinking I'd just throw myself at the Shriekers," Tallis forced a smile and elbowed him in the ribs.

"You did before," Finn reminded her.

"That was different," Tallis' smile faded.

"I'm sorry. I know why you did it."

"It's fine."

"I thought that, if we were just soldiers, maybe once all this was done," Finn said, "we could leave, go home together."

"Home?" Tallis glared at him. "Our home was burned to the ground. Almost everyone is dead. Here is the only home we have left now."

"Things could be rebuilt," Finn replied defensively.

"I can't go back," Tallis sighed, and the words felt like a dagger. "If I go back, I'll see Mama, Papa, Glynn, and everyone else who didn't make it here everywhere we went. Aiven told me she and Osind are the only refugees from Westham who made it to King's Harbor. There is no Westham without those people. Westham is as dead as they are."

Finn shrank back against the wall. The news that he, Tallis, and her siblings were all that were left of their entire village hit him like a fall from a horse. He felt as though all the breath had been knocked from his lungs and his stomach twisted into knots.

"I— I didn't know."

"I'm sorry, Finn," Tallis pulled him into a crushing hug. "I would have told you, but there's never any time."

Finn buried his face in her shoulder and he drew shuddering breaths. He wished he could weep, or scream, but his eyes remained dry and instead he felt only cold numbness seeping through his limbs. Sefton's face surfaced in his mind, and for a moment he felt guilty he felt more grief over Glynn than his own blood family. But Finn couldn't bring himself to feel anything but numbness that the man who'd housed and raised him was gone. Nevra and Glynn had done so much more for him than Sefton ever had.

"So, you'll leave for the luxury of the palace and I'll be left alone," Finn couldn't keep the bitterness from seeping into his voice.

"I'm doing it for Aiven and Osind," Tallis snapped. "I'm all they have and I'm going to do anything I can for them, and you don't get to make me feel guilty for that."

The bitterness continued to boil inside him, the only heat in the despair that had frozen through his body upon learning Westham's fate. Tallis was right, but that did nothing to soothe him. For as long as he could remember, he'd followed on Tallis' heel. Cut off from her, Finn felt lost, failing in the chaos that had torn their world apart.

"I understand," Finn said, but he couldn't make himself sound sincere. He pushed himself to his feet. Tallis grabbed for his hand and before he could think, he'd jerked it away as though she'd burnt him. "I have to go."

"Finn, please," Tallis' eyes swam with tears and Finn felt some small cracks in the ice around his heart. "I don't know if we'll get a chance to talk again. Just promise me you won't die out there? Then maybe when all of this is done, we can find some way to make a new life here."

"I won't if you don't," Finn sighed, his shoulders sagging with the heat of his anger dissipating.

"It's a deal."

Finn did not look back as he left her alone in the dark, as he felt she'd done to him. As he walked, he glanced up again at the sky. The Silver Fish was no longer a comforting beacon pointing the way home, but an omen of the terrors that now stalked the mainland. He wondered if somewhere up there the Protector was watching. It seemed to him that, if the Gods were watching, then they'd stopped caring. The Lady of the Waters and the Protector were meant to keep them safe, but so few had reached the refuge of Giant's Isle. If the Gods had abandoned them, then what hope did they have against the monsters from the West? He thought of the Nightmare Bridge's visions, and how one had already come to pass with the destruction of the Serpent's Mouth. With a shudder, he recalled the dark figure he'd glimpsed in the peaks of the Western Wilds and wondered if there were no gods to guide or protect, only monsters lurking in the shadows.

CHAPTER THIRTEEN

The Little Lion

Tallis sat with the twins at their quick breakfast. Finn had avoided her since their argument and sat with Cori somewhere else. The avoidance stung, but she couldn't blame him. If he'd been the one to choose to leave her behind, she'd have felt the same bitterness.

A messenger wearing royal livery strode into the hall, not something often seen on servants in the soldier's quarters. Curious heads turned toward the messenger.

"Tallis Larke?"

Tallis' heart froze and she raised her hand hesitantly, "That's me."

"Captain Eiran has summoned you," the messenger informed her. "Your quarters are to be moved to within the keep and the captain will be taking over your training, Commander."

Tallis could not respond for a moment. The shock of being called commander took her off guard. *Should have seen this coming,* she thought.

"Thank you," Tallis stuttered, not sure what else to say.

"I'll lead you to your quarters, then the captain wishes to see you," the messenger told her.

"I'll go get my things then."

Tallis rose from the bench and noticed the looks the twins were giving her, somewhere between disbelief and awe. She grimaced and gathered up her dishes as quickly as she could. They were under her command now and Tallis had no idea how that should change her behavior.

"Commander Tallis?" Harrin laughed, breaking the silence. "How'd you get so lucky?"

"I have no idea," Tallis forced a smile.

"How long have you known?" Hemma asked.

"A few days," Tallis said. "The captain asked me to keep it quiet."

"So you've actually met the captain then?" Hemma asked excitedly. "What's she like?"

"She's... intense?" Tallis shrugged, unable to think of a better way to describe the woman she'd met.

"So I suppose we won't be seeing you much anymore now you're rising up in the world," Harrin sighed.

"We will once we're moved to the ship," Tallis said. "Maybe too much."

"Well, till then, Commander," Hemma said with a grin and rose to salute her.

Tallis rolled her eyes. "See you soon, sailors."

The twins waved as Tallis followed the messenger out of the hall. Her smile faded the moment she turned away. She had been out of her depth enough so far from home and training to be a soldier. Now she'd be training for command.

As she left the mess hall, Tallis caught Finn's gaze. He seemed on the edge of saying something, but instead turned his gaze down toward his food and ignored her as she passed. Tallis wished there was the time or space to say something to him that might help, but she felt eyes on her from every direction, curious about the news and her departure. She hurried from the hall to escape their stares.

Tallis gathered her minimal belongings. Her spare uniform, her bed clothes, her father's sword, and the old clothes she'd worn to get here. They seemed even more meager all bundled up together rather than strewn around her bunk.

"I'm ready to go," Tallis told the messenger, fighting the shake in her voice.

The tower of the castle she was led to was finer than any part she'd seen yet. It was cleaner and was decorated with tapestries and paintings, in contrast to the bare stone walls of the barracks. She attracted curious stares from those she passed, most with indicators of command on their uniforms.

"This one is yours," the messenger pointed to a door and handed her a small key. "Captain Eiran's quarters are that next one down the hall. Report to her once you've dropped off your things. Good day, Commander."

"Thank you," Tallis nodded and took the key.

The room was small and furnished simply with plain wooden furniture. One narrow window looked out over the city below. Tallis guessed this might be a downgrade for some nobles, but for her it seemed like luxury. In Westham she'd slept in a loft over the kitchen with Aiven, listening to the dog snoring in his sleep below. She'd never had a whole room all to herself.

A new ceremonial coat of stiff blue fabric was laid out for her on the narrow bed. On one shoulder were two white stripes that marked her as a first officer. The king's Lion and Eiran's Rose were embroidered on the breast, larger and in more intricate detail than her old uniform. Beside it was another made of looser material for casual wear that was nearly identical to the one she already wore, except for the mark of rank.

Tallis dropped her small bundle of things beside the bed and replaced the plain coat of her old uniform with the new one. The fabric was softer and finer, but Tallis still felt less comfortable in it. Anyone who saw her now would know she was an officer and her presence would demand respect. It felt like lying.

Tallis examined herself as thoroughly as she could in a small mirror that hung from the wall. She hadn't seen herself since a brief glimpse when they'd taken her hair. The weeks of training had thinned her face and bulked up the rest of her. The woman in the glass was almost a stranger to the girl Tallis still felt she was.

A determined knock on the door made Tallis jump.

"Yes?"

The door opened and the captain entered. Apparently she'd grown impatient with waiting for her new first officer to report for duty. Eiran glanced around the room with a critical eye but didn't seem to find anything amiss. The captain stood as formidable as the day Tallis had first met her, if not more so, now Tallis knew just how much the woman expected of her.

"How do you find your new quarters?" Eiran asked after a moment.

"They're... luxurious, Captain," Tallis shrugged.

"Well you're one of the few to have said so," Eiran sighed. "At least you'll be more appreciative than others I might have chosen in your place."

"I hope to be more than appreciative, Captain," Tallis couldn't think of anything better to say.

"Good," Eiran nodded. "Come with me. I'd like to show you something. Can you ride?"

"Decently," Tallis said, but the memory of her last ride brought back images of fire eating her home and the screams of her family.

Eiran gestured toward the door. "Shall we?"

Tallis nodded and followed the captain out into the hall. The older woman said nothing as they descended the tower, then crossed an open courtyard where others with the marks of captains and officers dueled with blunted swords. The yard echoed with a familiar clang of metal on metal, but the faces were all strangers whose faces turned from confusion to indignation when they saw Tallis with her first officer's stripes. Tallis blushed and followed close on her captain's heels.

"Ignore them," Eiran said, meeting her fellow's glares. "I got the same when I first came here. Your actions will speak louder than their whispers, if you rise to the occasion."

"Why do they look so offended?" Tallis whispered as she did her best to ignore the others, but with little success.

"Because you're not one of them," Eiran told her bluntly. "You're a stranger, so they know you're not from a noble family, and that makes them feel threatened. The more people who earn their positions rather than being born into them, the more they fear losing what power they have."

Tallis supposed Eiran must be right. But that didn't make it any easier to meet their gazes. Eiran led Tallis into a stable where two horses were already waiting for them, saddled and chomping on their bits. They were sleeker and more spirited than the plow horses she was used to. A stable hand held out the reins of a storm gray mare and Tallis approached timidly.

"She won't bite," Eiran said. She'd already swung up into the saddle of the other horse, a gleaming chestnut. "They're both mine. That one's Mist; she's the gentle one. This one is the biter. His name is Lover. Won't let anyone mount him but me. He's a faithful lover that way."

Tallis led the mare to a mounting block and hoisted herself up into the saddle. She kept her eyes fixed on Eiran's back and tried her best not to look down as the captain spurred Lover out of the stable.

"I spoke to the king about your siblings."

"And?"

"He suddenly remembered there are two openings in the palace staff," Eiran turned in the saddle and winked. "It won't be glorious work by any means, but they'll have rooms in the servant's quarters, which are at least nicer than living in a tavern. They'll never go hungry, and no one will put a sword in their hands unless they ask for it."

It was the best Tallis could have hoped for given the circumstances. They'd never have anything like what they once had at home, but at least she'd know they were safe.

"Thank you, Captain."

"I wish I could have done more."

They passed through the keep's gate and into the main city. Eiran threaded her way down twisting streets that were unfamiliar to Tallis. They were narrower and more uneven than the one she'd taken up to the city on the day she'd arrived on Giant's Isle. But Mist seemed to know the streets as well as any urchin that begged on a corner for scraps and never lost her footing on the cobblestones.

Tallis was sure they must be lost, when they suddenly emerged from an alley into a bright and busy marketplace. A fountain carved in the shape of a man waltzing with a lion dominated the square. Women and children thronged around the fountain, the women with laundry and the children playing in the water despite the coming of autumn. Stalls lined the edges of the square, where merchants hawked their wares to a mass of people pushing carts or carrying baskets.

"Sit taller, Tallis," Eiran said as she fell back to ride beside her. "You're an officer now."

People stared here too. But here, the looks Tallis drew were more of respect and wonder than of scorn. The children grinned and pointed and their mothers hid smaller smiles.

"See?" Eiran leaned over to whisper to her. "At least in some places you'll be appreciated."

The two passed through the square and to another alley. Eiran took the lead again and urged her horse up to a trot. Tallis hardly had to nudge Mist before the mare was matching Lover stride for stride. Tallis' teeth chattered as she bounced along with Mist's gait.

"Here we are," Eiran announced as they approached a soldier's barrack at the base of the outer wall.

A man came for their horses and Tallis slid to the ground. Her steps were shaky and her knees felt stiffer than the sword that hung at her hip.

"Up," Eiran said, pointing toward a steep stairway cut into the stone of the wall.

Tallis groaned as she looked up at the summit of the wall that must be at least a hundred feet above them.

"You won't be complaining about its height when there are enemies on the sea beyond it," Eiran assured her and started up the stairs.

"If I was an enemy I'd probably just give up looking at this," Tallis muttered.

"You wouldn't be alone," Eiran said. "Many a fleet has taken one look at these walls and turned sail with the next outward wind. Something tells me the Shriekers won't do the same if they get here."

By the time they reached the top of the wall, Tallis was wishing for her horse again, no matter how stiff her knees would get. It certainly couldn't be worse than the way her calves burned now. Tallis leaned a moment against the cool stone before taking a look around.

"Well, what do you think?" Eiran asked.

Tallis could not help but gasp as she took in the view. From here, the entire city sprawled out below them. The statue of the giant man and the lion dancing in the square looked like nothing more than toys from here. In the distance, the tall towers of the castle glittered in the sun. Beyond that, fields of tall yellow grass billowed before disappearing over cliffs. All around, the ocean stretched blue and seemingly endless, flecked with white foam and liquid gold where it reflected the sun.

"Shall we walk?" Eiran asked. Tallis would sooner have stayed to rest by the stairs, but she held her tongue and followed the captain.

Gulls whirled overhead, crying out to one another in shrieking voices. Blue waves crashed up against the side of the wall. The walkway was wide enough for five men to walk comfortably side by side, but they passed only occasional soldiers who paused to salute them before marching on. Tallis followed Eiran in polite silence, wondering why the captain had brought her out here.

"How was it made?" Tallis ventured, finally breaking the silence. Looking down over the edge of the wall made her stomach lurch. It seemed impossible that people could build something so huge, and in the water too.

Eiran chuckled. "Some say the foundations were laid upon the Giant's arms that once encircled the bay, or long ago, wizards charmed the stones to build up from the ocean floor.

Others say bewitched workers who needed neither sleep nor food worked tirelessly until it was completed."

"Sounds like Shriekers," Tallis shuddered, imagining the monsters swarming over these stones.

"An interesting comparison," for a moment, Eiran looked troubled, but the expression faded quickly.

"So..." Tallis looked up at the captain for further explanation. "How was it really done?"

Eiran shook her head. "No one knows for sure. I say time, a determined king, or perhaps a few, with hundreds of underpaid hands at his command. On a still day, you can see great boulders scattered across the ocean floor from the deck of your boat. I imagine an attempt or two crumbled before the thing was finished."

Tallis nodded and forced herself to look down over the edge, trying to peer through the white-capped waves to find ancient rubble below, but all she could see was blue-green water. She raised her eyes to the walkway before them before her stomach could begin to churn again.

"I'm sure you're wondering why I brought you here," Eiran said.

"Well, yes, Captain."

"Look," Eiran pointed back toward the city.

By then they'd spanned enough of the wall to put part of the inner bay between them and the city. Tallis watched smaller craft crisscrossing the bay, back and forth between the docks and the larger warships moored in deeper water. Even at this distance, she could still make out tiny people working on the docks. From here she couldn't tell, but Tallis guessed that many of them were refugees like her, waiting and wondering if they would ever see their homes again.

"What do you see?" Eiran asked.

"I see the city?" Tallis ventured, wondering if the captain was looking for something more than that.

"You see what you're fighting for," Eiran said. "All those people down there just want to live, and it's our job to see that they do. Until we're back on my ship with my crew, you'll be among many people who will resent you for being a farm girl. Most would rather see you back in the barracks with the rest of the cannon fodder. But those people in the marketplace, the people you see down there on the docks, I want you to care about them. The moment you heed those who wouldn't shed a tear to see you fall, instead of those who smiled to watch you ride by, you are lost. Remember who you're protecting. Fight for them, and remember their faces when you're looking death in the eye."

Tallis looked down at the bay again and imagined she could see the people's faces. But all of them began to look like her parents, and other Westham villagers she'd grown up with who'd never made it to Giant's Isle and she turned away. Tallis wondered how easy it would be to remember strangers when many of the ones by her side would give her nothing but scorn. But Aiven and Osind were down there somewhere. She could fight for them.

"I'm not saying it'll be easy," Eiran said, as if she could read Tallis' mind. "I fought the same battle in my youth. Hell, I'm still fighting it. But if we refuse to surrender, maybe someday someone else like us won't have to fight. The Shriekers may be the enemy on the outside, but if we win, there will be another enemy on the outside to take their place. It's the enemies on the inside you should watch out for, because you can't just cut the heads off those ones and burn them."

"I'm still concerned about the ones whose heads I can cut off," Tallis cast a wary eye out to sea, as if there would be Shriekers striding across the water.

"Well, I never said not to be wary of those ones," Eiran laughed in a light way that reminded Tallis that under all the rough exterior, the captain was still an ordinary woman like her. Her laughter soon faded and her face turned serious again. "Your father. Was he happy with his life when he came home?"

Tallis was taken aback by the sudden change of subject. "I suppose he was. Why do you ask? Were you close?"

"Before I was captain," Eiran explained, "we served together under Leander. We were equals then, at least in rank. He was a good friend."

"I had no idea," Tallis admitted. "He never liked to talk much about his time during the war itself."

"I don't blame him," Eiran grimaced. "That war should never have been fought. Your father was a strong warrior though, and a good sailor. I offered him a permanent position on the *Storm Ghost* when I was made captain, but he refused. He preferred to go back to his farm, and his family. I resented it then, but I understand it now. I'm glad he got some years of joy before—"

Eiran broke off, bowing her head so Tallis couldn't see her face. Tallis didn't know what to say. She stared out to sea west toward the mainland and thought of home. Her father's time as a soldier was a part of his life she knew little about. Now, serving on the same ship, she wished she knew so much more. There were so many questions she wanted to ask.

"I'm sorry he's gone," Eiran said. "I could use him back on my ship again, but at least I have you. You earned my attention before I knew who you were, but I won't pretend I'm not glad to have a Larke in my crew again. I wish I could have seen him again before he died."

Eiran's words were cut short by a shout. Soldiers were gathering above the gate and pointing out to sea. They turned to see ships upon the horizon. Above white sails, flags flapped, but the glare of the afternoon sun and the distance made it impossible to discern what the sigils were. Tallis' thoughts of home were pushed aside by fear.

A horn blew one long blast then fell silent. Eiran sighed and relaxed.

"What is it, what does it mean?" Tallis asked.

"One blast for our ships," Eiran said, "two for friends, and three for foes."

"I didn't know there were still ships out there," Tallis looked out to sea again and watched the approaching ships.

"The king sent out scouts to see what the situation was," Eiran said. "We'll be called for a council to share whatever news they brought back. We must return."

Eiran started off down the wall the way they'd come at a brisk pace that left Tallis trotting to catch up. She stole glances at the ships as they went in hopes they'd come close enough for her to see the banners, but the sun kept the flags hidden from her sight.

The journey back passed in a blur. Tallis was lost in wondering what news the ships had brought. She hadn't heard anything since arriving in Giant's Isle. Behind the wall, it was almost possible to pretend the Shrieker threat didn't exist. But Tallis remembered the sounds of screams and cannon fire as the Serpent's Mouth was abandoned. She may have left the threat behind her, but it wasn't gone.

Like Eiran had predicted, a messenger was already waiting for them at the stables when they returned. Tallis followed Eiran into the castle to a large council chamber dominated by a massive oval table. A white lion was painted in the center and blue waves decorated its edges. At either end of the chamber stood a set of heavy wooden doors. One had been the entrance they'd come through and the other, Eiran told her, led to the king's private meeting rooms.

Around the edges of the room, the deep gold light of the setting sun streamed through panes of colored glass depicting seascapes, with ships riding the waves and seabirds in sunlit skies. Dozens of stiff wooden chairs surrounded the table, packed with captains and their first officers.

Tallis squirmed in her seat at Eiran's side. She imagined she stuck out like a beacon, no matter how small she tried to make herself seem in her chair. She could feel their wondering stares on her, despite their attempts to hide them. She felt she had no place here.

"Sit up, girl," Eiran hissed in her ear. "If you don't believe you belong here, they never will. You think I got them to respect me by slouching and looking like a lost pup?"

"Sorry, Captain."

Tallis sat up straight and did her best to ignore the whispers she was sure were all about her. She looked around the room and did her best to keep her face as still as stone as Eiran did. When she looked, she found not nearly as many eyes were on her as she'd felt. Most were turned toward the door at the end of the hall, waiting for the king to emerge. She felt foolish when she realized many of the whispers were likely wondering what the scouts had found, not about her.

"I've never seen this chamber so full," Eiran whispered to Tallis. "It's rare for so many of the fleet's ships to be gathered at once. Look, the latecomers missed the chance for seats."

At least as many of the captains and commanders present were standing in uneasy clumps around the edges of the room as were seated. Clearly this chamber hadn't been meant for a gathering of this magnitude.

"This will prove to be an interesting meeting," Eiran continued. "Attend well, it's sure to be educational."

Finally, King Leander arrived. They all rose and saluted while he took his seat. He waved for them to return to their own seats and waited for a moment before beginning. He surveyed them with ice-blue eyes. Tallis wondered if it was just her imagination that his gaze lingered a moment longer on her and Eiran.

The king was similar in age to Eiran, perhaps a few years older. Most of his hair was gone, but what was left formed a neatly cropped white ring around his head that was all but hidden beneath a golden crown with tines shaped like waves. Despite his age, Leander was still lean, and looked as though the sword was no long-lost friend to his hand, but a loyal companion.

"Welcome all," the king announced. It was a voice used to being obeyed, one that could compel others to fight, and win or die trying. "As you know, the last of our fleet has returned and the gate has been closed. I have gathered you here to hear the report from the front lines yourself. My cousin, the Lord Admiral Grayston, has brought back some disturbing news. Lord Grayston, if you would."

The man to Leander's right stood and cleared his throat. Tallis shuddered. She remembered overhearing Papa saying this man had been to the Western Wilds and back, losing all the soldier's he'd brought with him. There was nothing in his demeanor or appearance that hinted at the horrors he must have witnessed, and Tallis wondered what he'd seen beyond the Foggy River.

"The Shriekers have the shore," Grayston began. "We held them off as best we could but the loss of ships we suffered was unacceptable. I had thought the Shriekers would be unable to pursue us over sea, so I ordered a retreat to Giant's Isle, but it seems I was mistaken. The Shriekers have seemed to be mindless beasts, but their actions are becoming coordinated and militaristic. They make for tireless workers who will not hesitate or complain. When I left the shore behind, they were repairing ships damaged and left behind in the final fight to reclaim the harbors. I believe Giant's Isle will be their next target. They could be here ere autumn's end. Should they besiege us as winter approaches, many will not see another spring."

Mutters swept through the gathered commanders. Tallis sat rigid in her seat. She realized she was gripping the arms of her chair so tight the wood dug painfully into the palms of her hands. Even Eiran let out a colorful curse under her breath.

Leander held up a hand and stood as Grayston returned to his seat. The room fell silent in an instant and waited with bated breath for the king to speak.

"The fleet must prepare to sail," the king ordered. "Infantry will man the wall at all hours. The fleet will sail and meet these monsters at sea. They may have ships, but they cannot have the skill of our esteemed fleet. The Shriekers must not reach the city. The first attacks razed many crops, and now we are cut off from the mainland. Should they cut us off from our allies in the east, starvation will take more lives than blades. Many ships sustained considerable damage in defense of the harbors, but those able will sail within the week to form a barricade. The rest will join as soon as they can. Once the fleet is fully assembled, then, and only then, will an attack be made. Until that time you are out there only as a defense should the Shriekers reach you. Lord Grayston will have the command of the barricade."

Beside the king, Lord Grayston looked pleased. Tallis wondered how the man could possibly be pleased with the situation. The Shriekers were coming. Tallis wondered if she might have been better off lying about her experience as a sailor to be put with the footmen who'd be defending the wall.

"How soon do you want us to sail?" a captain asked.

"As soon as you are able," Leander said. "For those of you who just returned, I give you up to a week to rest. Those of you who've been here, I give you three days to stock your ships, assemble your crews, and set sail."

"But, pardon me saying this, Sire, many of us suffered considerable losses to our crews," another captain protested. "The replacements we've received are hardly seaworthy yet. Most have never even set foot on a craft larger than a rowboat, let alone a warship."

"Then let your senior crew sail the ship," Leander sighed. "Let your new recruits do their best, and if their best is not good enough for crewing the ship, they'll at least be more hands fighting."

"More hands to get in the way, more like," the captain next to Eiran muttered, but not quietly enough to avoid a glare from Leander.

"If the king says we must sail, then we'll sail," Eiran snapped, leaning forward to fix a dark glare on the other captains.

"Captain Eiran is right," Leander said. Tallis thought she caught the king giving Eiran the hint of a smile. "The Shriekers will not wait for your new hands to be fully trained. If any of you wish to wait for a better crew, I can grant that wish by giving the ship a new captain who understands what's at stake. Is that clear?"

The king's words were met with silence and averted eyes from captains around the room. It seemed only Eiran had the will now to meet Leander's gaze.

"Good," the king nodded. "This meeting is adjourned. Go and inform your crews of when you will be sailing. May the Lady and the Protector watch over you all."

"And you, Sire," the captains echoed.

The scraping of wood on stone filled the room as people filed out. The king singled out a handful of the senior captains and lords to accompany him to another meeting.

"Captain Eiran, with us," the king beckoned.

"Aye, Sire," Eiran bowed her head and turned to Tallis. "Go to the barracks, Tallis. Find a man called Alleto. He'll help you assemble our crew. You're in charge of informing them of the king's decision. Alleto will oversee preparations of the ship. Once you've done that, return to my chamber to meet with me."

"Yes, Captain," Tallis stuttered, though the thought of actually being responsible for something terrified her.

"Good," Eiran nodded. "I'll see you soon. And don't worry. Alleto knows what he's doing. He'll help you."

"I'll see you soon then," Tallis shrugged.

Eiran smiled and clapped a hand on her shoulder. "You'll do well."

The captain turned and followed the king to disappear through the other door. The moment Eiran left, Tallis felt defenseless. She looked around and felt eyes were on her again.

Tallis nearly jumped when she felt a hand on her shoulder.

"Tallis Larke," sounded a familiar voice. "I certainly did not expect to see you here."

Tallis turned to see Vaska, the captain she had met what felt like years, not months ago. His smile was bright enough to outshine even the darkest looks she'd gotten today.

"Nice to see a familiar face," Tallis admitted.

"And good to see you alive," Vaska's smile vanished. "When you were separated from the rest of Westham's refugees, I thought the worst. I'm sorry I wasn't able to protect your home, or see more of your fellow survivors to King's Harbor."

"You saved my siblings," Tallis said. "Thank you."

"I wish I could have done more," Vaska sighed. "But here you are, Eiran's first officer. Your father would be proud."

Tallis felt a lump form in her throat and found she couldn't form words. Imagining what her father would think to see her here made her heart ache.

"You're so like Nevra that I knew who you were the moment I met you," Vaska said. "You'll do well here."

"I hope to."

"I must attend the meeting of senior captains," Vaska said, glancing at the door at the back of the room. "I'm sorry to cut our meeting short, but I'm sure this won't be the last we'll be seeing of each other."

Vaska clasped his hand reassuringly on her shoulder. As he left, Tallis felt as though the mood of the room around her had changed. It was clear he was a man the other captains and officers respected, as she now saw fewer dark glances in her direction. Tallis made note that his good side was one she would do well to stay on, as she hurried to do as Eiran had bid her.

Tallis found the mood in the barracks changed even from just this morning. The soldiers that had once been her fellows in the yard now stood aside and saluted when she passed. There was a buzz of curiosity Tallis expected was sparked by the ships' returning. It died when she passed groups of recruits and soldiers and resumed once they were at her back.

"Where might I find a man named Alleto?" Tallis asked when she found a senior soldier who wasn't busy training new recruits.

"That's him there," the woman pointed to a man showing some of the younger recruits the tools and instruments of navigation.

"Thank you."

The soldier saluted her and Tallis gave the woman an awkward nod.

Tallis approached the man the woman had pointed out to her. He was younger than Eiran, but still much older than herself, with weather-worn and sun-darkened skin. His black beard was bushier even than the short-cropped hair on his head, which gave him a comically imbalanced look to his face. He looked to be twice her girth and had at least a foot on her in height, but not an ounce on him seemed to be fat.

"Alleto?" Tallis asked.

"Yes, Commander?" the man looked up from his work. His students bowed their heads and saluted.

"At ease, soldiers," Tallis did her best to sound confident giving the order, but the words still didn't fit in her mouth.

"Can I help you?" Alleto asked.

"I'm Captain Eiran's new First Officer," Tallis told him. "She sent me to find you."

"Ah yes," Alleto nodded. "She told me about you. You're younger than I thought you'd be."

"Is that a problem, sir?" Tallis snapped with unexpected ire rising in her chest.

Alleto laughed, but with no trace of malice. "No, Commander. I meant no offense. What does the captain require?"

"The captain wishes for you to assemble the crew," Tallis replied curtly. Alleto's relaxed attitude around her eased her irritation somewhat, but she didn't want his first impression of her to be of softness. "I have news for them."

"Aye, ma'am," Alleto turned to his students. "That'll be all for today. Report to the yard to join the others in swordplay."

The new recruits did their best to hide disappointment as they gathered their things and dragged themselves toward the yard. Tallis imagined the bruises and sore muscles they must be nursing. Navigation training might have been boring, but at least it didn't hurt.

"Wait for me here," Alleto said. "I'll send the crew, quick as I can. Some are down on the docks. We'll need to pass the news on to them secondhand, but that'll have to do."

"I'm sure it will," Tallis nodded.

Alleto lumbered off and Tallis took a seat on the bench. She examined the man's tools and maps, but navigation had never been something she'd gotten the hang of. The map made plenty of sense to her, but the instruments remained a mystery. If she'd known she'd be put in command she might have paid more attention during her lessons, but she supposed that would be Alleto's job, not hers, once they were aboard the ship.

Members of the crew began to filter in. They hovered at the edges of the room, eying her with curiosity and suspicion. The newer recruits huddled together separate from the veteran crew members. Tallis watched them all, trying to keep her face expressionless to hide her nerves.

"Hey, Tallis!"

The twins bounded up to her.

"Best call me 'Commander' now," she whispered to them. "At least around the rest of the crew."

"Aye, Commander," Hemma winked and gave her a salute.

"How's it been up in the grand world of the upper class?" Harrin whispered.

"I haven't even been gone a day," Tallis shrugged.

"And you're already back," Hemma teased. "That bad, huh?"

"You have no idea," Tallis grinned, but it soon faded when Alleto returned. Hemma and Harrin slunk back to the edge of the room.

"That's all of them that aren't down on the docks," Alleto told her. "Should be plenty to spread the word, Commander."

"Thank you," Tallis nodded and turned to the crew. "Good evening. My name is Tallis and I am the new First Officer for the *Storm Ghost*. I bring word from Captain Eiran. As I'm sure you know, the last of the fleet has returned. They bring word that the Shriekers have begun assembling a fleet of their own. It is estimated they'll arrive at Giant's Isle before winter."

Murmurs drifted through the crew. The newer ones looked shocked, but the rest seemed like they knew already. Rumors must have spread from the other ships already.

"A fleet of their own?" asked Fadren, who stood clumped with the other new recruits, eyes wide and a tremor in her voice.

"Lord Grayston reported they were repairing ships abandoned at the harbors," Tallis said, which was met with furtive glances between sailors and a few curses. "The king has ordered the fleet to sail and form a barricade to stop the Shriekers out at sea. We're to leave in three days. The Captain bid me tell you to make sure the *Storm Ghost* is ready to sail."

"Three days?" one piped up. "You think we can be ready in three days?"

"Those are the king's orders," Tallis asserted. "Three days is the time we have. The captain will expect her ship to be ready."

"Aye, Commander," the one who'd spoken bowed his head. At least they respected Eiran if they didn't respect her.

"How are we supposed to fight these things?" another voice chimed in. "They've advanced past every barrier we thought would hold them. And now even the sea itself isn't enough?"

Tallis drew in a deep breath, unsure how to answer the question, but knew she couldn't afford to show hesitation if she wanted the crew to believe she could do her job with confidence. "We fight them the way we've fought any enemy, with sword and cannon. We cannot underestimate the Shriekers. They are clearly not the mindless beasts we first thought, and so we must fight them with the same cunning and skill our fleet has protected this country with for generations. I know the *Storm Ghost* sailed in the Kerethi wars. Okaesa faced an enemy then who fought with pirate's honor and savvy, yet we prevailed."

"Something tells me we won't be making peace with Shriekers and doing trade with them years from now."

This voice was met with a few nervous chuckles. Tallis waited for them to dissipate.

"I'd wager you're right," Tallis conceded. "But that peace was negotiated because King Leander and Lord Grayston led the fleet into a gambit that left the Kerethi with no option but to surrender or lose more than they could afford. I trust they can do it again."

Finally, her words were answered with nods and silence. Tallis realized she'd done well to draw on their faith in the king and the admiral, something they could trust more than her until she proved herself.

"That will be all," Tallis said. "I'm sure there's much to do, so best get started as soon as possible. You may go."

The crew saluted her and filtered out of the room.

"You did well," Alleto came up to her after the rest of the crew had left.

"Did I?"

"It was certainly a good start," Alleto said. "It may not have seemed like it, but they did listen to you. That's no easy task."

"I see," Tallis nodded.

"Will you be needing anything else, Commander?"

"No, that will be all," Tallis said.

"I look forward to working with you," Alleto gave her a smile. "Until then, good luck. If I'm being honest, I'm a tad relieved the Captain picked you, not me. Not an easy job. But I'm here if you ever need help and don't want to bother the Captain."

"Thank you," Tallis said, taken aback. The way he said it sounded more comforting than demeaning. His offer felt genuine and kind.

Alleto saluted and left the room. Tallis returned to the yard and made toward the castle. The way back seemed to take longer than the way there. The courtyard and keep were clogged with soldiers and servants dashing about preparations for the fleet's imminent departure. Despite the number of people out, there was a hush over the city.

The sun was nearly below the horizon and the sky was turning a deep purple, though in the distance, Tallis could see clouds beginning to roll in from the open sea to the east. The air had the sharp scent of rain coming. The autumn storms were beginning and Tallis guessed this one would hit them soon. She wondered if the storms would impair the strike against the Shriekers.

Tallis hurried back to the tower that housed her and Eiran's quarters. She climbed the stairs slowly, afraid the captain would only have more orders for her. All she wanted to do was climb into bed and forget she'd be sailing off to battle so soon, or have a chance to say goodbye to Finn and clear the air before they left aboard separate ships.

When Tallis reached Eiran's quarters, she found the door opened just a crack. Voices filtered into the hall from within.

"A farm girl?" a man's voice Tallis recognized as the admiral's came through the partially open door. "What could a girl like her possibly know about command?"

Tallis halted. They were talking about her. She hesitated a moment, fist raised to knock, then lowered it and pressed her ear to the door, curiosity getting the better of her.

"Is that meant to insult her?" Eiran's voice was curt and cold.

"I'm only questioning if she's the wisest choice," Grayston responded. "It's unprecedented. Are you sure the king approves—"

"The king has approved my decision, as he once approved my own unprecedented appointment," Eiran snapped. "I recognize your concern, Admiral, but do not overstep your place. No matter how much you wave your 'cousin of the king' flag, I hope you haven't forgotten the king has a niece and two nephews in line for the throne before you. So don't question my decisions, nor King Leander's."

"I apologize for my frankness, Captain," Grayston said. "I just can't help but think your judgment may be biased. Can the girl even sail? Most of these villagers had never even seen the ocean before they'd been recruited."

"I sailed with her father, and he taught her to sail," Eiran said. "She's also repeatedly bested her peers on the training grounds. Believe me, my lord, my choice was entirely on merit."

"I'm sure it has nothing to do with her father having once been a friend of yours," Grayston scoffed.

"No more than your father had a part to play in your appointment, my *Lord*," Eiran retorted. "So if you would excuse me, I have more important things to worry about than your petty concerns about my first officer."

The admiral's doubt hurt more than all the bruises she'd gotten from the training grounds. Tallis' fists balled at her side. But the captain was defending her. Tallis figured she must have at least done something right for that.

"Very well, *Captain*," Grayston replied coolly. "Just know I'm not the only one with doubts."

"And she'll quell them just like I did," Eiran said. "Good day, Admiral."

Tallis pulled back from the door just as the admiral stormed out, nearly bowling her over.

"Well, well, what fortuitous timing," Grayston grinned, revealing clean white teeth. "I don't believe we've properly met. I am Lord Grayston Adamaris, captain of the *Lady's Kiss* and admiral of the fleet."

"I am honored, Admiral," Tallis bowed her head to hide her flushed cheeks.

"I wish you luck in your new position," Grayston's grin had faded and he scowled down at her. "We'll pray you do better than the last girl Eiran had in your place. Good evening."

The admiral swept down the hallway without a second glance. Tallis watched him go, teeth grinding against the temptation to yell after him.

"Tallis," the captain called from within. "Come."

Tallis sighed and entered Eiran's rooms, shutting the door fast behind her. The captain sat behind a desk covered in maps and papers. Behind her, the banner of the King was hung upon the wall. Besides the banner, the room was sparsely decorated and most of Eiran's possessions seemed to be packed away in boxes, as though the captain never really settled into this room and was always ready to go back to her ship.

"Have a seat," Eiran gestured to the seat across the desk from her.

Tallis sat and Eiran regarded her across the table.

"How did the crew take the orders?" Eiran asked after a moment.

"Not well," Tallis admitted.

"I assumed as much," Eiran said. "But they'll do as they're told."

"Captain," Tallis looked everywhere but at Eiran, unsure if it was her place to ask. "What did Lord Grayston mean when he mentioned the last girl you had as a first officer? I thought you said my predecessor was a man?"

Eiran's hands clenched into fists on the table and she stared at the papers in front of her without answering. The scar across her face stretched tight from the captain's furrowed brow and clenched jaw.

"I'm sorry... I shouldn't have asked—"

"Your predecessor was a man: Grovenor," Eiran said through gritted teeth. "Grayston referred to... the one before him. She..." Eiran closed her eyes and let her hands fall into her lap with a sigh. After a moment, she drew herself up again, her captain's wall reformed. "Pay no heed to Lord Grayston. He is proud of his Adamaris name and believes in upholding the standard of nobility serving as the fleet's officers. You should go get some sleep and try to forget about it. Once we set sail, we'll be seeing very little of him."

Tallis stood without a word. Though she'd only known the captain briefly, she could tell Eiran was not a woman to question. If Eiran didn't want to tell her something, she wouldn't, and Tallis would not press the matter. Tallis saluted and returned to her own chambers.

The sun had set and the clouds Tallis had seen earlier had rolled in to cover the stars. Tallis shut and locked her window against the coming rain before stripping out of her uniform and falling into her bed. She stared up at the ceiling and wondered if this room would begin to look like Eiran's; disorderly, with her things in a constant state of half-packed and ready to board the *Storm Ghost* at a moment's notice.

Lord Grayston's words played again and again in her mind. Even if Eiran was right and Grayston was the worst she'd have to deal with, Tallis guessed that there must be plenty of others thinking exactly what Grayston had the status to say aloud without repercussions. Eiran might not want to explain what he'd been referring to when he'd mentioned Eiran's other first officer, but Tallis couldn't imagine it was anything good.

The sky opened up with a torrent of rain and Tallis' thoughts were drowned by the roar of water on stone.

CHAPTER FOURTEEN

Eye of the Storm

Tallis wasn't the only one to disappear from the barracks. Not long after her departure, Vilmos, along with a handful of others, were fetched by messengers and never came back. Most called away were those born and raised in the noble families of the keep. None seemed to leave behind so cavernous a space as Tallis. Finn felt her absence like a deep splinter that he couldn't work out of his skin.

Finn took some small comfort that he was far from alone in his misery. It seemed that in almost the same breath that Commander Bevan had informed them of the king's orders to ship out, the wind had gusted, heavy with the smell of rain. All throughout their preparations, the storms raged, drenching them as they loaded the ships with the supplies they'd need.

The autumn tempests showed no sign of relenting as the storm green darkness of the day before their departure faded into the inky darkness of night. Finn sat on the edge of his cot, staring at the empty space at the foot of the bed where his small box of meager belongings had once sat. Everything had been moved to the hold of the *Lady's Kiss* except for a clean uniform and a water skin.

"You going to spend your last night on shore moping?" Harrin appeared at his side, followed by Cori. They both buzzed with nervous energy.

"We're going out," Cori informed him, reaching out a hand. "Fadren's invited us all to the Crow's Nest. You coming?"

Finn sighed, wanting nothing more than to stay in the dry warmth of the barracks and sleep through everything tomorrow. But Cori's eyes shone with a beckoning light. Finn reluctantly took his hand and let himself be pulled up and out into the pouring rain. Laughing, Cori began to run. Harrin caught Finn's gaze with a quick grin, before the two both sprinted after him.

Water poured all around them, slicking the cobblestones and sticking what little hair they had to the sides of their faces. As they ran, Finn couldn't help but feel his heart lighten. By the time they saw the sign of the Crow's Nest ahead of them, he wore a grin. They skidded to a halt by the door, panting and dripping. When they pushed inside, they found the room packed with soldiers, enjoying their last night of leave.

"Are you soldiers, or stray dogs that fell in the harbor?"

An older woman appraised them with a touch of both disapproval and amusement. Finn recognized the sharp features of Fadren's face, though this woman's hair was white, not brown.

"Sorry, ma'am," Finn was the first to speak.

"Over to the fire," she chuckled, then gestured at Harrin. "Don't need to ask your name, boy. You may as well be a copy of your sister. She's already by the fire with my Fadren. Go join them and dry up. I'll bring mulled wine for the lot of you. You need something hot or you'll catch a fever."

They moved into the crowded inn. A great hearth blazed on one side of the room, with a knot of sodden soldiers around it. To the other, tables had been cleared for a dance floor and a woman with a fiddle was charming the feet of soldiers to move. At her side, the lieutenant responsible for teaching knotwork sang with surprising skill. It stopped Finn in his tracks to see Lieutenant Charis, beaming bright and voice cutting high and sweet.

With the recruits, Charis was always short, to the point, and slow to praise. To receive an approving nod from them was like being showered with accolades. In Westham, people of a third gender, or no gender at all, were not unheard of, but Finn had never met anyone like Charis. He'd only made the mistake of referring to them as 'she' once, and the mistake had earned him an extra shift of cleaning out bedpans. The person whose voice now cut above the crowd seemed entirely unlike the one Finn knew from training.

Fadren and Hemma called to them, and Cori dragged Finn closer to the fire. Maija appeared with steaming mugs and Finn took his with a deep gratitude, letting his fingers, frozen from the autumn rain, begin to melt around its warmth.

"You managed to get Captain Cranky out of his brooding?" Hemma asked, feigning stunned disbelief. It took a moment for Finn to realize she was looking at him.

"Captain Cranky?" he asked incredulously.

"Ever since your lady love left us, you've been absolutely morose," Hemma taunted.

Finn rolled his eyes, attempting to look nonchalant, but inwardly he felt a touch of regret. Had he really been that bad?

"First of all, I am not a captain," Finn raised a finger accusingly at Hemma. "Second, Tallis is not my 'lady love'. I'm not particularly interested in ladies, and Tallis is not particularly interested in anyone."

Finn had meant to allude to Tallis' lack of desire to participate in any of the pairing off that had begun in recent years between the other youth in Westham they'd grown up with. But it had come out bitter, thinking of how she'd abandoned any friends she had in Giant's Isle to take her new position as an officer.

"But you *are* cranky," Harrin raised his mug in mock toast.

"Guilty." Finn grinned and raised his own mug, draining a long gulp that burned his throat and made his head swim.

Gradually, as their clothes began to dry, more wine went down, and the jovial mood of the inn around them began to seep in with the alcohol, Finn relaxed. He couldn't remember the last time he'd had the chance. He was sure it had been before the Shriekers had assaulted the western villages. Likely it had been a night at the Coat of Arms in Westham, with Tallis.

Finn's smile faded as soon as he had the thought. The Coat of Arms was likely little more than broken timbers and ash now. Its owners, Quillon and Genecia, would have died along with the rest of Westham's refugees on their flight to King's Harbor.

"Oh no you don't," Cori grabbed his wrist. "Not tonight."

"Sorry," Finn shook his head. "Just… thinking of home."

"So don't think," Cori threw back the last of his wine. "Come on, dance with me."

"I don't—"

"Do not say you don't dance," Cori fixed him with a stern gaze.

"I don't think there's anything I'd like more," Finn changed course.

"That's better," Cori gave him a wink and pulled him to the open floor.

The dancers whirled in patterns that Finn recognized. From the fiddle flowed a familiar tune that set their feet flying. Cori took the lead, pulling him through the weave of dancers, passing under the arched arms of another pair, before being swept down the line. Finn had never had the confidence to do much dancing, never understanding the steps well enough to lead. But he felt swept up in the whirling patterns like he was caught in a riptide, and he had to either tread water, or drown. Charis' voice rose above the chaos.

Fall like the leaves
And rise like the tide.
Winter winds slip in like thieves
But we've got hot wine inside!
Come dance the last summer's dance.

There was something about the way Cori moved that reminded Finn of another boy he'd once known. Nothing else about their appearance was the same, but the way Cori seemed to always flit one step ahead, while dragging him along, was identical in an almost uncanny way. Finn hadn't thought about Kaif in years, and the memories tugged at his heart in a way he'd thought he'd buried. Finn had spent long months trying to make himself forget; the golden gleam of sunlight on hair as rich as summer soil, soft lips on his hidden in a barn, a note left but nothing more.

Kaif had given the note to Tallis, not even having the dignity to deliver it to Finn himself, or say goodbye. Like Nevra, Kaif's father delivered crops downriver to the Serpents Mouth. The four of them had gone together, and only three returned. A Kerethi ship had offered him a place, and he'd leapt at the opportunity to see the world. Finn almost couldn't blame him. Almost.

Cori pulled Finn close, hand on his waist and Finn's heart raced as fast as his feet moved through the swinging spin.

"You're doing it again, *Captain*," Cori whispered in his ear tauntingly.

Before Finn had a chance to retort, Cori had broken away, turning over his shoulder to exchange partners with the pair beside them. Finn was pulled into another swing by a soldier he didn't know, then he and Cori were off again, weaving in and out of the lines of dancers.

The dance found Finn facing the door of the inn, and the music seemed to fade into silence and though the dancing continued to swirl around him like eddies around a shoal, he stood frozen. Tallis was there. It was the first time he'd seen her since they'd argued. With the day of their departure looming, he'd begun to think he wouldn't even have the chance to say goodbye.

"Finn, what—?" Cori was at his side, but his words broke off when he followed Finn's gaze and saw Tallis. "Oh."

Cori tensed at his side, looking both resigned and disappointed. Finn gave him an apologetic look.

"It's fine," Cori said in a clipped tone. "I'll go back and join the others."

"Cori, I—" Finn felt torn apart. In the currents of the dance with Cori was the first time he'd managed to feel something other than fear or heartache since he'd fled Westham. But if this might be the last chance he had to see Tallis, he couldn't let it slip from his grasp.

"I understand," Cori took his hand and squeezed. "Go."

Finn slipped away from the dancers, weaving now between clumps of drinkers and onlookers. Tallis hadn't yet noticed him and was starting to move away from him in the crowd.

"Tallis!" he shouted, unable to keep the desperation from his voice.

She turned, looking startled. Finn pushed the rest of the way to her side. She'd left her uniform jacket, the one with her stripes of rank, behind. In its place she wore the same plain brown coat she'd worn when they'd left Westham. Without the uniform, she could have been anyone. She blended in with the crowd, rank and command left behind.

"Finn? What are you doing here?"

"Came here with Cori and the twins," Finn explained. "Fadren invited us. One last night to ourselves before setting sail."

Tallis nodded. "I just came to see Aiven and Osind before we left."

"Oh," Finn's heart sank. He'd begun to hope that somehow Fadren had invited her too, that she'd come to share their last night with them, like she would have if she hadn't been promoted.

"It's good to see you," Tallis smiled but it looked forced.

"I wondered if you'd come to say goodbye before we left," Finn said, more sharply than he'd intended.

"I've been busy," Tallis mumbled, and Finn immediately felt guilty for his bitterness.

Silence stretched to fill the void between them. There had been a time they could spend hours without saying a word and it never felt strange, but now it was strained. There was too much to say and not the right words or enough time to say it.

"I wish I was on the *Storm Ghost* with you," Finn said.

"Me too," Tallis sighed, and he believed her. Again, the wordless void stretched, and Finn knew he'd brave any bridge if it meant he could cross it. Tallis finally broke the silence first. "Are you still angry with me?"

Finn remained silent. He wished he could say no, but resentment still lingered, not boiling as it had the last time they'd spoken, but it still simmered.

"You are," Tallis sighed, and Finn said nothing to deny it. "I'm sorry. I wish…"

Tallis did not finish her sentence. Finn filled the silence, imagining everything either of them could wish for, a home unburnt, a village still filled with people, and monsters still a thing of stories. But none of that would change.

"Can you do something for me, Finn?" Tallis said, taking his hand in hers.

"What's that?"

"Let me go," her words were earnest and struck Finn like a blow. "I don't know if either of us will come back. Even if I do, it won't be over for me. This isn't a post I can just abandon. I want to know that if something happens to me, in this war or another, you'll keep going. Maybe even go home without me when this is done."

"And where is home exactly?" Finn demanded, the anger bubbling again to the surface. "I'm not going back to a burnt and crumbling husk of a town without you. You can't ask me to do that. You're still my friend, and the only piece I have left of home, so home is wherever you are. Where you go, I go. That much at least hasn't changed, and never will."

Tallis buried her face in Finn's chest and wrapped her arms around him. He melted into her embrace and clung to her, as though if he held on tight enough, they could keep out the rest of the world. The dawn would never come, and the fleet would never sail.

"I need to find my siblings," Tallis said, breaking the spell and pulling away. Around them, time continued to move. The dancers whirled, soldiers drank and laughed, and the night wore on ever closer to sunrise. "We'll see each other again soon."

Her voice held a conviction that almost made Finn believe it would be true.

"Goodbye, Tallis."

She disappeared into the crowd, and Finn watched her go. He glanced to where his friends were still drinking and laughing and found he couldn't bear the idea of rejoining them. The little cheer he'd managed to take from the evening was drained, and he didn't want his mood to ruin their night. Finn slipped out of the Crow's Nest to return to the barracks.

The clouds above had parted. In their place, the stars glittered, and the moon lit up the wet street with glowing silver beams. When he reached the main road, Finn could see the harbor, the water dark as ink. Already, the ships that were to embark in the morning were moored at the docks, ready to carry them away.

Though the storms had subsided for the moment, the absence of warm, wet air coming from the east gave way for a vicious wind blowing piercing cold blades from the northwest. It brought with it the warning of winter from the western mountains, where it was already driving summer away. It drove the flags atop their masts to whip and snap. Finn fled the new chill up the hill to the barracks for the last time, wondering which, if any, of his visions from the Nightmare Bridge would come to pass once they sailed.

CHAPTER FIFTEEN

Hoist the Sails

The morning of their departure dawned cold and bright. Captains and first officers gathered in the castle courtyard, garbed in ceremonial attire. When Tallis entered the courtyard, a stablehand approached her, holding Mist's reins. Tallis thanked him and scanned the crowd for Eiran. She found her captain standing in a corner, ignoring the rest of the people gathering.

"Haven't you got any family to see you off?" Tallis asked when she approached. Looking around, she could see other captains bidding farewell to families. But Eiran stood alone beside her horse.

"My father was hanged for crimes against the kingdom," Eiran grimaced. "My brother took his ship, sailed east, and has not been heard from since. And my mother threw herself into the sea to escape the shame my father's actions brought upon the Garray name. So, no, I do not have any family."

"I'm sorry," Tallis said, wishing she hadn't asked.

"Don't be," Eiran sighed. "My father only ever saw me as a tool to marry off as close to the throne as he could, but he never knew just how close he got. If my father hadn't seen better opportunities elsewhere, I might have been one of those women seeing off a husband, not one of the ones going."

Eiran watched the crowd. Tallis followed the direction of her gaze and saw the king scoop his niece up in his arms to plant a kiss on her forehead. Before Tallis could ask any more questions, Leander swung up into his saddle and held up a hand for silence.

"Captains and Commanders," Leander addressed them. "It is time for the fleet to depart. Move out."

Tallis hoisted herself up into Mist's saddle. Leander led them down the street of the upper city. Lords and ladies, wealthy merchants, and retired officers rained flowers down on the soldiers. They beamed and shouted, as though the fleet was departing for adventure, not war. Tallis waved back and did her best to mimic Eiran's smile.

When they passed through the wall to the lower ring of the city, the silence hit them louder than all of the triumphant noise of the upper ring. The streets here were lined with solemn faces. Common folk stared, hands over their hearts, still and noiseless as statues.

Here and there, a crack in the stone could be seen. A child would gape and point as the king rode by, only to be pulled back a moment later by a parent. A mother would call out to her child marching by, putting on a proud face until they passed, then the tears would return. These people knew only death waited beyond the walls of Giant's Isle.

The procession stopped when it reached the docks. Tallis dismounted and followed Eiran to the dock where the *Storm Ghost* was moored. For now, the sails were furled, but the banners atop the tallest mast flapped in the wind. Like all the other ships of the fleet, her prow was set with a silver lion figurehead, though hers seemed more weather-worn than many of the others.

The king walked down the line of docks, pausing briefly at each captain. When he reached Eiran, a look passed between them that suggested familiarity, and Tallis thought Leander stood much closer to Eiran than he had to the other captains.

"Captain Eiran, Commander Tallis," the king nodded to each of them. "May the Lady grant you kind winds and gentle waves, and may the Protector guide you home safe and victorious."

"The *Storm Ghost* will come home, your Grace," Eiran bowed her head. "She always does."

"I'm sure she will," King Leander's smile faded and he shook Eiran's hand, holding it a moment longer than a formal gesture from king to captain. "You just make sure you come home with her."

When he let her go, his gaze lingered on Eiran, and when his polite smile returned, it looked forced. Leander gave Tallis a salute and a nod before moving on. Tallis wanted to ask what that exchange had been about, but after Eiran's response when she'd asked about her family, Tallis kept her mouth shut. She wondered just how close Eiran had been set to marry to the throne, and if there'd been a chance Eiran might have been commanding from a throne, rather than from the helm of a ship.

Leander remounted his horse and swept his gaze over the crowd.

"Brave soldiers and captains, we face a foe greater than any Okaesa has ever faced. The Shriekers threaten the very roots of our country, and if we do not stand strong, they may threaten the whole world. There will be no negotiations, no truce, and no mercy. Go forth and send those beasts down into the Lady's domain. May the waves take your bones should you fall. Farewell."

Tallis saluted the king along with the rest of the captains and crews, then followed Eiran up the gangplank to the deck of the ship. The moment Eiran stepped on board, the crew sprang into action. The sound of sails snapping in the wind and the creak of wood and rope filled the harbor as the two dozen ships of the king's fleet made their way one by one toward the Lion Gate.

Tallis marveled at the coordination of the veteran crew. With only a few words from Cara—the bosun who'd been one of her overseers before she'd been promoted—and guidance from Alleto for navigation, they took to the rigging and set the course westward. On her journey to Giant's Isle, Tallis had spent most of her time below deck, and hadn't had the opportunity to watch the crew work. Eiran took up her place at the helm where she could observe everything and quickly change course if necessary.

The newest recruits, however, were all doing their best to stay out of the way. Most milled toward the aft of the ship, away from the stairs up to the helm, where the least activity crisscrossed the deck. Of them, only Harrin had leapt into his duties, scrambling with the efficiency of a squirrel to the crow's nest high above. Tallis made a mental note of his readiness to act, and that he was someone who could be relied on.

Tallis now understood why Eiran had chosen her. With the veteran crew busy keeping the ship running, and Eiran overseeing them all at the helm, it was up to her to manage anything else. As they sailed on, the new recruits would have more to do. But having just set out, there was little need for cooking, cleaning, or minor repairs, and Tallis hoped it would be some time before they were needed as soldiers.

"You lot," Tallis approached the knot of recruits, most looking nervous and lost. Tallis tried not to think about how many of them were younger even than herself. With a gesture, she split the group down the middle and addressed each group. "One group for the gunnery and steerage deck, the other for the hold. Check everything is in place and lashed down."

Tallis scanned both groups. Most avoided her gaze or looked queasy. Only Hemma and a boy she didn't recognize met her gaze without hesitation. Tallis beckoned them both forward.

"Hemma, you lead the gunnery and steerage group," Tallis turned to the other boy. "And you are?"

"Jayim Tomei," the boy bowed his head.

"Jayim, you'll lead the hold group," Tallis instructed, again making a mental note of who were the more confident among the new recruits she might rely on. "Both of you report back to me when you're finished and satisfied all is in order."

"Aye, Commander," Jayim saluted first, and Hemma echoed him a moment after.

The two began shuffling their groups to the hatch that would lead them below deck. As the recruits disappeared from the main deck, there was an almost imperceptible easing of the chaos. Sailors moved into the space they'd occupied, and operations became less cramped. Tallis was sure the job she'd sent the recruits to do had already been done, but it would give them something to do out of the way.

Tallis caught Eiran gazing down on her from the helm. The captain beckoned to her with a quick gesture and Tallis hurried up the stairs, eager for direction herself now that she'd taken care of her fellows. Inside, she felt just as lost as they had looked, and almost wished she could have followed them below deck and out of the way.

"Well done," Eiran gave her an approving nod when Tallis joined her by the wheel. "It's good to see you have good instincts."

"Thank you, Captain."

"How are you feeling now that you're aboard?" Eiran lowered her voice to ask, though Tallis felt it was hardly necessary as the crew were all absorbed in their tasks.

"You want the honest answer or how I should be feeling?" Tallis asked, surveying the deck from the vantage of the helm. From here, she could begin to see the order to the chaos, the crew bustling in organized teams, not a rush of bodies jostling around aimlessly.

"I can know the honest answer," Eiran said. "Just so long as no one else does."

"I'm terrified," Tallis admitted.

"You should be," Eiran put a hand on Tallis' shoulder. "And you know what, so am I. But the crew need to believe that we're not afraid. Giving the new recruits something to do did more than get them out of the way, it gave them something to take their minds off what we're sailing toward, and showed them your authority. Keep it up, and we might just make a solid officer out of you before this fight is done."

"I'll do my best, Captain," Tallis promised.

"Good," Eiran straightened to attention as a series of whistles sounded from Cara's bosun pipe. Immediately, the crew fell still and silent.

"Signal from the *Lady's Kiss*," Cara called. "The fleet is clear of Giant's Isle. Line ahead formation."

Eiran nodded acknowledgement, and with another series of whistles, Cara sent the crew back to their work. Tallis watched as the ships around them began to move, slowly falling into formation one by one. The *Lady's Kiss* led with the rest of the ships of the line—the strongest ships carrying the most cannons—spread out in two columns behind her. Eiran steered the *Storm Ghost* to the side of one of the columns, toward the front but still allowing the *Lady's Kiss* to lead. Other smaller ships like the *Storm Ghost* spread themselves to either side of the line, ready to scout or carry messages as needed.

The sun had already passed its highest point and was slowly arcing over in front of them, as though the Protector himself was leading the way. Giant's Isle quickly shrank into the distance as the fleet picked up speed toward the mainland.

CHAPTER SIXTEEN

Cormorant's Feathers

Frigid wind from the west slowed their forward progress. The sky was emptied of clouds, and waves washed by below like frightened horses, frothing in the wake of the ship as it plowed west. Finn peered across the dark water. In the night, the other ships following behind the *Lady's Kiss* could only be seen as vague dark silhouettes sliding silently over the water. Stars winked out and rekindled as the ships passed before them, as wavering as his courage. He wondered which of the smaller ships sailing to the side of the line was the *Storm Ghost*, but it was impossible to see their flags in the darkness.

Finn shivered and pulled his coat tighter around his frame. The night watch was always cold and lonely. At least during the day, there was the bustle of activity and distraction of the crew, but now he stood with nothing but his anxiety for company.

They were going the wrong way. Finn knew this deep in his bones. As the fleet surged away from Giant's Isle, his heart was an anchor caught upon the sharp rocky outcroppings of terror, knowing even more treacherous waters lay ahead. The further they went, the closer he felt to tearing. He and Tallis had fought and suffered their way to Giant's Isle, and now they were being swept back toward the horrors they'd so narrowly escaped.

Finn paced across the deck as though in that small space, he could leave any of his worries behind. He shook his hands for warmth and focused on the sea beyond the rail. The empty expanse of water told him nothing, and given how difficult it was to see even the ships that sailed alongside and behind the *Lady's Kiss*, he doubted he'd spot an enemy ship if it was there.

The click of boots against wood drew Finn's attention away from the ocean and back to the deck of the *Lady's Kiss*. Cori emerged from the stairs that led below deck, and Finn's heart leapt to see the two steaming bowls he carried.

"Thought I'd join you," Cori said, holding out a bowl of stew to Finn. "If you don't mind."

"Please," Finn eagerly took the stew and nearly scalded the roof of his mouth in his haste. "It's too quiet out here."

The two found a crate by the rail. They sat in silence until they'd both cleaned out their bowls. With half his shift left to go, Finn was grateful for its heat.

"Finn, there's something I need to tell you," Cori broke the silence. When Finn turned to him, he saw Cori's face was uncharacteristically somber.

"What is it?" Finn's brow creased, wondering what had Cori so worried.

"Remember how I told you about how the Brothers of the Sky and Daughters of the Sea choose their names? You noted how a cormorant is both"

Finn hesitated, wondering where this was going. "Yes, I remember."

"Well," Cori lowered his voice. "You were close to the mark. My mother was one of the Daughters. That's all I know about her. When she knew she was dying, she gave me to them so that I'd have a family like she had."

"Gave you to the Brothers?"

"No," Cori's hands twisted in his lap. "To the Daughters, like her, where she thought I would belong."

"So… you're a girl?" Finn's brow creased, wondering what reason Cori had to hide this, since girls and boys alike could have enlisted to escape the mainland.

"I—no," Cori shook his head. "I never felt like I belonged with the Daughters. I remember being young and watching the Sons, wishing I could be one of them instead, not really understanding why. By the time I was old enough to choose my name, I understood it was because in my heart, I wasn't a Daughter, but a Son. I chose to take the name of a bird who dives in the sea to honor my mother and the time I spent with the Daughters, then I left for the Sons and never regretted that choice."

"Why hide it?" Finn asked, thinking of Lieutenant Charis and the casual ease with which they moved through their world. In Westham, such a choice might have sparked some disgruntled confusion, but he'd never seen anyone question Charis.

"It's different in the harbors," Cori shrugged. "King's Harbor especially has traders coming through from every corner of the world. Sometimes it seemed there were as many different ways of seeing and judging the world as stars in the sky. It was safer and easier to keep it hidden. Sometimes I thought of running off with the Kerethi. They always seemed to care the least about that sort of thing."

"I'm glad you didn't," Finn couldn't stop himself from saying. "Or we'd never have met."

Cori laughed quietly, lost for words for a few moments before continuing his story. "I didn't know Giant's Isle would be different, so I kept it hidden when I got there. Out of habit, I suppose. But that's much easier to do in the barracks than the cramped quarters of the ship. I knew it would come out before long and wanted to tell you, not have you hear from someone else or by accident."

Finn shifted across the space between them where they leant on the ship rail to bump his shoulder against Cori's.

"I'm glad you told me," Finn said.

"It doesn't change how you feel about me?"

"Not at all," Finn replied automatically, though he wasn't sure yet what it was he felt for Cori. It was different from what he'd felt with Kaif, which had flared bright and fast as a match, but had snuffed out again just as quickly. The feelings surfacing seemed similar, but moved with the almost imperceptible inevitability of the tide.

"Good," Cori leaned his head against Finn's shoulder and Finn did not flinch away. Instead, he melted into the touch, the warmth of it comforting against the chill night air.

"What do you think you'll do once all this is over?" Finn asked, thinking of his argument with Tallis.

"I haven't given it much thought," Cori sighed. "It's been enough just trying to get through each day."

"Would you go back to King's Harbor?"

Cori pushed his spoon around his bowl. Finn was beginning to regret having asked by the time he finally responded.

"If there's a King's Harbor to go back to," Cori said. "Perhaps? But I'm not certain that will be an option for some time. There will be much rebuilding to do if we manage to eliminate the Shrieker threat. I'm the eldest survivor of the Sons. I feel some responsibility to help reestablish the organization for my last two brothers, and I imagine by the time this is done there will be many more children needing a place to go."

Finn found himself again thinking of the Guardian's words. *How many people have you outlived, Finley?* A stab of envy twisted in his guts, and he thought back to his argument with Tallis. He'd been so focused on the path immediately in front of his feet that he hadn't considered what might come after. Tallis had her siblings and was building a new life with her position on the *Storm Ghost*. Cori had the Sons and his brothers there to give him something to keep fighting for.

"And you?" Cori asked. "What will you do when this is all over?"

"I don't know," Finn admitted. Growing up, he'd dreamed as much as any child in Westham of adventure beyond their small town's borders. But in those dreams, he'd always followed Tallis. Without her, he felt adrift. He'd never considered what he might want for himself separate from her.

"Well, it could be nice to not have to try rebuilding the Sons alone," Cori offered.

Despite the chill of the night and the impending devastation they sailed toward, Finn felt warmed. A cold resignation had seeped into him when Tallis had told him the fate of Westham's other refugees. While the buildings and land may still be there, Westham's heart was gone, and he had no home to return to. Trying to imagine surviving this fight had ended in visions as blank as fog, but with Cori's offer, that fog began to lift. Finn could see himself at Cori's side, working to rebuild what the Shriekers had destroyed. That alone was enough to begin to dispel the numbness he'd felt at losing Westham and all who'd lived there.

"I think I'd like that."

Though Finn had never seen it, he tried to picture King's Harbor in his mind. Having never seen another mainland harbor, the image that came to him was of the Serpent's Mouth. With that image came the memories of pillars of black smoke and a cacophony of screaming and cannon fire. The warmth that had begun to fill him quickly ebbed away. After witnessing the Serpent's Mouth demolished under cannon fire, it was hard to imagine rebuilding anything.

"Have a quiet shift," Cori said, taking Finn's silence as an end to the conversation.

As Cori took his bowl, Finn almost asked him to stay, dreading facing the dark alone. But he only half-mumbled a good night and watched Cori walk away, disappearing into the hold below. Finn stood and resumed his pacing to keep out the night's chill, trying not to imagine Cori, black eyes staring at him blankly as flames consumed King's Harbor around him.

CHAPTER SEVENTEEN

Strong as the Sea

For several days, they sailed on open waters, without any sign hinting they were headed for war. The fair weather held and a steady wind pushed them closer each day to the mainland. Tallis spent her time becoming better acquainted with the ship, learning to work the rigging and the wheel. Though she'd already learned much of what she needed to know, being told something and actually doing it were far different things. But each day, she became more familiar with the ship, and the language she'd need to know as an officer. She even started to understand some of the messages sent from the *Lady's Kiss* by a system of flags, though mostly that was handled by their own messenger.

In the beginning, the newest recruits spent much of their time clinging to the sides of the ships, doing their best to keep their meals inside them. Though Tallis was used to the rocking of her father's ship, the river never came close to the swells of the sea. She was able to keep a calm face in front of the crew, but that didn't stop her from suffering through the night and eating very little until she got used to the swell of the waves. Soon enough, she, and even the weakeststomached of the new recruits were walking around confidently and managing to eat just as much as they liked.

Eiran said nothing about it, but Tallis could tell the captain was worried they had yet to encounter anything out of the ordinary. Every day, Eiran spent her time anxiously watching the horizon and frequently calling to either Hemma or Harrin in the crow's nest, asking if they saw anything. Finally, on the sixth day, the messenger on the *Lady's Kiss* raised his flags calling "Captain's meeting", one of the few phrases Tallis had been careful to learn.

"Ready a rowboat and bring the *Storm Ghost* closer to the *Lady's Kiss*," Eiran ordered.

Tallis stood at the rail, fingers tapping on the wood in anticipation as they drew closer to the *Lady's Kiss*, wondering if she'd get the chance to see Finn. Other ships were beginning to cluster around Lord Grayston's ship. A rowboat was untied from the side of the ship and lowered to the water.

"About time he called a meeting," Eiran said.

"What do you think he wants?" Tallis asked.

"He wants to make it seem like we're doing something other than just sailing without direction," Eiran said. "That we haven't seen any sign of our enemy is unsettling. I expect he'll want to send out a few ships for reconnaissance. It's what I'd do. If so, we should expect to be sent ahead."

"Why us?"

"Grayston and I may have our differences," Eiran shrugged. "He never approved of my initial appointment. He claimed it had nothing to do with my being a woman, and that anyone who joined the army under false pretenses deserved at least dismissal, if not harsher punishment. But the king overruled his objections. I never approved of his promotion either, but my reasons were too personal to feel they were worth voicing. Despite our history, however, I recognize Grayston is a shrewd and practical man. And he recognizes I am reliable, and the *Storm Ghost* can be trusted to get things done. If there are to be scouts, the *Storm Ghost* is a practical choice with her speed."

"Ready when you are, Captain," a sailor shouted from the rowboat below. Eiran gave him a curt nod before turning back to Tallis.

"You stay here and take charge while I'm gone."

Tallis opened her mouth to protest, but Eiran swung herself over the rail to the ladder without waiting for a response. Before beginning her descent, Eiran fixed her with a gaze of cold determination that stilled any argument. Tallis watched Eiran's boat as she was rowed to the *Lady's Kiss*. She longed to be going with her, if only for the chance she'd see Finn. There'd be no chance to speak, she knew, but even just a glance to see how he fared would be some comfort. She'd urged him to let go, but once she'd realized this was the longest she'd gone in her life without seeing him, a pang of guilt and homesickness had risen in her heart.

Time seemed to drag almost to a standstill as Tallis waited for Eiran. There was little to do with the fleet sitting unmoving. Most of the crew took the unexpected pause to rest. A few broke out cards, some went below deck to sleep. Tallis made her way to the helm, not knowing what else to do.

Harrin remained at his post in the crow's nest, but Hemma broke away from the milling crew and climbed up to join Tallis at the helm. Tallis felt a touch of relief. Since they'd sailed, she'd had little time outside of her duties, and as an officer she'd felt removed from the rest of the crew.

"Did the captain tell you anything about what we're stopping for?" Hemma asked.

"She had guesses, but wasn't sure," Tallis shrugged, not wanting to dwell on what was happening in the meeting.

"How are you holding up?" Hemma asked, taking the hint to change the subject.

"Well, I'm keeping my food down now and not nearly falling over every time there's a large wave," Tallis tried to sound lighthearted, but it came out dry and humorless.

"It's a start," Hemma smiled brightly. "I'm not feeling like I'm going to lose my bladder every time I look down from the crow's nest anymore. I didn't even know I was scared of heights until I was up there. Harrin and I used to play on the cliffs overlooking the ocean near the harbor. It was a long drop from the top to the water. But that was nothing compared to being up a swaying mast, clinging to nothing but ropes as you climb."

"How's the view from up there?" Tallis asked, relieved to be talking about anything but the mission before them. She hadn't yet dared to climb the mast, for once grateful that her officer appointment meant most of her duties kept her strictly on the deck.

"Much the same as from down here," Hemma's brow furrowed. "Just water as far as you can see. Sometimes there's an island, or flocks of birds, if it's an exciting day. But that's the problem, isn't it."

Hemma glanced over to the *Lady's Kiss*, moored at the head of the fleet.

"That was Eiran's guess," Tallis' heart fell as the conversation turned back to the captain and the fleet's task.

"If we just keep going like this, we'll end up right back where we started," Hemma's brightness was gone, replaced with a dark trepidation. Tallis shuddered, not wanting to think about the Serpent's Mouth or the day they'd left it.

"Look," Tallis nodded in the direction of the *Lady's Kiss*. "The rowboats are coming back. We'll find out soon enough."

"Don't be a stranger, Tallis," Hemma reached out and gave her arm a squeeze.

The girl disappeared off among the crew, who were hurriedly packing away their leisure activities and making themselves look busy again. Tallis descended from the helm to await the captain at the rail.

When at last Eiran clambered back on deck, her face was grim. She met Tallis' eyes and the look was tired. The captain quickly shook off her grave mood and straightened to address the crew, who were already beginning to mill around them, eager to hear Eiran's news.

"We have a mission," Eiran began. The mood of the crew tensed. "Admiral Grayston is concerned we've yet to encounter any enemy ships. He wants more information to strengthen our position. To that purpose, he is sending out three ships to scout the way ahead. The two others will go north and south. The *Storm Ghost* will sail west."

"Is he mad?" one of the older, seasoned sailors shouted. "Sailing by ourselves due west? That'll bring us straight to the Serpent's Mouth. We were there, you know full well what happened. The admiral destroyed the harbor, so what more could we possibly learn?"

"Some of us suffered much trying to escape that harbor," another said. "It's the last place we should be returning to."

More shouts of agreement followed, but most came from those who'd also come to Giant's Isle via the Serpent's Mouth.

Eiran held up a hand and silence fell. "We need only sail far enough to bring back word of the state of things at the harbor, or return with an estimate of the enemy's numbers if we encounter them. We are not to engage in combat without the rest of the fleet."

"And what if there's no choice?" the first sailor who'd spoken asked, and a few voices echoed his with support. "What if we can't run? Are we expected to sacrifice ourselves for the sake of information? The last time we sailed west, we lost a lot of good sailors. Now he wants to send us back?"

"I volunteered," Eiran snarled, her face a dark mask, daring them to question her choice. "The admiral is right. The fleet cannot continue to sail blindly."

"We should never have come back from the East," another man said. "We escaped the viper's nest, only to jump right back into it."

Eiran advanced on the man, a look of hot fury on her face. Others backed away, and the man blanched, but she grabbed him by the collar before he could escape her wrath.

"You'll want me to forget those words, Islewec," Eiran growled, the fresh scar across her face pulled taut by her enraged expression. "For you speak dangerously close to treason. Do you think I've forgotten the cost in lives we paid? I follow the orders of the admiral. Anyone here who would do otherwise can start swimming."

Islewec's mouth opened and closed like a fish as he struggled to stammer out an answer. "I'm sorry, Captain."

Eiran's sudden outburst seemed to subdue the crew, for they stared at her in silence. She released Islewec's collar and he sagged, falling back in with the others.

"What does happen though?" a soft voice spoke up. Tallis looked around to see it had come from Hemma. "If we meet the Shriekers, I mean. What if we can't make it back to the fleet?"

Eiran looked lost for words for a moment. Coming from Hemma, the words sounded less like the defiance of the other protests, and more like legitimate fear. The captain's face softened and the anger faded as storm clouds when their rain was spent.

"Then we fight back and take as many of their ships down with us as we can," she said, the edge gone from her voice. "Many of you have family and people you care about left behind on Giant's Isle. I don't follow orders blindly and without question, and I don't expect you to either. This is for those we've left behind, and for those we've already lost, so their deaths may be avenged."

Her speech seemed to calm the fear of the younger soldiers, and put to rest the protests of those who'd served long enough to dare defiance.

"You have your orders," Eiran stated. "Now go. This ship sails west."

The captain's gray eyes were hard as stone and difficult to read. With a jerk of her head, Eiran bid Tallis follow her and briskly turned on her heel to stride to her cabin. Tallis obediently followed, countless thoughts of what was ahead of them swirling in her mind, too many to make sense of or formulate into something coherent to ask the captain.

"They didn't take that well, did they?" Eiran said once the door of the cabin closed behind them. She dropped into the seat at her desk, shoulders heavy and face weary.

"Will Islewec be a problem?" Tallis asked.

Eiran barked a bitter, cheerless laugh. "He'll fall in line. Always has. He's served on this ship longer than I have.

Islewec is all bark and no bite. If I show my teeth, he'll cower with his tail between his legs. He was resistant when I was made captain, stuck in old ways. And it still shows sometimes that he's of a dying breed."

"How do you stand it?" Tallis knew if she'd faced the same onslaught of doubt and outright defiance, she'd have crumpled, where Eiran had stood firm as a rock buffeted by waves.

Eiran sighed and stood up to look out one of the small windows at the rough gray waves. She beckoned for Tallis to join her. Tallis moved to stand by the window, doubtful that she'd find any answers out on the never-ending water.

"Men call both ships and the sea 'she'," Eiran said after a moment. "Look out there, Tallis. Do you think the men scorn the orders of that woman?"

Tallis shook her head.

"If they ignore the signs of the ship and the sea and think their own ideas are better," Eiran continued, "then the ship will sink and every single one of them will drown. Already they are at the mercy of two women the moment they step on board."

Eiran paused and turned to look Tallis in the eye. Tallis did her best to hold the captain's gaze and not squirm in discomfort.

"Tell me, Tallis," Eiran said. "What do you see when you look at me?"

Tallis examined her captain, trying to see beyond the angry red scar and tangled black mat of hair to the woman beneath the wild exterior.

"I see a captain," Tallis ventured after a moment. "I see someone who people will follow when the seas get rough and it seems like we'll never see land again."

Eiran nodded. "Because that's how I want to be seen. You think that's all there is?"

Tallis shook her head. There were cracks in the captain's facade, small and easy to overlook, but she'd caught glimpses.

Eiran unclasped the top button of her uniform jacket and drew a silver locket in the shape of a shell out of her shirt. Beside it hung a silver ring with a lion's head holding a pearl. She opened the locket to reveal a painting of a younger version of herself. Tallis could hardly recognize her captain without the scar, and her now wild, unkempt hair was instead neatly arranged around her unmarred face. The young woman in the painting was beautiful in every way Tallis had imagined the ladies of the court would be when she was a child. Beside Eiran in the picture was a young girl, perhaps only a handful of years younger than Tallis.

"I found this girl in the streets of the city," Eiran explained. "She was nine, maybe ten, she'd lost her parents too young to be certain. I found her begging on a street corner and couldn't turn my back on her. I raised her as my own daughter, brought her on board the *Storm Ghost* and taught her everything I knew about sailing. When she was old enough, I made her my first officer."

"She's the one Grayston mentioned..." Tallis trailed off, not sure if it was a subject Eiran wanted to go into.

Eiran slipped the locket back under her shirt and returned to her seat behind the table littered with maps and charts. For the first time, Tallis thought the captain looked her age.

"I lost her in a storm," Eiran said, not lifting her gaze from the maps to look at Tallis. "I failed her. A soldier cannot also be a mother. Tallis, the sea is a woman who has chosen the life of a soldier over the life of a mother. You want the men to heed your orders? You must be as strong as the sea."

But the sea is not always rough, Tallis thought, though she did not find the voice to say it aloud. Eiran returned to her seat and went back to examining her maps.

"What was her name?"

Eiran looked up but said nothing. The soldier's face fell away to reveal the mother.

"Della," the name fell out of Eiran's lips as barely more than an escaped breath. Eiran's face hardened back to the mask of the strong captain Tallis was used to. "We've all lost someone, and if we fail now, we'll lose more. It's a heavy burden of command, to feel responsible for the death of someone you loved. I pray it is one you never need to carry."

Tallis' jaw clenched, thinking of her father and how she'd cut him down with his own blade. Eiran's brow furrowed, reading the look on Tallis' face as though she'd already spoken the truth aloud.

"I already understand," Tallis admitted, heart in her throat and words spilling out like blood from a wound. "It's my fault Papa is dead. They turned him and I killed him."

"No, Tallis," Eiran interrupted her sharply. She reached across the table and laid a hand on Tallis' arm. Her firm grip calmed the burning heat of untold truths in Tallis' throat. When Eiran spoke, it was with the same tone she used when issuing commands to the crew, a voice that left no room for questions. "You did not kill him. He was already dead. You simply put him to rest. Having seen what that disease does to people, it's not a fate I'd wish on even my worst enemy."

"But we hardly know anything about it," Tallis said. "What if there's a cure?"

Eiran leaned back in her chair and hid her face with her hands. "Tallis, there's something you should know. The whole kingdom only became aware of the Shrieker threat this past spring. But the first rumors of Shriekers that seemed more than wild tales began to surface close to a year ago, and Leander's sister fell sick with some mysterious illness no one had ever seen before around the same time."

"A year ago?" Tallis was incredulous. "Why wasn't anything done?"

"Leander didn't want the people to panic, but he didn't do nothing," Eiran explained. "He sent me to look for answers. I sailed the *Storm Ghost* further than any Okaesan ship in living memory. Do you want to know what I found?"

Tallis nodded. This was the first she'd heard of anything being done about the Shrieker threat before soldiers had been sent to defend the crossing of the Foggy River. Eiran got up from her chair again and spread out a well-worn map of the known world on the table between them. The mountains of the Western Wilds spread alongside one edge of the map, with Okaesa and the Isles of Kereth in the northwest, the only settled lands on their side of the great ocean that split the map down the middle. On the other side, and slightly south was their closest neighbor, Sabutia. Tallis remembered that a younger Sabutian prince had married Leander's sister. She also remembered a rare foreign trader in Westham telling Finn he had a Sabutian complexion, and perhaps his family had originated there. Many smaller kingdoms and provinces dotted the coast of the eastern continent. But continuing east and south, the land turned to sparsely populated desert that faded into the opposite edge of the map.

"I spent weeks in Sabutia's famed library, pouring over old texts. What I found led me so far to the southeast it was difficult to find anyone who spoke a language I know," Eiran explained, pointing to a region near the bottom corner of the map, where a river larger than the Serpent wound its way from the ocean to the eastern edge of the map. "We sailed up the Gartuan river, to inland cities never visited by our explorers. I spoke to merchant caravans that had traveled so deep into the desert that the ocean is little more than a myth to the people there, but their myths also contained monsters similar to Shriekers. A Sabutian scholar who accompanied us spoke of a theory that there aren't, in fact, two continents, but one."

Eiran picked up the map and wrapped it into a tube so that the vast desert on the eastern edge met the Western Wilds. "The theory proposes one vast continent stretches from the unexplored east to the Western Wilds on the borders of Okaesa. No one has ever returned from ventures beyond the mountains in the west, and none have ever found an end to the desert. The creatures invading our land and those found in the east could then be coming from the same place beyond the edges of the known world. I don't know that I believe this idea, but there's too much we don't know. All the major countries we know of have grown along the coastlines. What lies on the far side of the world is a mystery it seems none know the answer to."

As she spoke, Eiran's voice became more agitated. She dropped the map back on the table and began to pace. "All the scholars could tell me was there were records of experiments performed, but none had found any cure. The caravans that traveled inland had heard of a way to kill them; burn them, or remove the head. I hurried home with that news. My haste cost me Della's life. I knew we should have dropped sail and taken shelter, but I thought every moment lost was another soldier taken by the Shriekers. Even so, I was too late, and the infection had already spread to outlying farms and villages. What little I'd learned turned out to be useless. The soldiers had already figured out how to kill the beasts on their own."

Eiran stopped pacing and turned to Tallis. "Trust me, Tallis, the moment you let guilt start worming its way into your heart, it is nearly impossible to get it to let go. You did your father a favor by killing him. That disease is unnatural and cruel."

Tallis stared at Eiran, stunned. This sudden outburst was so unlike the hard-shelled captain she was used to. To see Eiran as an ordinary woman with just as much fear, worry, and grief as her came as a bit of a shock.

"I'm sorry," Eiran said and collapsed back into her chair. "I've wanted to get all that out but had no one I trusted enough to do so with. I failed Leander. And though he's never shown a hint of anger or even disappointment, I have been unable to forgive myself. He sent me to find answers to save the kingdom, and all I did was come back too late with more questions."

"I didn't even know anything had been done," Tallis told her. "Knowing someone was sent, even if not much was found, is better than believing the king did nothing."

Eiran regarded her with an appreciative eye. "I hadn't thought of it that way before. Leander wanted my mission secret because he didn't want to spread panic." Eiran ran a hand over a map of Okaesa's mainland, her fingers resting over Westham. "I wish I could have brought back something that could have saved your home. I wanted a chance to see

Nevra again, tell him I understood why he left the *Storm Ghost*. I know your assignment to my ship was random, but I cannot help but feel it was fate. For whatever reason, the Gods want you here."

Tallis did not know how to respond to that. She hadn't felt like anything was the work of the Gods since the Shriekers invaded. But perhaps being alive at all to be fighting back was their doing.

"Do you really think the lands beyond the eastern kingdoms and the Western Wilds are the same?" Tallis asked, changing the subject back to Eiran's journeys. She stared in wonder at the maps on the table between them. All of them ended in blank, uncharted edges.

"It's possible," Eiran said, seeming relieved to discuss something else. "No one's traveled far enough to find out. There must be something in between the two. Whether it's ocean or land is unknown. But either way, if they're connected somehow, it would explain how Shriekers have been found on the outer edges of kingdoms on both the eastern and western shores of the ocean."

"There could be anything out there," Tallis mused.

"Perhaps, but that is a matter for another time," Eiran said. "If we can fend off this attack, then we can worry about ensuring it never happens again. For now, we must focus on the task at hand. Go and get some rest. We'll all need to be alert on this mission."

"So long as you do the same, Captain," Tallis said. It seemed Eiran might need the reminder based on how worried she seemed.

"Thank you, Tallis."

Tallis left the captain's cabin, unsure whether the conversation had consoled her, or only added more to worry about. The captain was clearly concerned about what lay ahead, and there were more questions than answers about their foe. Tallis returned to her own cabin, avoiding the gaze of the crewmembers to hide her growing anxiety. Her mind raced across Eiran's maps, frustrated by how incomplete they all were, so often ending with embellishments depicting strange creatures and cryptic messages of 'here be monsters'. Now that she knew that message to be true, she ached to fill in those blank edges, but Eiran was right. If they couldn't push back the Shriekers, there would be no chance to pursue the questions Eiran's journeys had raised. Tallis tried to shove these questions to the back of her mind for now, but a seed had been planted she couldn't stop from growing.

Black Sails

Three sets of sails faded away toward a horizon that blazed fiery orange with the sun dipping ever closer to the water's edge. Finn watched the Rose banner, eyes straining as long as he could still see it, wondering if this would be the last time he'd see it. Silhouetted against the glare of the sun, the ships' white sails looked almost black. Finn shivered, remembering visions of black-sailed ships, crewed by Shriekers.

With the fleet holding position, there was little to do aboard the *Lady's Kiss*. Finn wished he had something to take his mind off worrying about what the *Storm Ghost* would find, and whether she would return to report her findings. Most of the crew were already taking advantage of the stop to take extra rest time, and had disappeared to the cabins below. Only Rohya, on watch in the crow's nest, remained above deck. Finn contemplated following the rest of the off-duty crew. Cori had challenged Tarsi to some kind of dice game that was popular in King's Harbor after learning she'd also grown up there. Maybe Finn could join them and learn the game, instead of continuing to earn his 'Captain Cranky' nickname.

Finn had just about convinced himself to join his friends when the admiral suddenly appeared at his side. Grayston didn't look at him, but also had his gaze fixed on the western horizon.

"Finley, isn't it?" Grayston asked, still not taking his eyes off the place where the *Storm Ghost* had faded from view.

"Yes, sir," Finn stood tall at attention, his throat as tight as his posture, wondering what the admiral could possibly want with him.

Grayston finally turned his gaze on Finn and appraised him. Under the scrutiny from Grayston's icy blue eyes, Finn shifted from foot to foot anxiously, and wished the admiral would go back to watching the horizon.

"You were at the Serpent's Mouth," Grayston noted. "You impressed me that day. A raw recruit fresh off the docks, but you answered the call to arms. It's why I requested you be appointed to my ship. I need soldiers who won't hesitate to follow orders in this war."

"I—" Finn fished for something to say, knowing he shouldn't remain silent. "Thank you, sir?"

"You may not be thanking me by the time all this is over," Grayston scoffed. "You know what's out there, what happened to the harbors. You've seen them, what they can do to a man."

"I have, sir," Finn replied, his voice barely more than a whisper.

"Your accent is mainland," Grayston observed. "Was the Serpent's Mouth your home?"

"No. I fled there from Westham."

"Then I offer my condolences," Grayston said flatly, then his tone became distant again, as if he was speaking to the sea and not to Finn. "All that raw, bestial power. What can we possibly do to stop it? If it could be controlled, if we could harness it..."

Grayston trailed off and straightened, turning his attention again to Finn. "Westham was the first of the villages east of the Foggy river to fall. You were lucky to survive. You and Eiran's new first officer."

Finn's throat tightened at the mention of Tallis, so callous in Graystons' mouth. "We grew up together, and fled to the Serpent's Mouth together."

"It was my impression that Westham's few survivors had escaped to King's Harbor with Captain Vaska," Grayston said. "Yet you and Commander Tallis arrived in the Serpent's Mouth. How did that come to pass?"

Finn remembered the lie Tallis had come up with about getting separated and sailing her father's boat to the Serpent's Mouth. But Tallis had always been a better and quicker liar than him. It had gotten them out of all sorts of trouble. Finn felt the admiral could see right through him and would see the lie before he could even finish the words.

"We got separated," Finn said, hoping that might be the end of the questions. "We weren't fast enough to cross the bridge before it was destroyed."

"Oh?" Grayston raised an eyebrow. "So how did you cross?"

Finn inwardly cursed. So much for keeping it to himself. He could have left out how they were separated, but he was too nervous in Grayston's presence to think clearly.

"We crossed the Nightmare Bridge," Finn admitted.

Grayston's brow furrowed. "If you'd told me that a year ago, I'd have thought you were lying. Only someone with nothing to lose would venture there. But faced with the Shriekers... I understand the choice." Grayston trailed off, his gaze turning west, his eyes narrowed and his expression grim as though he could see the Nightmare Bridge and, beyond, the mountains that had spawned the Shriekers. "Tell me, Finley, what did you see?"

Finn was taken aback by the question. "Sir, how do you know I saw anything?"

Grayston was silent for a moment, jaw clenched. Finn wished he'd held his tongue, and feared the admiral would reprimand him for questioning a superior officer.

"Perhaps an admiral hears more detailed reports than the rumors spread in the villages," Grayston said finally. "Those that have survived the crossing are rarely lucid, and most don't survive for long after their encounter. But to see the Shriekers first must make one more resilient to visions of horror."

"Things I saw keep happening," Finn admitted, and even though he barely knew the admiral, it was a relief to finally tell someone. Perhaps if he warned Grayston of what he'd seen, the admiral would be able to do something to stop his other visions from coming to pass. "I saw Shriekers overrun the Serpent's Mouth, and ships firing on the harbor. I saw the fleet sailing out from Giant's Isle to meet a fleet of ships with black sails."

"Was that all you saw?" Grayston asked.

"No," Finn gripped the rail so tightly his knuckles turned white. "I saw ships burning, I saw the fleet scattered and black-sailed ships surrounding Giant's Isle."

Grayston's face remained placid and unreadable as he gazed out at the sea. "And you fear those visions will come to pass as well?"

"Yes," Finn's voice came out as barely more than a whisper, choked by the terror he'd been struggling to keep contained.

"Did you see anything else? Think carefully, and leave nothing out that could still come to pass."

Finn thought back to the visions he'd tried so hard to repress. He'd thought if he refused to replay those memories, perhaps they'd disappear. But as he reflected back on his crossing, the visions returned just as clearly as though they'd been shown to him hours, and not weeks before. He shuddered and gritted his teeth, determined not to let the fear get the better of him. If there was anyone who could do something about what he'd seen, it would be Grayston.

"From there the visions became a blur," Finn said. "They came one after another so fast I could barely comprehend them. The Guardian wanted me to lose hope, so all I saw was devastation. The last thing I remember clearly was seeing the mountains of the Western Wilds. There was a figure standing there. I couldn't see their face, but they had long hair of a white that made me think of bones."

Grayston hissed a word under his breath that Finn couldn't understand, perhaps a curse in a language Finn had never heard. Or a name.

"It makes sense," Grayston's fingers tapped on the rail of the ship. "I knew something must be controlling them when I saw them building ships."

"You think there's something else out there? Something more than the Shriekers?" Finn shivered. The Shriekers were bad enough, but the dread he'd felt seeing the figure in the mountains was greater even than what a Shrieker's call evoked. "Do you think the Guardian might know something about it?"

"Perhaps," Grayston's fingers began tapping faster. "It is uncertain where the Guardian came from. His bridge is on every map of Okaesa I have ever seen, save for one. In the king's quarters, there's a map so ancient it's nearly too faded to read. Many of the mainland villages west of the Serpent had already been founded. You can find Westham on this map, but the Nightmare Bridge is missing. In its place is an unmarked road that does not exist on any other map I've seen. So the Guardian was not already there when the first explorers founded Okaesa, as some other stories claim."

The drumming of Grayston's fingers suddenly ceased. "Have you told anyone else what you saw? Commander Tallis perhaps?"

"No, sir," Finn stammered, head reeling with everything Grayston had told him, and what it might mean about the visions the Guardian had shown him.

"Good," Grayston breathed a sigh. "Keep it that way, for now. Should you recall any other details, report them directly to me."

"Of course, sir," Finn felt as though a burden had been lifted from his shoulders. Someone else knew of the terrible things he'd seen, someone who could do something about them.

Grayston's demeanor relaxed, shoulders easing and posture softening. "It never gets easier to watch a ship sail toward danger, carrying people you care about aboard."

The admiral placed a hand on Finn's shoulder with a firm grip. The small gesture of comfort made Finn think of Nevra, and a sudden wave of homesickness crashed over him.

"Reserve your fear for when it is warranted," Grayston said. "The *Storm Ghost* always returns."

With a nod of his head, Grayston turned his back on Finn and strode across the deck toward his cabin. Finn glanced once more toward the western horizon, where the last light of the sun was now fading and the stars were slowly awakening in the sky. The brightest star of the Silver Fish, its eye, was now shining clearly where the scouts had disappeared. Finn imagined it gazing down on the *Storm Ghost*, and although Tallis had passed far beyond his sight, it comforted him to know they were still both watched by the same eye of the Silver Fish, and the eyes of the Protector. As the evening chill began to creep across the deck of the ship, Finn turned away from the horizon to join the rest of the crew in the warmth below deck.

CHAPTER NINETEEN

The Bloody Shoals

The closer they drew to the Serpent's Mouth, the more nervous the whole crew became. They would reach the harbor by morning. Tallis tossed and turned late into the night before finally giving up and getting dressed again. There was no point in her lying awake and doing nothing. She may as well go relieve someone above and let them sleep.

The night was unusually quiet for the season. The water was calm, and the wind barely moved the sails. But it was much colder than any of the previous nights had been. Tallis' breath fogged in the frosty air. The stars shone bright in the clear cold air and the still ocean reflected them with near mirror-like quality, making it look as though both sea and sky were flecked with frost.

Tallis went up to the helm to find Fadren at the wheel. The girl looked up, startled, and wiped away tears too late for Tallis to not notice.

"Are you alright?" Tallis asked.

"Sorry, Commander," she said. "I thought I'd be alone for a while."

"It's fine," Tallis said. "Do you want to talk? Or would you rather go rest? I couldn't sleep so I was going to relieve you."

"I'm not sure I'd be able to sleep either."

"Something bothering you?"

"I'm almost as worried we've seen nothing as I am nervous we'll encounter the Shriekers," Fadren admitted, words spilling out of her, clear she'd been holding them in for too long. "And I miss my little sister. I've never been away from her this long. And I can't stop thinking about my father. We don't know he's dead, but if he isn't then that's probably worse. I suppose I wanted a chance to find him, if he's alive, and if he's not... I don't know why I'm telling you this. You must have better things you could be doing than listening to my problems, Commander."

"My job isn't just bossing you all around when the captain needs me to," Tallis said. "The captain needs everyone on this crew to do their jobs, so if there's anything I can do to help make that happen, I should do it. You seemed upset. If it'd help to have someone to talk to, I can listen. I understand wanting to help your family. Even if circumstances hadn't forced me here, I may have joined anyway to keep them safe."

"I know your siblings were staying at the Crow's Nest with my mother," Fadren asked. "What happened to your parents?"

"They never left the mainland."

"Oh," Fadren looked embarrassed, realizing what that meant. "I'm sorry."

"It's alright," Tallis lied. Nothing about this whole war was alright. "At least I know they're dead. It must be hard not knowing."

"I keep hoping maybe my father's ship will turn up," Fadren said. "But the Star Bird was last seen when the fleet abandoned King's Harbor. Unless they ran instead of returning to Giant's Isle, they probably either sank or were taken. The Star Bird's captain isn't the type to abandon his duty."

"Perhaps this scouting mission will allow us to find out one way or the other," Tallis offered, but it was little in the way of comfort.

"I hope so," Fadren said. "Before I left, I promised my mother I'd do what I could to find out what happened. And if the Star Bird was taken by the Shriekers, I'd give my father the rest he deserves. But I've never been in a real battle before, just training. I'm not sure I can kill anyone, let alone my own father."

"The Shriekers won't give you a choice," Tallis said, her father's deformed face surfacing in her mind. "It'll be you or them. And it's not like killing a person. To kill a Shrieker is mercy. I was forced to kill my father, but it wasn't him anymore. There was nothing in those black eyes that reflected who he used to be."

"You were able to do it though?" Fadren asked.

"I had to," Tallis gritted her teeth, remembering how Papa had rushed at her, mouth dripping with black poison.

"So you understand," Fadren said. "If we find the Star Bird, I have to do something, even if I don't know what that will be."

Tallis stared up at the Silver Fish constellation the *Storm Ghost* was sailing toward. Tallis remembered her father teaching her the constellations, telling stories about what they meant, and how they could be used for navigation. Nevra had always spoken of the Silver Fish as a comforting companion to Okaesan sailors, pointing the way home. But for her, the Silver Fish had only ever pointed toward darkness and danger. As a child, it had hovered above the peaks of the Western Wilds, and now it pointed to a mainland that was no longer theirs.

"I understand," Tallis said finally. "If there was any chance my parents could be alive, I'd be searching for them too."

"What are they like?" Fadren's voice was quiet, and there was a dark shadow of fear in her eyes. "The Shriekers, I mean. Everyone talks about them, but it's hard to know what's real and what's exaggerated."

Tallis had spent so much time trying not to think about her few confrontations with the monsters that it was strange to recall it now. All the time between fleeing Westham and arriving at Giant's Isle was a nightmarish blur, simultaneously vivid and unreal.

"It's true they're dangerous," Tallis said. "But they aren't invulnerable. We have a chance of destroying them. They fear fire, and that is a weapon the Okaesan fleet is renowned for. I can't imagine Shrieker ships standing up against explosive cannon fire."

Tallis spoke with conviction in her voice, but inwardly she thought of how the Shriekers had advanced past every barricade that had been raised against them. Despite Tallis' internal worries, a faint smile played across Fadren's face, and the fear had faded from her eyes. Eiran's words echoed in her mind. *Strong as the sea.* It would have to be enough that Fadren took comfort from her words, even if she didn't feel that conviction herself.

"Why don't you try to get some rest, Fadren," Tallis said. "I can take care of the helm. We don't know what we'll find in the morning. You should be well rested."

"Aye, Commander," Fadren gave a small salute. "Thank you."

The girl left the helm and Tallis watched her disappear below deck. Behind the *Storm Ghost* to the east, the sky was beginning to lighten with the first whisperings of dawn. It wouldn't be long now before the deck was bustling with activity. The sunrise chased away the night, and Tallis could see the faint outlines of the mountains against the sky. The shore was close.

Before the sun was fully up, Eiran emerged from her cabin. Without a word, she joined Tallis at the helm. Tallis didn't need to ask to know the captain had slept no better than herself. Eiran's eyes were lined with exhaustion. Together, they stood in silence as the sun painted the sky with deep red, golden light casting long shadows on the deck of the ship. Gradually, more crew members rose from sleep and came up to the deck. Alleto ascended to the helm to stand beside Tallis and Eiran. They all watched as the lightening sky revealed what lay before them.

The view of the Serpent's Mouth was dismal. The buildings were charred and broken, and the docks and streets were deserted. The harbor looked nothing like Tallis remembered it from her childhood, or even from the last time she'd been here. She thought of the day they'd fled, listening to the sound of cannon fire from the darkness of a ship's hold.

"I would have done the same thing in Grayston's place," Eiran sighed. "But to fire on our own city... I don't envy him that moment of choice."

"Where are the ships?" Tallis asked.

Eiran shook her head. "It doesn't make any sense. Clearly Grayston wasn't lying about them making repairs, otherwise the wrecks of the ships that didn't make it back would still be in the harbor."

"It's too quiet," Alleto said. "Have you noticed? This place should be crawling with gulls scavenging what was left behind. So why is the sky empty?"

"You're right," Eiran scanned the sky. "Not a bird or other beast in sight. Tallis, give the order to ready the cannons. I have a bad feeling about this."

Tallis nodded. "Aye, Captain."

Most of the crew milled about on deck, cautiously watching the shoreline and waiting for orders. Tallis hurried down the stairs from the helm to address them.

"To battle posts," Tallis ordered. "Load the cannons and be ready to fire. Something's not right here and the captain wants us prepared. Go."

Some urgency in her voice must have carried. There were a handful of tired grumbles, but no one protested, and the crew quickly set about their work.

"Captain!" Hemma shouted from the crow's nest. "There's ships coming from the east!"

Tallis ran to rejoin Eiran.

"The east?" Eiran turned her scope back the way they'd come and cursed. She tossed the scope to Tallis. "Try to get a count of their number. They're not ours, and I don't know of any fleet with black sails."

"Aye," Tallis raised the scope to her eye and understood why Eiran looked so worried. Somehow, an entire fleet of ships had gotten between them and the way back to the rest of the fleet.

"We've been outflanked!" Eiran shouted and sprang down to the deck. She strode among the crew, shouting orders. "Bring her around. We can't get caught here. Aim for the Bloody Shoals to the south. If we can lose them in the shallow water, we can outrun them back to the fleet. Hurry!"

The sailors jumped to their posts with a haste Tallis had never seen before. Within moments, the sails were raised and the *Storm Ghost* was turning toward the islands in the distance that were little more than rocks jutting from the surface of the water.

Tallis counted near a dozen ships behind them. They were picking up speed and headed straight for the *Storm Ghost*.

"Eiran, they've spotted us," Tallis shouted.

"They're gaining on us," Hemma called almost simultaneously.

Eiran dashed back up to the helm and took the wheel from Alleto.

"We can outpace them," Eiran said. "We just need to pick up speed."

"Captain, the rocks," Alleto's voice trembled. "We should be dropping speed, not increasing it. They're not called the 'Bloody' Shoals for nothing. They'll kill us just as sure as those ships."

"Come now, Alleto," Eiran grinned. "I thought you'd have more faith in me than that. There's a way through. The king himself taught me how to navigate it during the Kerethi war. It saved us then and it can save us now. This is why I'd choose the *Storm Ghost* over a grand ship like the *Lady's Kiss* any day. Only she can pull this off."

"But the tide is low," Alleto protested.

"Then lighten the ship if it makes you feel better," Eiran snapped "Tallis, have you got numbers for me?"

"It's hard to tell," Tallis said. "But it's near a dozen."

"You're sure?" Eiran asked and Tallis nodded. "Where'd they get all those ships? Only a few could be ours and there's no way they could have built ships in that short of a time."

"A few look like the Kerethi style," Tallis said.

Eiran frowned. "The Kerethi color their sails red and gold."

"The sails are different, but I've seen Kerethi ships at the Serpent's Mouth," Tallis said. "My father would point them out to me. He fought in the Kerethi wars. He'd know what a Kerethi ship looked like. Their hulls are Kerethi style with gull figureheads."

Eiran looked worried. "Is there one with a wolf on its flag?"

Tallis looked through the scope again. "I don't see flags on any of them."

Eiran bowed her head and her knuckles were white on the wheel. "Damn pirates. Plenty of good ones. But a few probably saw the abandoned harbors as a chance for easy loot and didn't give a thought as to why we'd left in the first place."

"I thought the Kerethi were on our side now?" Tallis asked.

Eiran laughed. "The only side the Kerethi are on is their own. The only reason we have peace with them is that, usually, we outgun them, and they see more profit trading with us than stealing from us. They have a leader, called the Kerr, but the position holds less authority than our king. Their captains operate more independently than ours, often acting without the authorization of the Kerr. There are some for whom an empty harbor's too tempting a prize, treaty or not. I only hope my friend, the Wolf, is smarter than that."

"Doesn't really matter whose ships they used to be," Tallis said, wanting to ask about the Wolf, but there wasn't the time. "They're all the same now."

"Are we certain they're Shriekers?" Alleto chimed in. "I know Grayston reported seeing them repairing ships, but how could a mindless horde become a fleet?"

Eiran glanced behind. The ships were close enough now to see without the scope, but not close enough even with it to make out details of the crew. Tallis wished Alleto could be right, and that there was a chance the fleet following them were crewed by ordinary people. Eiran grabbed the scope again and peered through it. Every moment of her silence stretched, and Tallis wished she knew what the captain was seeing.

"No banners," Eiran sighed, lowering the scope to her side. "And no other signals to speak of. I don't know who'd be sailing those ships if not Shriekers, but whoever they are, they aren't friendly. They'd be making some kind of signal if they were."

By now, they now sailed almost equidistant between their pursuers and the Bloody Shoals. Tallis wondered which was the deadlier foe.

"Find me Harrin," Eiran commanded. "I need his keen eyes in the bow as much if not more than his sister's above right now. Tell him, if he sees a rock ahead, to raise a hand for which direction I should turn to go around. Tell the crew to be ready to douse the sails on my order. Momentum will carry us through the rocks."

Tallis nodded and ran off down the deck, seeking the boy among the chaos.

"Alleto!" Tallis called and the man turned to her. "Make ready to take in the sails. Eiran will give the word when it is time. And I need to find Harrin."

"Below deck, Commander," Alleto told her. "I wanted the less experienced fighters below, in case it comes to arms."

"Let's hope it doesn't," Tallis said before leaving Alleto to arrange the sails. She dashed down the stairs. Harrin was waiting beside a cannon.

"Harrin," Tallis called, "you're needed above."

The boy jumped on hearing his name, but relaxed when he saw it was her. He followed her back up to the deck.

"You're needed as a lookout," Tallis explained as she led the way. "The captain's leading us into the rocks. It seems dangerous, but she says she's done it before."

Harrin's eyes widened as she conveyed Eiran's orders for him. When they reached the bow and saw exactly what the *Storm Ghost* was headed for, he hesitated, fear evident on his face. Ahead, sharp rocks jutted from the water, none large enough to even be called an isle, but plenty large enough to sink a ship.

"That's a lot on me," Harrin sounded nervous and Tallis laid a hand on his shoulder.

"You and your sister are the best eyes we've got and she's busy above," Tallis said. "The captain needs you and she wouldn't have asked if she didn't trust you. If all goes well, you won't even have to do anything. You're the back-up."

"I'll do my best, Commander," Harrin promised. His jaw set and the fear in his eyes began to dissipate.

"I'm sure you will," Tallis said. "I must return to the captain. If you want to start praying to the Lady and the Protector that this escape plan works, I'm sure it won't hurt."

"Let's hope they hear us."

Tallis turned from Harrin and dashed back across the deck, dodging sailors who were scrambling to be ready to either fight or flee. Everywhere she looked, she saw terror in the crew's eyes, but Eiran stood steadfast at the helm, outwardly calm despite the chaos on deck.

"Is everything prepared?" Eiran asked when Tallis rejoined her.

"Aye," Tallis said and glanced behind the ship. "And it seems you're right about the *Storm Ghost*'s speed. They're not gaining on us anymore."

"Now we just need to get back to the fleet in time to warn them," Eiran said.

"Eiran, we're coming into those rocks very fast," Tallis noticed. "Should we strike the sails yet?"

"Give it another few moments," Eiran said. "I want them to try to chase us through the rocks. With some luck, we can sink a few of their ships in this escape."

"It won't be any use if we're lost too," Tallis said.

Eiran glanced over at Tallis, a wild look in her eyes. "You're about to see why the *Storm Ghost* has a reputation for always coming home."

Tallis knew better than to try to argue with the captain. Instead, she kept an eye on the ships behind them, to see if they were either managing to outpace them. She was tempted to keep glancing toward the rocks, but it only made her more nervous. It would be better to just trust Eiran.

"Take in the sails!" Eiran finally shouted after long minutes that had stretched into ages. "Be ready to hoist them again once we're clear of the shoals."

The sailors up on the masts pulled the white sails up and tied them off. With the sails up and the ship running on momentum and the rudder, the chaos on deck subsided. A quiet stillness took over. The crew stood at their posts, silently waiting for further orders from Eiran. Some watched the rocks ahead, and some stared behind at the enemy ships. The air was thick with the anxious energy of everyone on board the *Storm Ghost*, like the air before a thunderstorm.

Only Eiran seemed to be unaffected by the mood on the ship. She steered with a calm confidence, deftly maneuvering around the first rocks and keeping to the deeper water in between. It was clear she had indeed done this before, as Harrin remained motionless in the prow.

It was difficult to gauge how much water separated the *Storm Ghost* from the rocks below. The clear water made it easy to see the bottom, but the clarity also deceived the eye and made it unclear what was the seabed and what was rock closer to the surface. However deep the water was, it was much too shallow for Tallis' taste. Though wrecking the ship here was unlikely to kill them with the mainland so close, the *Storm Ghost* was their only hope of escape. They might not drown, but reaching the mainland might turn out to be a worse fate.

Harrin raised his left hand and Eiran turned the ship to port. For a moment, the captain looked worried, but the calm mask quickly returned. Tallis looked over the starboard side of the ship to see the hull barely slide past a giant submerged rock.

"How are the ships behind us responding?" Eiran asked.

Tallis held up the scope to look behind.

"They're dropping canvas," Tallis said. "Much further back than we did. They're clearly more nervous of the rocks than you."

"Good," Eiran grinned. "Though let's hope they're not too nervous to follow us in."

Harrin raised his left hand again and Eiran turned the wheel. The boy began waving his hand more urgently.

"We can't keep going to port or we'll be off the safe route," Eiran growled, but Harrin's frantic waving clearly worried her and she turned the nose of the ship harder to port.

A dull scraping noise preceded a shudder that reverberated through the beams of the ship and the *Storm Ghost* was knocked sideways with a great force that made Tallis stumble. No one on the deck moved while the scraping sound grated across the length of the ship.

CHAPTER TWENTY

Red Sky at Morning

Finn watched the horizon. To stand watch while the *Lady's Kiss* was moored at the center of the fleet felt unnecessary, but he performed his duty with rapt attention. His gaze was fixed due west, the direction the *Storm Ghost* had been sent. He'd watched her go until her sails disappeared over the line of the sea, and now he watched, aching with hope he'd see her coming back, despite what he knew waited at the Serpent's Mouth.

Light began to creep into the edges of the world behind him, but Finn remained fixated on the west, where the sky remained inky black. A shout from the crow's nest split the night air like a knife. Finn jumped, heart leaping to his throat.

"Smoke and fire!" cried the voice from above. "To the north!"

Finn turned his gaze northward. From where he stood, he could barely see an orange glow upon the horizon, and dark, billowing smoke only visible by how it blocked out the stars. Finn sprang to action, sprinting across the deck to the admiral's cabin. Whatever was happening, he was sure Grayston would want to know, and as the nightwatch on deck, it was his duty to wake him. Though, Finn did not relish the idea of rousing the man from his rest.

The admiral appeared only a few moments after Finn pounded on his door, scowling, but fully dressed as though he'd already been awake.

"Sir," Finn saluted, before hurrying with the report, "to the north, something is happening. There's fire."

Without a word, Grayston strode to the prow. Unsure what else to do, Finn followed, in case the admiral needed something, or if anyone else needed to be roused. The admiral withdrew a scope from an inner pocket of his jacket and raised it to his eye. He stood without sound or movement for a few moments. Finn realized he was holding his breath.

"To the south!" the voice from the crow's nest called again. "More fire!"

Grayston's face darkened and he turned his scope southward.

"Salt and rotting fish," Grayston murmured almost imperceptibly, along with a few more colorful curses that bled together in one breath.

"Sir?" Finn spoke tentatively, wishing he could disappear. "Orders, sir? Should I fetch Commander Bevan for you?"

Grayston's hands fell to his sides, the scope hanging limply, as if forgotten, in one loose fist. For the first time, the admiral turned his gaze to Finn. His cold eyes looked as though they could freeze even salt water, and Finn trembled.

"No," Grayston shook his head. "There's nothing that can be done but wait. When the sun rises, perhaps we will be able to see and learn more."

"Is it the scouts?" Finn asked before he could think, his worry about Tallis overtaking his fear.

Grayston regarded him in silence and Finn sucked in his breath, as though he could suck his words out of the air along with it.

"I'd imagine so," Grayston said at last, returning his gaze to the horizon, not to the barely visible fires, but to the west. He raised the scope again, scanning the western horizon. He dropped it with a sigh and Finn could not tell if it was from frustration or relief. "For us to be able to see the smoke, they were either already on their way back, or never managed to reach King's Harbor at all. That means the Shriekers have mobilized and are no longer confined to the harbors. There's no sign of the third scout. Though is that good or bad?"

The question was not directed at Finn, so he gave no answer. The admiral returned the scope to his jacket pocket and leaned forward, both hands upon the rail, still gazing westward, as though his naked eyes could tell him more than the scope could.

"I imagine you share my anxiety over the absence of the third scout," Grayston's jaw clenched. "If we lose the *Storm Ghost*... it's a heavier loss than just a ship."

Finn wanted to point out that any ship lost also meant the loss of dozens of lives; people who mattered, had family, and yearned for the chance to go home. But he couldn't deny his own concern for the *Storm Ghost*.

"You must have known Commander Tallis since you were very young," Grayston said. Finn was taken aback by the statement. The admiral's moods were still a mystery to him, and Finn wondered what had brought this on.

"As long as I can remember," Finn admitted. "She's a year older than me. Tallis was always a leader. I followed her around wherever she'd go. Until now."

The hint of a smile played across Grayston's face, though he kept his gaze fixed westward, not once turning to look at Finn.

"Eiran has three years on me," Grayston said. "I suppose you had fewer choices for companions. Growing up in Giant's Isle together, I think Eiran hardly noticed me. Of course she knew who I was, but she kept the company of other nobles' daughters her own age. She played the part of a proper lady well, but I could see even when we were children that role didn't fit her. She was always sneaking off to ride across the bluffs or explore the lower city."

"She sounds like Tallis."

Grayston let out a soft laugh. "I didn't understand why Eiran chose Tallis. I still have doubts about choosing someone with so little experience. But perhaps it was not such a mysterious choice for Eiran."

The smile faded from Grayston's face as quickly as it had appeared. His brow furrowed as he continued to watch the horizon.

"It wasn't supposed to happen this way," Grayston muttered, almost too softly for Finn to hear.

"Sir?" Finn could not fathom what the admiral meant.

"I'd never have risked Eiran if..." Grayston continued as though he'd forgotten Finn was there, his voice low and agitated. "I should have been able to stop this. I *could* stop this."

A wild look had come into Grayston's eyes, and Finn took a step back. This was a side of Grayston he'd never seen, and a terror Finn couldn't explain welled in his gut.

"Admiral?"

Grayston straightened and tore his gaze from the horizon, glancing down at Finn as though surprised to find him there. His eyes were again clear and hard as ice, with no trace of the brewing wild storm of just moments before.

"Tell me, Finley," Grayston's voice had returned to its regular, even tone of authority. "What price would you be willing to pay for the safety of Okaesa?"

"I—I don't know," Finn stammered, unable to guess what kind of answer Grayston was looking for.

"I see," Grayston nodded, as though Finn's answer had given him information Finn was unaware of himself.

The admiral turned away and it was like a curtain being drawn over a window he'd briefly allowed Finn to see through. He'd been shown a glimpse at what lay beneath Grayston's role as admiral, and his answer had somehow meant that window was now closed. What he'd seen left a haze of unease.

As they'd talked, edges of dawn's light had begun to creep ever higher. Finn did his best to shake off his unease at Grayston's sudden change of tone and turned his gaze at last away from the west. Behind the ship, the sky and sea were a deep, rosy red, as if blood had been spilled from the sun onto the water.

"Red sky at morning," Finn recited in a hushed tone.

"Sailors take warning," Grayston finished for him. "It seems our luck with the weather is running out. It bodes ill for whatever news we will receive from the scouts today, if we receive any."

As if to affirm the admiral's words, a call came again from the crow's nest. Boats had been spotted, but not the scouts returning. The glaring sunrise behind them had masked their approach, but now Finn could see them, even without Grayston's scope or the height of the mast. Three rowboats cut through the water toward them from the south.

As they drew closer, Finn could see the number of sailors in the boats was nowhere near the number that would have made up the crew of even the smallest of the fleet's ships. They all looked exhausted, some were injured, but all were still human. The boats drew up alongside the *Lady's Kiss*. Grayston hurried to the side, no trace of the mood Finn had glimpsed left on his face.

"Drop them the ladders," he commanded. By now, many of the crew of the *Lady's Kiss* had emerged from the sleeping quarters below deck. The admiral's command was answered quickly. More slowly, the sailors in the boats began to ascend.

Finn barely recognized the first man to come over the rail. He nearly collapsed when he put his feet on the deck, but Grayston caught him by the arm.

"Commander Avedis," Grayston addressed him. "Where is your captain? And where is the Elk Horn?"

Avedis was breathing heavily, and struggled to speak. When he'd been in charge of their training, he'd been proud and stern, with an air that nothing could faze him. Now, his eyes were dark with exhaustion, and looked bloodshot with tears and terror. He held his right arm close to his side, and his coat was stained heavily with blood, both red and black. But through a tear in the sleeve, Finn could see a long, deep gash in his shoulder. The wound looked grave, possibly enough to rob Avedis of the use of his arm, but it bled with red blood. He was uninfected.

"Ambush," Avedis panted. "We were overwhelmed. Many of our crew were infected, Markence among them. He ordered anyone who hadn't been bitten to the rowboats, and those who were already lost remained behind with him. They kept fighting as long as they could, so we might have a chance to escape. The Elk Horn is either at the bottom of the sea, or in the hands of the Shriekers now."

"The rest of your report can wait," Grayston said. "Finish it after you've been seen to by our healer. You and your crew will have to be inspected, of course, you understand."

"Of course," Avedis agreed. "Even the most honest man can turn to lies in the face of death."

Grayston led Avedis and what remained of the crew of the Elk Horn below deck. Finn was locked where he stood, reeling from Avedis' words. The unease he'd felt after speaking with the admiral was washed away by this new revelation. He'd heard the rumors and prayed they were false, but this was proof the Shriekers had the ability to sail. How many ships did they have to cause such a catastrophe? The fleet had yet to launch an attack, and already they'd lost at least one ship, perhaps more given the smoke to the north during the night, and the absence of the *Storm Ghost*.

Instead of the usual bustle of activity, the crew on deck all stood in similar, shocked silence to Finn. Some whispered to each other, others simply stood and stared out to sea. Finn noticed many of the newest recruits, those who'd come from Giant's Isle, with their faces pale and eyes wide with horror. They'd now seen first-hand what the Shriekers could wreak, and Finn knew exactly how they felt. He remembered when battalions had crossed the Foggy, only to return, broken and with such small fractions of the numbers they'd left with. They'd stumble, dazed, into Westham, as if they didn't remember where they were. Many didn't make it. Finn thought of how much blood was on Avedis' jacket, and wondered if he would make it.

"Finn?" Cori appeared at his side, laying a light hand upon his arm. "You alright?"

"No." Finn couldn't muster the energy to lie, or to say anything more.

"We still don't know what happened to the *Storm Ghost*," Cori said, and clearly meant it as a comfort. "She could still come back."

Finn nodded, not knowing if "she" was meant to refer to the ship, or to Tallis. It almost didn't matter. So few of the crew of the Elk Horn had returned without their ship. He didn't dare imagine how many had been left behind, choosing to fight to the last, knowing they were already dead.

"Seems like it was a long night watch," Cori's eyes were full of sympathy. Finn wanted to fall into those eyes and never get up, sudden exhaustion taking over from the adrenaline that had powered him through the night and the morning. "Let's get you some food and some sleep."

Finn let himself be steered away from the deck, and the group of tattered, unmoored sailors who'd survived one night of horror, but were still so far from the chance of going home. To the east, the sun had cleared the horizon, but the gathering clouds around it were still the red of clean blood. The bank of thick, red clouds promised a brewing storm, and more blood yet to be spilled.

CHAPTER TWENTY-ONE

Star Bird

There was a collective sigh of relief when the grinding scrape of the hull on ground stopped and the ship began to move freely again in the deeper water. Tallis checked over the edge to see what they'd hit. The water looked deceptively deep, but a hidden shoal lurked just beneath the surface. They'd just barely missed an outcrop that jutted up to the surface and had instead run over the shelf that sprawled out from it.

Tallis shuddered when she noticed the old bones of a shipwreck. It was ancient, engulfed in barnacles and seaweed. It was hard to tell if the other ship had merely not turned away as quickly as Eiran had, or if it had the misfortune of a lower tide or a heavier cargo. But whatever the case, it was clear Eiran barely steered them clear of suffering the same fate.

"There's a wreck down there," Tallis informed Eiran.

"Yes," she nodded. "And there will be more the further we go until we reach the other side. Especially if we can't find a way back to the deeper route I was trying to keep to before this shoal turned us the wrong way. The tide must be lower than I anticipated."

"We will make it through, right?" Tallis asked. "We're not too far off course, are we?"

Eiran turned to look at her. The captain's face was grim, but she broke out her grin anyway.

"The *Storm Ghost* and I have survived worse than this together," she said. "Now get below deck and bring me a damage report. I need to know if the hull is cracked or broken. If she's taking in any water we need to do something about it now, or we might never make it out of this labyrinth. And, if there is water getting in, make sure the cannon powder stores are clear of it. We're going to need those dry."

"Aye, Captain," Tallis hurried down to the lower levels of the ship. The younger recruits still waited nervously by the cannons.

"Is everything alright up there, Commander?" Jayim asked, stepping out of the group toward her.

Tallis thought about Eiran's worried face, and about her advice, *Strong as the sea.*

"We're back on course now," Tallis assured them. "There was a hidden shoal, but we missed the worst of it. The captain wants a report on the hull. Could I have a few volunteers to help me check the storage and sleeping quarters below?"

Jayim was the first to raise his hand, along with Fadren and a few others who seemed eager to do something other than wait, not knowing what was ahead.

"Come on then," Tallis led them down to the bottom level of the ship.

It was always damp where the ship sat below the water, and it was difficult to tell what was normal and what was potential leakage.

"Spread out," Tallis ordered. "I want the whole hull inspected. Eiran needs to know if there's even the tiniest crack letting water in."

The sailors did as she asked and Tallis went to inspect the powder hold herself. The room where the barrels were stored seemed dry enough. Tallis carefully examined the floor for any signs of a leak.

A loud boom made Tallis jump. There were shouts from above. The group of volunteers all came running.

"What was that?" one asked.

"Keep up the work on the hull," Tallis said. "I need the inspection finished. I will go find out what's going on."

"That wasn't a rock," Fadren spoke up. "I was only a kid when the Kerethi attacked Giant's Isle, but I still know cannon fire when I hear it."

"Stay down here," Tallis said, trying to appear calmer than she felt. Most of these sailors were younger than her. Tallis was suddenly struck by the same desire as Alleto to keep the youngest of the crew below deck. Another boom of cannon fire sounded, this time from directly above.

"That was one of ours," Jayim said.

"The captain will want me above," Tallis said. "Stay alert. The hull is important, but your lives are more so. Keep your weapons ready and listen for orders from above. Now, keep looking for leaks. Go."

Tallis drew her sword and dashed back up the stairs. The cannons were being fired on the starboard side. Tallis hurried up to the deck.

A black-sailed ship was emerging from the shelter of a natural rock formation. The rock must have hid it until it was too late to change course. Now, it blocked the way forward and the momentum of the *Storm Ghost* was carrying them toward it.

Eiran had turned the *Storm Ghost* to return fire and to make for a narrow gap between two tall rocks ahead. The enemy ship had also seen the gap and was moving to cut them off. Eiran was shouting orders and sailors were drawing swords as the *Storm Ghost* drew nearer to the other ship.

A chorus of shrieks sent a shiver down Tallis' spine. The faint hope that Grayston's reports had been wrong, and their pursuers were some unknown, but ordinary fleet evaporated. On the deck of the other ship, Shriekers were preparing to swing over and board the *Storm Ghost*.

"It's the Shriekers!" a sailor shouted.

"Lady, preserve us," another prayed.

Tallis felt frozen in place as she watched the other ship approach. Papa was the only Shrieker she'd seen. Finn had told her the horde that had descended on Westham had moved like a herd of deer scattered by the howl of a wolf, each one for themselves. Now they moved like the wolf pack, calculated and predatory, ready to strike as one. Tallis wondered what had changed, but had no time now to ponder.

Beside her, a new recruit's sword dropped from his hand and clattered to the deck. His eyes were white with terror. He backed away from the starboard side, as though there were anywhere he could run. Tallis broke herself free of her own initial shock and strode forward, scooping the sword from the deck. She grabbed the man by the shoulder and pressed his sword back into his hand.

"You'll be needing this," she said, looking him squarely in the eye. "What's your name?"

"Mirrus, Commander," he stuttered.

Tallis looked to Harrin in the bow, and Eiran at the helm. If they wanted to escape, both needed to be safe from the impending fight to navigate out of the trap they'd fallen into.

"Mirrus, go to the bow," Tallis ordered. "Take a couple more fighters with you and protect Harrin. The captain needs the boy for navigating out of here and fighting will distract him from his duty. Make sure no Shriekers reach that boy, or the rocks may doom us just as much as that ship. Understand?"

"Aye, Commander," Mirrus saluted, and straightened. His grip on his sword tightened, and some of the fear faded from his eyes as he focused on the task she'd given him. Mirrus hurried off, grabbing a few more along the way to form a perimeter around Harrin.

Tallis met Harrin's eyes. He looked scared and confused. Tallis gestured to the rocks, hoping he'd understand his job hadn't changed. He nodded and turned back to scanning the water. Tallis then swept her gaze across the deck, seeing similar horror to Mirrus' in many of the other crew members' eyes. She remembered that, for most of the crew, this was their first time seeing Shriekers. Tallis took a deep breath and braced herself to attempt to rally the crew, but Eiran's voice rang out across the deck first.

"Hold your positions!" Eiran called. "Remind these monsters that they're dead, and we'll get to see Giant's Isle again. Waves take their bones!"

Eiran's speech was cut short as the *Storm Ghost* drifted within range and the Shriekers swung over. The moments stretched as they hung, suspended over the water. One by one, they dropped, hitting the deck hard enough that Tallis heard bones crunch, but this did little to even slow them.

Time resumed its pace like a wave crashing as the Shriekers rushed the crew. Before she could think and let terror take hold again, Tallis raised her father's sword and charged forward to meet them. She cut the line of one that had landed, tottering, on the rail. Rather than swinging back for another attempt at boarding, the creature plummeted to the clear blue water below.

Around her, the clash of metal on metal rang a dissonant cacophony with the bone-chilling shrieks of their assailants. Tallis gritted her teeth and rushed at the next Shrieker nearest her, taking off its head with a clean blow of her sword. The next came at her too fast to give her time for a swift cut to its neck and instead she raised her sword to stop the downswing of its blade. The impact knocked her backward.

In training, very few of her opponents had come at her in earnest, often pulling their blows at the last moment. She regained her footing and turned its next blow aside, but rather than responding with another blow of the sword like a human opponent might, it bent nearly double, broken jaw yawning wide so Tallis could see the razor-sharp fangs, dripping with black poison. It lunged with such speed all she could do was raise her off hand. The jaws closed around her wrist, and Tallis screamed, anticipating the sharp bite of teeth that would mean her end, but it didn't come. The Shrieker's jaws had closed around the thick leather of her bracers and hadn't pierced skin. As it struggled to bite down harder, Tallis hacked at its neck with her sword, too close to give it a quick end. The first time she hit, it shrieked, releasing her wrist. Her second blow broke the spine and it dropped to the deck.

"Commander!" Alleto was at her side. He grabbed her by the wrist and pulled her away from the fray. Other sailors poured around them, cutting them off from the Shriekers.

"I'm fine," Tallis protested, but raised her arm to inspect it anyway. She hadn't felt anything pierce her skin, but needed to be sure. There were teeth marks in the leather, but no blood.

"Thought we'd lost you," Alleto sighed with relief.

"Not yet."

Tallis took the brief moment of calm to survey the chaos on the deck. She glanced between the stairs to the lower decks and the ones that led up to the helm. Jayim and other newer recruits were still below, and Eiran was focused on steering. Tallis felt torn between protecting her captain or the younger sailors.

Tallis noticed a knot of soldiers hesitating to join the fray.

"You lot!" Tallis rounded on them and they looked startled to be singled out. "Protect the stairs to the lower decks. Don't let them down to the cannons. Come on, don't just stand there, protect the ship!"

Unwilling to ignore direct orders, they did as they were told. Tallis turned to Alleto, still at her side.

"Go with them," Tallis told him. "We can't let the Shriekers pass beyond the main deck."

"Aye, Commander," Alleto saluted and followed the group, organizing them into a line to guard the stairs.

Tallis turned from the group and hurried to Eiran's side just in time to cut down a Shrieker that had broken through a wall of fighters on the starboard side of the deck. Tallis wrenched her sword free of the creature's neck and leapt up the stairs to join the captain.

"The hull?" Eiran asked when Tallis joined her.

"I wasn't able to finish the work, but the powder is dry and there wasn't any major damage that I noticed," Tallis said.

"Well at least that's one good thing."

Tallis lunged at a Shrieker making for the stairs. It put up more of a fight than the first, but Tallis managed to get in a cut at its arm that made it drop its sword. She swung her sword hard down on its neck and kicked it overboard. Shrieks cut through the air and set Tallis' teeth on edge. It was hard to focus on anything through the din.

Fadren appeared suddenly at Tallis' side.

"I thought I told you all to stay below deck," Tallis said.

"I came up to see what was going on," Fadren said. Her voice was flat and her eyes were glistening. "I was going to go back down to tell the others, but then I saw the ship. Commander, it's the Star Bird."

Tallis' heart sank, and she looked over to the black-sailed ship. "You're sure?"

"I'd know that ship anywhere," Fadren asserted. "I need to stay and fight. For my father."

"Fine, then," Tallis sighed. She couldn't take this chance away from Fadren. "You defend the port stairs, and I'll defend the starboard."

Fadren nodded and the two of them together kept the stern clear for Eiran to continue steering them toward escape.

"We're not going to make it," Eiran said suddenly.

Tallis looked up to the gap they were making for and realized the captain was right. They'd lost too much speed when they'd hit the shoal and the Shrieker ship was keeping pace with them. Unless the *Storm Ghost* reached the gap first, the Shrieker ship could push them onto the rocks and break them.

"Look," Fadren pointed. "We blew a decent chunk out of the hull there. My father was the Star Bird's navigator. He let me tour it once. Unless the Shriekers have changed things around, that hole is near where the powder is stored. It's hard to tell from this distance, but it looks like the hole's big enough for me to get through. If I can get through and ignite their powder…"

"Absolutely not," Tallis interrupted, seeing where Fadren's line of thought was headed. Tallis' thoughts went to Maija, and the little sister she knew Fadren had left behind at the Crow's Nest. "You'd be lost with the ship."

"But you'd escape," Fadren said, a determined gleam in her eye. "And you'd make it out to warn the fleet and protect Giant's Isle. I'm small enough to get through that hole. Who else is? Maybe Hemma or Harrin, but they're both busy now. Besides, neither of them know the Star Bird like I do. I'm willing to bet no one on this ship does."

"Eiran, you can't let her," Tallis begged, her voice cracking with barely contained desperation.

Eiran was silent and refused to look at either of them.

"We could loose the sails again," Tallis suggested. "Pick up speed to carry us out to deeper waters ahead of the Star Bird."

"The shoals block too much of the wind," Eiran stated, her voice flat and expressionless. "It wouldn't be enough. That ship is going to cut us off. If we're lucky, the Lady gives us the grace to drown us. If not, we'll be more swords in the Shrieker horde."

"Commander Tallis, I'm not asking you to let me," Fadren said through gritted teeth. "My father's likely still on that ship, and I have to protect my sister. I'm going, and you have to promise you'll get out and make sure the Shriekers don't get to the city. Don't let them get to my family."

Tallis looked to Eiran, hoping that she would stop Fadren, that she would come up with some other way out. But the captain remained silent, eyes fixed on the closing gap between them and the way out. Tallis thought of her promise to help Fadren, but could think of no way to honor that promise but to physically restrain the girl.

Fadren stripped off her coat and sword belt and threw them down on the deck. Without them, she looked even smaller, barely any larger than Aiven. Tallis shuddered when she thought of her sister, and how soon she could be recruited. The thought led her to Osind, and Fadren's family, all of them at the Crow's Nest, and she knew there was nothing she could do to stop Fadren.

"I'm sorry, Commander," Fadren said. "I don't expect you to understand."

"I do, though," Tallis' shoulders sank and she bowed her head, defeated. "I was also ready to die to do the same for my father."

Fadren's earth rich brown eyes looked on the point of brimming with tears, but she blinked them away. Without hesitation, she wrapped her arms around Tallis in a tight embrace. Tallis drew in a shaking breath as she clung to the girl, wishing she could hold on forever and keep her safe.

"Thank you," Fadren whispered into her ear before pulling away. Tallis let her arms fall to her side, though they screamed to be vises anchoring Fadren to the *Storm Ghost*'s deck. Fadren climbed up onto the railing of the ship. The girl was shivering, though Tallis could not tell if it was from fear or the cold.

"Waves take your bones," Eiran finally broke her silence. Her voice quavered, lacking its normal icy determination.

"May the Lady grant you smooth waters, Captain," Fadren looked back at them, and Tallis could see tears glistening in her eyes. "Tallis, tell my mother how I died. You tell her I did it to keep her and Micha safe."

"I will, Fadren," Tallis promised, choking back tears of her own.

Fadren dove off the edge. Unwittingly, Tallis rushed to the rail, stretching an arm out toward the girl as if to pull her back, but was far too late. Tallis watched her cut through the water, keeping below the surface to avoid being noticed by the Shriekers. She didn't resurface until she reached the other ship. Using the broken boards, Fadren climbed up the side of the ship and disappeared into the breach.

The moments stretched out. Tallis could feel her heart pounding in her ears. The battle on deck continued to rage. Shriekers swarmed across the deck like locusts on a harvest, and Tallis' skin crawled. There were bodies on the deck, and some of them had roses on their uniforms. She saw Alleto still holding the line protecting the lower decks. He fought with a two-handed axe rather than a sword. The way he swung it reminded Tallis of Papa with his scythe, hewing the summer wheat. He led a line, swinging the great axe in long sweeping arcs, pushing the Shriekers back toward the side of the ship. His efforts meant none broke through to attack the stern, for which Tallis was grateful. She turned her gaze back to the Star Bird.

Just as Tallis was beginning to fear Fadren had failed, the air burst with a boom that rippled the water. The Shrieker ship exploded open with fire and shot shattered planks of wood high into the air. Shattered wood hit the water and the Star Bird began to sink. Time stretched, freezing the crew and Shriekers where they stood, the fighting forgotten for a moment. The Shriekers seemed more drawn by the noise and distraction than anything like despair at losing their ship. Like a second explosion, the shock wore off and monsters shrieked with rage, falling upon the crew in a chaotic frenzy.

Tallis rushed down the steps to join the fray, a cry almost like a Shrieker's escaping her. Her vision blurred with tears and she blinked them back. Her throat felt raw and her shoulders ached from the fighting, but she threw herself at the remaining monsters, determined to make them pay for every member of the crew that lay motionless on the deck. Tallis reached Alleto's side and raised her sword.

"Push them back!" she called to the crew. "Drive them to the Lady's embrace."

The line advanced, overwhelming the remaining Shriekers. Some met their ends at the edges of blades, and some were pushed over the rail to plunge into the cold waters below. Tallis tried not to think of Fadren, dripping and freezing from the autumn sea, until the fire was lit in the Star Bird's hold.

At last, the grating sound of shrieks ceased. The silence that followed was broken only by the splash of waves against the hull and the rocks beyond, and the panting of tired fighters. The *Storm Ghost* passed through the gap between the rocks and open ocean greeted them on the other side.

"Hoist the sails," Eiran called, the vigor was gone from her voice and she sounded tired. "Set a course to rendezvous with the rest of the fleet. Alleto, take the helm."

Eiran gave the wheel over and descended to the main deck, her footfalls heavy and her shoulders slumped. She surveyed the deck and the bodies strewn across it, her face blank and unreadable. All eyes were on her, waiting for orders.

Eiran knelt beside a fallen sailor and reached out to touch the rose embroidered on his uniform. She bowed her head and closed her eyes.

"Waves take your bones," she murmured, almost too faint to be heard. When she rose, her blank expression had crumbled into pieces of anger and grief. "Throw the Shriekers overboard and gather our fallen. Cara!"

The bosun pushed through the crowd of sailors to Eiran's side. "Yes, Captain?"

"Note the names of our fallen so we can report to their families," Eiran ordered. "Then have them given to the waves as well. Tallis, you and I will oversee examining the crew for bites ourselves."

"Captain, none of us would hide a bite," a sailor spoke up in protest.

Tallis stepped forward, starting to unlace the bracer on her left arm where she'd been nearly bitten. "*All* of us will be inspected."

Eiran gave her an approving nod as Tallis shrugged out of her uniform jacket and submitted herself for inspection first. Tallis pulled up the sleeve of her white undershirt and ran her fingers over the skin of her wrist, shivering when she thought of how close she'd been to becoming the very thing they were fighting. Eiran made a show of looking her over from all sides, focusing for several moments on her eyes, before nodding in satisfaction.

There were no more protests from the crew, and they set to the task of clearing the deck and submitting themselves one by one for inspection. Tallis cringed any time she saw red blood among the black stains, but each time it was a benign cut from a Shrieker's blade, and not the marks of teeth. They had a medic who could treat those sorts of wounds. But nothing in the medic's supplies would help a bite.

Tallis caught sight of Harrin in the prow. He had sunk to the floor, shaking, whether from relief they'd made it, or being overwhelmed by how much had been put on him, Tallis couldn't tell. Hemma had come down from the crow's nest and had her arms wrapped around him in a tight embrace.

Jayim approached Tallis for inspection. There was black blood on his face, but his eyes were a natural dark, not the black of an infected. He sheepishly stood before her, taking a moment to collect himself.

"Should we—should I—" Jayim stuttered. "We never finished checking the hull."

The hull seemed like such a mundane concern after all that had just happened. But in her heart, she knew it was still a pressing matter. Their escape would mean nothing if they were too damaged to make it back to the fleet.

"Have a damage assessment done," Tallis nodded.

"Aye, Commander," Jayim gave her a quick salute before hurrying down the stairs to the lower decks.

When the inspection of the crew was finally complete, Eiran turned to her. "You did well today. Go and rest, now. You've earned it."

"I can still help," Tallis protested.

"Go," Eiran insisted.

Tallis felt the weariness she'd been ignoring settle heavily across her shoulders and relented. With one glance back to the fire she could now barely see between the gaps in the rocks behind them, Tallis descended to the lower deck where her cabin was tucked near the prow, smaller than Eiran's, but at least private, unlike the rest of the crew's bunks.

Tallis watched the waves through the window of her cabin as they crashed against the side of the ship. The *Storm Ghost* was cutting through the water, making for the rendezvous point with the rest of the fleet at full speed. Hours passed, but she found herself unable to rest. Several times, Tallis had considered going up to help the crew, but found that she couldn't stand to face them. She wasn't ready to find out who else they'd left behind with Fadren. Jayim came and went, quickly letting her know the hull was intact. Likely it would need some work on the exterior when they docked again, but that was a problem for another day.

The light steadily faded. Tallis could hear the shuffling of non-essential crew as they made their way to their bunks. The ship would sail through the night, and members of the crew would take turns sleeping and sailing. Usually, lights out was accompanied by talk and laughter, but tonight they were silent, likely just as weary in both mind and body as Tallis felt. Tallis wished she could sleep, but any time she tried, she saw Fadren's determined face as she leapt over the side of the *Storm Ghost*.

Someone knocked on her door, so softly Tallis nearly mistook it for just another creak of the ship.

"Tallis?"

Tallis was surprised to hear Eiran's voice. For a moment, she considered not answering and pretending to be asleep. There was a part of her that resented the captain for allowing Fadren to die. No matter how much she tried to tell herself that no one was to blame but the Shriekers, Tallis couldn't help herself from feeling that both Eiran and herself were partly to blame.

"Tallis, I need to talk to you."

There was a fear and an urgency in Eiran's voice that softened Tallis' anger. Reluctantly, she got up to open the door. Duty came first, and she couldn't ignore her captain.

Eiran quickly entered the cabin and shut the door behind her. Without a word, she took a seat on the trunk next to Tallis' bed. She looked older and more tired than Tallis had ever seen her, and her brow was creased in worry, stretching at the edges of the scar that cut across her face. She sat rigidly, hands clutching at the edges of the trunk. Tallis sat down opposite her on the bed.

"Why didn't you summon me to your cabin?" Tallis asked. "There's much more space there to meet."

Eiran shook her head and closed her eyes.

"What's wrong, Captain?"

Instead of answering, Eiran stared out the window at the now black water. The night was cloudy and moonless, so there was little to see beyond the glass but darkness. Even the horizon was nearly invisible, the sky blending almost seamlessly with the water.

"Wasn't there something you wanted to talk about?" Tallis asked, beginning to worry. She'd never seen Eiran so agitated before.

Finally, Eiran turned her attention away from the window and back to Tallis.

"Tallis, I understand if you're angry with me, but I..." Eiran bowed her head and a strained noise escaped her throat, somewhere between a sigh and a sob. Her words fell out in a rapid jumble. "I'm sorry. I didn't know what else to do. If we'd had to take down that whole ship by fighting, so many lives would have been lost, and we might not have even made it. Even if we'd survived, the *Storm Ghost* might have been so damaged that we'd have never made it back to the fleet."

Eiran stopped, out of breath and avoided eye contact with Tallis, keeping her gaze fixed on the floor. "She reminded me of—" Eiran's eyes blurred with tears and her hand went to her chest where Tallis knew the locket with the painting of her and Della hung. "So young, and so brave. And I didn't even know her name before today."

Tallis looked at the floor, unable to find words to respond. A part of her wanted to scream, as if screaming loud enough could reach the ears of the drowned through the deafening weight of water and call Fadren back. But Fadren had made her choice, and directing her anger at Eiran would change nothing.

Eiran seemed to crumple, her composure breaking. Her shoulders sank and her head bowed. A sound of frustration and despair tore itself from Eiran's throat.

"Tallis, they knew."

"Knew what?"

"They knew I'd flee into the shoals," Eiran explained, finally looking up at Tallis. "They flanked us and knew what way I'd try to escape and waited to ambush us. Tallis, how could they know I'd go that way? How did they know where to wait?"

"They probably just guessed you'd try to escape, rather than stand and fight," Tallis shrugged. "Through the shoals was the only way out."

"But they knew the route," Eiran said. "They knew exactly where to hide where we wouldn't see them until we were right on top of them. The king himself taught me that route, and only a handful of other captains know it."

"Maybe the Kerethi knew it," Tallis suggested. "There were Kerethi ships following us."

Eiran leaned forward and grabbed a hold of Tallis' wrist with an uncomfortable strength. "You don't understand. I used that route to escape Kerethi. Their ships crashed upon the rocks trying to follow me."

"That war was years ago," Tallis said, trying to pull back from the captain's grip. "Maybe they learned it."

Eiran realized she was hurting Tallis and let go.

"I don't understand," Eiran said. "When they first started attacking, it was random. Uncoordinated. Now they're matching us in tactics. It's like something took control of them."

"What could be controlling them?"

"I don't know," Eiran shook her head. "But however they're being coordinated, they somehow have knowledge of our strategies. They knew I'd be at the Serpent's Mouth and so hid to flank us. They knew I'd try to escape through the rocks and so set an ambush. How could they know these things?"

"They had the strategy to use the landscape to their advantage," Tallis said. "That doesn't mean they somehow have inside knowledge."

"I hope you're right," Eiran sighed and relaxed slightly. "Maybe I'm just being paranoid. But still, I can't shake this feeling."

"It's probably just nerves," Tallis said. "It's been a long day."

"I know," Eiran nodded. "It's just been that everything seems to have been against us since the moment this whole war started. Any time it seems we've finally gained an advantage, they're somehow still a step ahead of us."

Tallis couldn't argue with that. In all the time since the Shriekers had come out of the west, it seemed as though nothing had gone right. Eiran went back to staring out the window at the dark nothingness beyond. Tallis wondered what she was thinking about.

"It never gets easier," Eiran said, as though reading Tallis' thoughts. "You'd think that after all these years, it would. But every time I lose a crew member, it's just as difficult as the first time. I've never been able to stop from blaming myself. This ship is my responsibility, and that includes the lives of everyone on board."

"I'm sorry," Tallis couldn't think of what else to say. She had seen Eiran vulnerable before, but this was beyond when Eiran had told her about Della. All the years Eiran had been a captain were evident on her lined face and in the streaks of white in her otherwise night black hair. If Tallis could feel the weight of command after only a few weeks, she couldn't imagine what it must feel like after years.

"No, Tallis, I'm sorry," Eiran said. "I brought you into this. If you decide this isn't for you, and you want to leave the *Storm Ghost* when this is all over, I won't blame you. The life of a captain isn't for everyone."

"Eiran, I'm not going to abandon you," Tallis assured her.

The captain gave her a look that Tallis couldn't read. It seemed to be a mix of pride and worry.

"You have your father's loyalty, and his strength, it seems," Eiran said, with the shadow of her usual grin. "You will make a fine captain for the *Storm Ghost*. Perhaps even better than I am."

"*If* I become captain, you mean," Tallis said.

"Yes, of course," Eiran looked as though there was more she wanted to say, but left it at that. "I should let you rest. Goodnight, Tallis."

"Goodnight, Captain."

Eiran left Tallis' cabin without another word. Tallis didn't know what to make of the conversation. It seemed there was something Eiran was keeping from her, but she couldn't think of what it could be. Tallis tried to settle down to sleep, but the thought kept nagging at the back of her mind. Tallis forced herself to put it out of her head and focused instead on the rhythm of the waves against the side of the ship. The steady beat of water against wood slowly calmed her and pulled her to sleep.

CHAPTER TWENTY-TWO

The Gathering Storm

The energy aboard the *Lady's Kiss* was tense after the survivors of the Elk Horn returned. The survivors did their best to integrate into Grayston's crew, but they moved about the ship as though lost, rarely speaking to anyone other than themselves. As time stretched with no sign of the *Storm Ghost*, the mood grew more nervous. Finn was not the only one with an eye on the horizon. Everyone always seemed to have one eye on their job, and the other on the water, not sure whether it'd be Shrieker ships or the final missing scout they'd see first.

"Ship approaching! I see the rose banner!"

Hyval's call from the crow's nest sent the crew on board into a frenzy. Sailors crowded to the rail, straining their eyes to spot the *Storm Ghost*'s return. Finn rushed to the prow, leaning as far out as he dared over the rail and shading his eyes against the afternoon sun. Without the height of the crow's nest or a scope, she was barely more than a dark blur against the glare of the sun on the sea.

Cori and Tarsi joined Finn at the prow, drawn by the commotion.

"There, you see?" Cori punched Finn playfully on the arm. "Captain Eiran's not famous for nothing."

"You can stop your worrying," Tarsi rolled her eyes.

Finn gritted his teeth, thinking of the news he'd overheard delivered by Commander Avedis. The *Storm Ghost* might have survived, but that didn't mean Tallis had. He knew the worry gnawing at his guts would not abate until he knew for certain nothing had happened to her. The anxiety grew, twisting in his throat as they watched the *Storm Ghost* approach, finally resolving into the clear shape of a ship. It wasn't long before even he could make out the rose on her banner.

When the *Storm Ghost* pulled up at last alongside the *Lady's Kiss*, Finn dashed toward where a gangplank was being lowered across the span between the two ships. The admiral was waiting there too, pacing in agitation.

Captain Eiran stepped first onto the gangplank and strode across to the *Lady's Kiss*. Tallis followed close on her heels and Finn was barely able to restrain himself from crying out to her. Without thinking, he began to step toward her, but Cori placed a hand on his arm and held him back. Finn ached to run to her, but knew Cori was right and he should keep his space from the officers. Tallis met his gaze and gave him a subtle nod. Her eyes were red and swollen as though from lack of sleep, but she appeared otherwise unharmed.

"You should have been back before now, what happened?" Grayston demanded almost as soon as Eiran's boots hit the deck.

"We were ambushed at the Serpent's Mouth," Eiran explained. "Near a dozen ships outflanked us and drove us into the shoals, where what was once the Star Bird was waiting to attack. They have taken some Kerethi ships, and they're clearly not as mindless as we thought them to be. They're intelligent, and dangerous."

Grayston nodded and glanced at his crew, looking as though he was trying to make a decision. After a moment, he sighed.

"No use keeping it from the crew," Grayston said. "They'll find out soon enough."

"Find out what?" Eiran asked.

"Unless your attackers were the same as those that the Elk Horn encountered, we're outnumbered. And even if they were the same, it's a near even match, I'd estimate."

"What are you talking about?" Eiran asked.

"The *Storm Ghost* is the only one of the three ships I sent out to return," Grayston explained. "In the same night, we spotted fires to the north and the south. Commander Avedis of the Elk Horn came back with a handful of his crew in rowboats. Captain Markence went down with his ship, and we've had no word from the Lion's Pride. I fear they suffered the same fate, but with no survivors. Commander Avedis' report was much the same as yours, which leads me to hope you were attacked by the same group of ships. But for both the Lion's Pride and the Elk Horn to go down in the same night, there must be more ships than the ones you saw."

Eiran cursed loud enough for all the nearby crew to hear. Finn felt his momentary relief at seeing Tallis evaporate, replaced by a knot of panic in his stomach. Around him, Finn heard whispers spreading among the crew, and saw the same panic he felt in their eyes.

"Did you lose many of your crew?" Grayston asked, heedless of the stir his words had caused.

"Six," Eiran said through gritted teeth.

"Well, it could have been worse," Grayston sighed and Eiran glared at him with a terrifying coldness, but he continued as though oblivious to her ire. "The *Storm Ghost* is still sailing, and it appears to me that no one important was lost."

Finn could see the anger in Eiran's eyes as she opened her mouth to retaliate.

"How do we plan to respond to this threat?" Tallis interrupted.

Both Grayston and Eiran looked at Tallis with surprise, but Finn couldn't help a small grin. Her tone was the same as any time he'd heard her jump in to take charge of a situation she saw falling apart when they were children. Eiran took a deep breath, and her face returned to a calm mask.

"An excellent question," Grayston said. "I have been considering that. We must do whatever we can to prevent the Shriekers from reaching Giant's Isle. But if we are outnumbered, the risk of the fleet remaining outside the walls of Giant's Isle may become too great. I have called the captains to join us so we can decide our next move. You may wait below in the meeting room."

"Aye, Admiral," Eiran nodded.

"Commander Tallis," Grayston turned ice-blue eyes on her, "you should join the meeting. You've now seen more of our enemy than most of the captains. Any insight from those who've experienced what we may face will be valuable."

"As you will, Admiral," Tallis answered in a steady tone.

Without a word, Eiran led Tallis to the steps that descended to the lower levels of the ship. In the helm, their flag bearer sent the message for captains to gather, and Finn watched as flags went up on ship after ship, acknowledging the command. The crew of the *Lady's Kiss* loitered near the rail where arriving rowboats pulled alongside her and ascended to the deck. Finn guessed they were as eager to overhear any scrap of conversation or news they could as he was.

Captains filed onto the *Lady's Kiss* one by one. Finn watched them disappear down the stairs to the large meeting room on the deck below. Grayston was the last to descend once all the captains had boarded. As soon as he was out of sight, the crew on the main deck began to break away from the clump that had formed around the gangplank.

Finn made his way back toward the prow with Cori and Tarsi. They gazed out over the water towards the empty western horizon. The late afternoon sun bathed the world with gold. The rich wood of the *Lady's Kiss* and the fleet surrounding her gleamed in the light and the sea that stretched between them and the western horizon glittered. Adrift with nothing to see except water in all directions, it was almost possible to forget what lurked beyond their range of sight.

"I was wondering why we hadn't heard or seen anything of the Kerethi this whole time," Tarsi mused. "I guess now we know why."

"They can't all have been taken by the Shriekers," Cori asserted, but the confidence quickly faded from his voice. "Could they?"

"Their ships are never all in this region at once," Tarsi said. "And the Kerethi Isles are even further east than Giant's Isle. The Shriekers couldn't have made it that far without us knowing. Though how many people or ships are moored there at any time is never consistent."

"The Shriekers threaten everyone," Finn said. "Someone should go to the Isles to warn them. Maybe they could even help."

"You feel like going down and suggesting that to all the captains below?" Tarsi scoffed. "Couldn't pay me enough to walk into that room. One captain is about all I can handle. So long as he continues pretending we lowly rabble don't exist."

"He makes me feel like part of the scenery," Cori grimaced. "I'd feel insulted except I think only doing something wrong would make him notice someone like us. Probably better to be ignored."

"He's spoken to me," Finn frowned, remembering his conversations with Grayston and his curious interest in what he'd seen on the Nightmare Bridge. "Several times in fact."

"Well aren't you special," Tarsi rolled her eyes. "What, did you trip into him to make him realize you weren't another figurehead?"

"He just... talked to me?" Finn shrugged, wondering what had set him apart from the other new recruits that the admiral had treated him so much differently. His pondering was cut short by another cry from Hyval in the crow's nest.

"Black-sailed ships to the west!"

Finn immediately stood to attention. Backlit by the brightness of the sinking sun, a black mass stretched across much of the western horizon. A cold dread settled in the pit of Finn's stomach. Suddenly, a strong wind whipped across the deck, causing the sails to flap loudly and tugging at Finn's jacket.

"Storm clouds to the east!" came Hyval's call.

"We're caught between the two," Cori's eyes were turned eastward. Finn followed his gaze to see a great bank of gray and green clouds roiling behind the fleet. From the looks of it, the storm would be one of the worst they'd seen yet this season.

"Someone needs to tell the captains!" came a shout from another sailor on the deck.

Without thinking, Finn strode toward the center of the deck. "I'll go."

He regretted the words almost as soon as they were out of his mouth. His first thought had been of Tallis, and that bringing this news would mean seeing her. But now that all eyes were on him with looks of relief, Finn wondered if he'd made a mistake. The thought of going below to interrupt a room full of captains to bring them bad news was almost as chilling as the ships on the horizon.

Finn took a deep breath, steeling himself. He couldn't take back the words that had flown from his mouth faster than his senses. Delaying would only give the storm and the Shrieker fleet the chance to tighten the net they were snared in.

"Are you sure about this?" Cori asked, placing a hand on his arm. "I could—"

"No," Finn shook his head. "Like I said, I've at least had a conversation with the admiral. I can do this."

Before he could rethink Cori's offer, Finn strode toward the stairs. The first level below the main deck was split into two sections. Most of this deck was devoted to rows of cannons, but toward the prow was a large meeting chamber. The door was shut tight, but Finn swallowed the rising anxiety in his throat and rapped softly on it.

"Enter," came the admiral's voice from within.

Finn pushed his way into the chamber. He'd never had cause or permission to enter this room before. It was dominated by a great table covered with maps and charts. Around it sat the assembled captains, and Finn trembled under their combined gazes.

"Finley," Grayston's eyes narrowed and his voice was cold.

Finn spotted Tallis among the group at Eiran's side. She sat tall at attention, her demeanor matching her fellow officers now more than his own. She again gave him a slight nod, but it was less comforting now. This was her place, and she'd managed to fit into her new role seemingly with ease. But from the irritated looks he was receiving from other captains, this was definitely not his place.

"Well?" Grayston leaned forward, clasping his hands before him on the table.

"Sir," the word nearly lodged in Finn's throat and he had to cough to continue. "A fleet of black-sailed ships has appeared to the west, and what looks to be a mighty storm is brewing at our backs to the east. We're trapped between the two, and the winds are picking up. If we don't take action now, we'll be caught out of formation."

"The Shrieker ships all had black sails," Eiran thumped a fist on the table with urgency. "There's no time for more debates, we must form up and be ready."

"With a storm brewing, should we be sailing into battle?" a captain Finn didn't recognize spoke up.

"We are out here to hold a line between the Shriekers and Giant's Isle," this time, Finn recognized the captain who spoke as Vaska. It felt like it had been years, not months, since Vaska had warned him and Tallis to enlist and prepare to flee Westham. "We either hold the line or run. And where could we run now with a storm brewing at our backs?"

"Vaska is right," Grayston nodded.

Finn began to wonder if he should leave. It seemed like the captains had returned to the business of deciding what to do, a conversation he shouldn't be a part of. But no one had dismissed him, and it seemed now that no one even remembered he was standing there. As suddenly as all the attention had turned to him, it was now all back on the admiral.

"If we mobilize quickly, we can use the storm to our advantage," Grayston continued. As he spoke, he leaned forward, arranging clay disks each painted with a captain's sigil. Finn guessed these represented their ships. He took an equal number of blank disks and looked up at Finn. "You said 'ships' not 'ship'. So they sail side by side and not in a line?"

"It was difficult to see, sir," Finn hesitated, suddenly overwhelmed that he was being brought into Grayston's strategizing. "But they spanned much of the horizon, so I would guess so."

Grayston's mouth quirked in close to a smile. "Then they aren't quite so advanced at sea tactics as we might have feared. Their methods are outdated. Now that is an interesting fact to ponder at some later date."

Grayston arranged the blank disks side by side and began to arrange a line of Okaesan ships perpendicular to it with the *Lady's Kiss* at the head of the line. "They'll be sailing against the wind, but we could sail with. Half of the ships of the line can break through their center and divide their forces. Our fastest ships can use the winds of the storm to go around to flank them. These were our ships and Kerethi ships. Their guns will be fewer from behind, making it safer for our lighter ships to broadside them from the rear."

Finn noticed Grayston take the disk painted with Eiran's rose and move it around to the other side of the Shrieker line, along with a handful of others. The rest, he arranged in two more lines parallel to the first, but set further back so they'd reach the Shrieker fleet later than the first line.

"Our second and third lines will fan out to broadside them from the front," Grayston said. "The risk is greater from the front. But our ships of the line can take some beating from their forward guns. Once the ships of the first line break through, they can divide in the same way. If all goes well, we'll have the Shrieker fleet flanked, divided, and surrounded."

"If all goes well," another captain intoned. "But we cannot predict what this storm will do."

"No," Grayston shook his head. "We cannot be assured our formation will work. But we can be assured that we do not want to be caught between a storm and an enemy fleet with no plan. If you have a better idea, by all means, share it."

The captain who'd spoken remained silent, and her silence stretched out across the room until Tallis raised a hand.

"Yes, Commander Tallis?"

All eyes turned to her, and Finn didn't envy her the attention.

"Our goal is to protect Giant's Isle," Tallis began. "If our ships are taken, we may only make things worse. Their numbers have already been swollen by Kerethi ships."

"And do you have any suggestions to prevent this?" Grayston looked doubtful, but awaited her answer.

"We were nearly trapped in the Bloody Shoals by one of our own ships," Tallis continued. "One of our crew sacrificed her life to take it down. We would not have escaped if not for her. I suggest we follow her example. Rig our spare powder to destroy our ships. If a ship is overrun, all it takes is a single soldier waiting and ready to blow it to a useless wreck."

Her words were met with a tense silence. The other captains looked unnerved by her words. Finn was unsurprised by her boldness, but the dark tone in her voice was one he'd never heard.

Grayston broke the silence with a deep sigh. "I regret that you are right. Our first priority is to protect Giant's Isle. We must do all it takes to be sure that we are hindering our enemy, not helping them. What you suggest should be done on all ships. Now, if there are no further questions, I call this meeting to an end. Let us begin the strike."

The captains exchanged glances filled with apprehension, but none spoke. After a moment, they began to stand. Finn scurried out of the door and off to the side, hoping to avoid further attention. None of them paid him any mind. Finn saw Eiran reach the door, Tallis close on her heels, but Grayston stopped Eiran with a hand on her arm.

"Be careful out there," he said, his usual formality dropped. "We almost lost the *Storm Ghost* once. I would hate to have to deliver word to the king that we lost the ship that once was his, or her captain."

"Perhaps you should have thought about that before you sent us to the Serpent's Mouth," Eiran growled.

"Who would you have sent in your stead?" Grayston demanded. "Tell me, who could have done what you did? The *Storm Ghost* came back when neither of the other two ships I sent did. If I'd picked someone else, I wager we'd have lost three ships, not two."

Eiran had no answer for the admiral, but continued to glare at him with fire in her eyes. Finn shrank further back into the shadows, terrified he was overhearing something he shouldn't and would be scolded for eavesdropping.

"I thought so," Grayston's tone softened. "Do not think me cruel, Eiran. I sent the ships that were best for the job, and do not think I am ungrateful that yours was the one to return. If we make it back to Giant's Isle, my offer still stands."

"And my answer remains the same, Admiral," Eiran said, her voice icy.

Grayston let go of Eiran's arm and stepped back. Finn wondered what this offer could be that it turned Eiran's voice so cold.

"May the Lady's grace and the Protector's strength be with you tonight," he said.

"And with you," Eiran replied.

Eiran hurried toward the stairs with a pace that Tallis struggled to match. Finn knew this might be his last chance to speak to Tallis and decided it was worth the risk. He trotted to catch up with them.

"Tallis," Finn called softly. Both she and Eiran turned. Tallis exchanged a glance with her captain, who nodded. Finn wished more than anything that he had all the time in the world to say all the things on his mind.

"Gods be with you, Captain Eiran," Finn saluted to them. "And to you, Commander Tallis."

"And with you," Eiran acknowledged his salute.

Tallis took a step toward him, beginning to reach out a hand, but her gaze focused over his shoulder and let it fall. Finn quickly glanced behind to see Grayston was watching them.

"Be safe, Finn," Tallis whispered, her eyes boring into his.

"You too, Tallis," Finn fought the urge to throw his arms around her neck despite Grayston's eyes on his back, unsure if he would ever see his friend again. "Are you... alright?"

Tallis sighed, again glancing quickly behind him. "I'll be better once this is over. You?"

"I'm alright," Finn lied, not wanting to add to the stress that was written clearly in the lines furrowed into her brow. It seemed to be the first time Tallis believed one of his lies as a faint smile spread across her face and the creases in her brow eased slightly.

"I'll see you on the other side," Tallis took a reluctant step backward toward the stairs.

"Is that a promise?" Finn blurted and Tallis' smile grew.

"It's a promise," Tallis gave him a final nod and turned away, disappearing up the steps.

Finn balled his fists at his side and focused on willing his feet not to move to chase after Tallis. He knew that if he did, there would be nothing he could do to stem the tide of words that longed to pour forth. With the impending battle, there was no guarantee he'd ever see her again. He pictured the clay disk painted with Eiran's rose, circling to flank the Shriekers, and the disk with Grayston's lion at the head of the line. Both of their ships would be in some of the most precarious places in the formation.

"There's never enough time."

Finn jumped and turned to Grayston behind him. The admiral stood in the shadows beyond the square of late afternoon light filtering down from the stairs, but a faint beam of light from one of the cannon holes shined across his face. There was a gleam in his eye that reminded Finn of the brief moment he'd glimpsed of the man beneath the admiral's facade. He remembered Tarsi and Cori's assertion that Grayston paid the new recruits as much mind as the shoals and clouds beyond the deck of the ship. Again, he wondered what had made him different.

"To your post, Finley," Grayston ordered, no trace of that moment of vulnerability left in his voice. "The strike will come sooner than any of us would like."

Finn saluted and was grateful to turn away and dash up the stairs to his assigned battle station on the main deck. Sailors crisscrossed the deck in a frenzy of preparations for the fight to come. On the eastern horizon, the storm clouds loomed, dark and heavy with the threat of the tempest to come. On the western horizon, the black silhouettes that were now clear as individual ships mirrored the brewing storm, and the sun sinking low behind them cast a final furtive beam across the water. Finn rested a hand on the hilt of the sword that hung at his hip and steeled himself for the moment these two forces would collide around them.

The Lady's Grace

Turning her back on Finn felt like trying to force a door shut against a hurricane's winds. But Tallis ascended the steps and crossed the plank back to the *Storm Ghost* where Eiran was waiting for her.

"Friend of yours?"

"We grew up together."

Eiran sighed and looked back to the *Lady's Kiss*. "It's difficult to have to hide what you really feel, and stay silent when there are so many things to say."

"At least I got to see him one last time before the battle," Tallis said. "If you hadn't chosen me as your first officer, my last time seeing him would have been on Giant's Isle."

Eiran did not respond. It was clear that something was bothering her.

"What was Grayston talking about?" Tallis changed the subject. "What did he offer you?"

"Tallis, I want you to go and do a survey of the ship to make sure we are ready for battle," Eiran ordered, ignoring the question. "Be sure Cara has all she needs."

"Aye, Captain," Tallis said, taking the hint, but her curiosity only increased.

Blackened sails could be seen on the horizon. At this distance, it was difficult to distinguish them from the swells of the sea. The light was fading quickly from the sky and Tallis dreaded the prospect of facing another battle in the dark and in a storm.

As Tallis strode across the deck to find the bosun, Eiran ascended to the helm. Her voice boomed out across the deck and all hands aboard froze in their tracks.

"The time has come," Eiran called. "The Lady has forced our hand. This storm shows her displeasure with these monsters, and these winds are her will that we be the instrument of their destruction. The *Storm Ghost* will circle wide of the Shriekers' right flank to strike from behind. All hands to battle stations. Go!"

Immediately, the deck descended into chaos of preparations. Tallis pushed her way through the crowd toward where Cara stood near the prow, her gaze fixed on the horizon.

"The captain wanted me to check in with you," Tallis said, and Cara drew a shuddering breath.

"You can tell the captain I'll be ready," Cara wiped at her eyes, not meeting Tallis' gaze.

"Are you alright?"

"I thought I was ready for anything after the things I've been through on this ship," Cara sighed. "But nothing could have prepared me for those monsters. I had hoped we wouldn't be facing them again so soon."

Tallis placed her hand on Cara's shoulder and squeezed. "If we play things right tonight, we may never need to face them again."

"I hope you're right."

Tallis wished she could believe her own words, but nothing they'd encountered thus far gave her any real hope of ending this here and now.

"I will be ready to direct the crew," Cara said, her hand going to the bosun's whistle that hung at her belt.

"Good," Tallis gave her a nod and strode back toward the helm. The captain stood gazing off into the distance toward the approaching enemy ships.

"The crew is ready, Captain," Tallis said. Eiran turned to regard her.

"Are you?" Eiran asked.

"As ready as I could be," Tallis said.

"Do you ever wish your life had gone a different direction?" Eiran asked.

"Any other direction would probably have left me behind to die on the mainland," Tallis said, then pointed to the Shrieker ships. "Or I'd be sailing on one of those ships instead of the *Storm Ghost*."

"Consider yourself lucky then," Eiran said and bowed her head. "My alternative could certainly be considered better. Regret is as dangerous a weapon as a sword sometimes."

"If you hadn't become Captain, where would you be?" Tallis asked, expecting Eiran not to answer.

"Back on Giant's Isle," Eiran said, surprising Tallis. "Serving my king still, but in a much different way."

A flag went up on the *Lady's Kiss*, signaling the fleet to begin moving into position.

"Hard to port!" Eiran shouted. "Stay out of range of those ships until we come around behind."

Cara's whistle blew, and sails unfurled. Eiran turned the wheel, and the *Storm Ghost* began to move away from the *Lady's Kiss*. Tallis glanced back toward the rest of the fleet. The *Lady's Kiss* began to surge straight forward toward the approaching line of Shrieker ships. As the ships steadily picked up speed and distance opened up between them, the other ships of the line fell in behind the *Lady's Kiss*. Other light ships like the *Storm Ghost* also broke away toward either side of the Shriekers' flanks.

"That storm is coming in fast," Tallis observed as she watched the fleet begin to move in formation in their wake.

"Perhaps the Lady has answered our prayers and will be on our side," Eiran mused. "Or perhaps her rage will take the Shriekers down, and us with them."

Though the fleet was sailing at full speed, advancing on the Shrieker ships, the storm outpaced them. Soon, the last lingering hint of light disappeared, and clouds swirled above. The *Lady's Kiss* surged ahead, rising and falling with the growing waves. The Shrieker ships drew closer, as undeterred by the storm as Grayston. It wasn't long before the tempest was upon them. Tallis guessed by the strength of the wind that this would be one of the worst storms they'd had yet this autumn.

The sea roiled gray beneath a green sky. Waves crashed up against the sides of the ship and the prow reared up out of the water like a frightened horse. The sails cracked and snapped, swelling in the wind and pulling them steadily onward toward the enemy. Salt spray mixed with the first drops of rain to sting skin and burn eyes.

Soldiers and sailors barked orders and shouted to each other over the roar of the wind. Their leather boots slipped on the slick wet wood and the sway of the ship tossed them on jagged paths across the deck. Some of the less willing recruits had found secure corners that offered some small shelter from the wind and the spray and clung to ropes and posts.

"Take the helm, Tallis," Eiran said. "I need all hands on deck before we reach the enemy lines. Let's see if I can coax some courage out of these sailors."

Tallis nodded and took the wheel from Eiran. It pulled at her, wanting to give into the wind and the waves, but she threw her weight into it and forced it to keep the ship on a straight course. Once Eiran was confident that she had control of the helm, she left, shouting orders and scolding those who'd abandoned their posts. Her voice was soon lost to the jumble of noise and Tallis kept her focus on keeping the course.

Squinting her eyes against the salt, Tallis peered out across the open water around them. The late afternoon sky had turned near as dark as night, and she could only see the rest of the fleet as faint silhouettes. Occasional flashes of lightning illuminated white sails rising up out of the sea. The blue flags atop the masts flapped high and the white lions upon them danced, each captain's own crest flying below. Out beyond the line of the fleet, all she could see were the deep green and black thunder clouds forming. The black-sailed ships of the Shriekers had disappeared almost entirely into the darkness.

"Commander!" a voice shouted out from the wind. Alleto stood at the bottom of the stairs leading to the deck. "Commander, the wind is picking up! Do we stay the course?"

Tallis looked to where Eiran stood at the prow, sword in hand and wished she hadn't left the helm to her. Eiran was still barking orders to the soldiers. Tallis wondered what Eiran would do in her place. The captain had trusted her with the ship while she managed the soldiers, Tallis couldn't let her down.

"Our orders are to sail forth and meet these monsters before they have the chance to reach the city," Tallis reminded him.

"Our orders are to protect the city," Alleto protested. "We can't protect the city if we're shipwrecked by this storm."

Tallis looked around. The sails were straining against their ropes and her crew struggled to fight against them. The majority of the other ships assigned to attack this flank continued to surge forward, but a handful were beginning to fall behind. Tallis could recognize a few of those ships. The Salt Gull, the Bloody Lady, the Enduring. Tallis knew their captains, many were older sailors, ones that knew storms and ships like she never would. Though the *Lady's Kiss* was still flying full sails, she was a larger ship and could take a heavier beating than the *Storm Ghost* could. If Tallis managed to sink the ship on her first time commanding her, Eiran would haunt her for eternity down in the depths of the Lady's halls.

"Strike the royals and topgallant sails," Tallis ordered. "Raise the storm jib. The wind is still on our side. We could end this tonight and save the city."

"Or this storm could destroy the fleet," Alleto cast a wary look at the swirling clouds.

"We keep going until the captain or the admiral signals otherwise."

"Aye, Commander," Alleto nodded reluctantly before going off to give her orders to the crew.

Suddenly, out of the dark, the enemy fleet loomed. In the confusion of the storm it was difficult to get a count, but they at least equaled the king's fleet. Though the topmost sails had been struck, they'd hardly lost any speed and were almost at the head of the ships that had been sent to flank the Shriekers. At the edge of the enemy line, a couple smaller vessels were being tossed like toy boats on the waves and had broken off from the main line.

"Alleto!" Tallis called, an idea forming in her mind that went against what Eiran had ordered, but she'd left Tallis in command of the helm. Alleto appeared at the stairs. "Reckon we can take those stragglers there?"

Alleto looked where she pointed, shielding his eyes against the rain with a hand, "Aye, Commander, I say we can. These waves are nearly doing the job for us."

"I'll bring her through," Tallis said. "We take them down and then come round to take the line from behind."

"I like the way you think, Commander," Alleto said. "I'll give the order and tell the captain. Don't wait for approval. It's what she'd do."

Tallis nodded and turned the wheel hard to starboard, taking them off of their original wide path around the Shrieker fleet to aim for the gap between the enemy ships. She prayed they were too busy fighting the waves to mark the *Storm Ghost*'s path. To go between the ships would allow them to send a crossfire, but the enemy ships were small and the *Storm Ghost* was fast enough that she might have a chance to slip through without taking too hard of a hit. With the wind and the rain in their eyes and against their sails, they may not even have the opportunity to react to the attack.

The storm did its best to shake them off their course, but Tallis fought the wheel and they kept up the advance on the enemy ships. The closer they got, the clearer it was that their targets were barely making any headway. Each high wave that buffeted the smaller ships nearly knocked them over. Any sane, human captain would have turned tail to run from the assault of both the fleet and the storm, but clearly these creatures did not have the self-preservation instinct or free will to make that call.

"Waves take their bones!" a bloodthirsty scream was carried on the wind, but Tallis couldn't tell whose voice it was.

A brief moment of calm took hold before the *Storm Ghost* slid into the gap between the two ships. Though the storm still raged, the chaos of shouting and soldiers running paused. Tallis could hear nothing but her own heart beating and the wind roaring in her ears.

"Fire!"

The shout broke the calm. Both the starboard and port cannons exploded and sent flashes of red out into the darkness. A few shots fired back, but before they could launch an effective counterattack, the two ships exploded into splinters. The *Storm Ghost* sailed unharmed through the gap.

Tallis glanced off to her right toward the ships of the line and saw more flashes of cannons and ships going up in flames. In the middle of it all, the *Lady's Kiss* was cutting through the center of the Shrieker fleet as planned. Tallis took it as a sign to continue the advance. Without pausing to ask advice this time, Tallis turned the *Storm Ghost* to run behind the line of Shrieker ships.

"Behind!" one of the twins called from the crow's nest.

Tallis glanced behind to see a Shrieker ship approaching fast on their tail, likely another small and fast ship that operated out of the main formation like the *Storm Ghost*. She wrenched the wheel to widen the gap of water between the two ships, but there was no time to evade its attack, and it pulled up alongside. Before Tallis had the chance to think, Shriekers were swinging over on ropes. The clang of swords added to the din of the storm and Tallis pulled her own sword free, keeping hold of the wheel with one hand and preparing to defend herself with the other.

The Shriekers that swarmed the deck were a mix of former soldiers, still dressed in ragged uniforms, and ordinary citizens, likely from either King's Harbor or the Serpent's Mouth. Tallis did her best not to think about who they used to be. Few made it past the soldiers that defended the helm, but some did. Even in the darkness, their black eyes stood out as wrong in their pale faces. Tallis did her best to keep a hand on the wheel at all times, but sometimes the fight forced her away.

A well-aimed shot from the *Storm Ghost*'s cannons cracked the mast of the Shrieker's ship at their side, and it crashed down with a sound like thunder. Another shot burst through its hull and the combined weight of the mast and the breach in the hull split the ship in half. The waves swallowed the bones of the ship. Though there were still Shriekers on the deck, Tallis was able to direct the *Storm Ghost* toward open water again and take stock of the battle.

Tallis could see no sign of the *Lady's Kiss*, but other ships were still engaged in the fight. Shrieker and Okaesan ships alike burned and sank. It seemed as though there were some who had already given up. Tallis watched as one of their ships burst open in a flash of fire that could only have been caused by the powder lighting, and she felt a pang of guilt that it was her idea that had destroyed that ship. But it was surrounded by Shrieker ships and took several of them out with it, renewing her confidence that it hadn't been a terrible idea. Tallis gave the wreckage a wide berth.

"The *Lady's Kiss* is assaulted! Off to starboard!"

Tallis looked and a flash of lightning briefly illuminated the admiral's flag flying high amid a wall of black sails. She had broken through the line of Shrieker ships as planned, but was now beset on both sides by ships like the one that had pulled alongside the *Storm Ghost*.

Through the rain, Tallis could see Eiran on the deck, statue still as she weighed her choices. To help the *Lady's Kiss* would endanger the *Storm Ghost*, but she was the flagship, and Grayston was Leander's family. Loyalty and duty urged them to help. The image of Finn, fighting on the deck of the *Lady's Kiss* and swarmed by Shriekers came unbidden to Tallis' mind. Control of the *Storm Ghost* was hers, but she awaited the captain's word.

"Defend the admiral," Eiran gave the order. Tallis breathed a sigh of relief and turned the wheel toward the *Lady's Kiss*. "Tallis! Take her to broadside the ship to the *Lady's Kiss'* starboard. Ready the port cannons."

Tallis took the *Storm Ghost* in an arc to give the port cannons a clear shot at the enemy ship, but kept them out of range of boarders. The *Lady's Kiss* was hard pressed on all sides, and it seemed they'd been boarded. A wall of noise hit her as thunder boomed overheard just as the cannons fired. A giant swell rocked the deck and most of the second volley of cannons shot into the water.

Tallis could see Grayston at the helm of the *Lady's Kiss*, but he was busy fighting off an attack and wasn't at the wheel. A third round of cannon fire burst from the *Storm Ghost* and these hit their mark, tearing open gaping holes near the waterline of the Shrieker ship sending boarders over to the *Lady's Kiss*. The swells of waves rose up and through these holes, and the ship began to list to the side as it took on water. A round of fire from the *Lady's Kiss'* port side cannons ripped through the ship at its other side. Soon, both were falling behind and sinking into the depths.

A knot of soldiers broke through to the helm and opened space for Grayston to get to the helm. The admiral turned to see who'd come to his aid. Through the torrents of rain, Tallis could hardly see his face, but he gave her a nod and turned back to the task of navigating his ship.

Tallis maintained course with the *Lady's Kiss*, and the two ships sailed side by side for a time. It seemed Grayston's plan had worked, and the ships of the line had broken the Shrieker formation. Together, they caught straggling ships in their crossfire. Tallis strained to catch a glimpse of Finn or Cori, but in the mass of uniformed soldiers, she couldn't tell one from another.

The wind and the waves fought her, and each swell seemed to push the *Storm Ghost* further away from the *Lady's Kiss*. The waves had grown so each time the ship swayed, Tallis' heart leapt to her throat to see how far to the side the mast dipped. It was all she could do to maintain her footing and keep her hands on the wheel. A massive wave rocked the *Storm Ghost* so violently that Tallis staggered down to her knees, barely keeping a hold of the wheel to keep from sliding away. Down shifted suddenly to her side and not toward her feet. Tallis glanced over her shoulder to see roiling water thick with foam.

The ship righted itself, and Tallis struggled back to her feet. There was a surge of motion at the rails and at first, she thought they'd taken on water. But rather than flowing out and off the deck, the wave surged up. Hands with torn flesh clawed up the wood, dragging bodies behind. What she'd taken for a wave resolved into a sudden wave of Shriekers swarming over the deck. Tallis readied her sword, confused as to where they'd come from.

"The water!" someone called. "They're in the water!"

Tallis looked around and realized they were sailing over the wreckage of a ship. The Shriekers must have climbed up the side of the ship when they'd passed. Shaken by the swells of waves and certain they were out of boarding range of any ships, the soldiers on deck had been taken unprepared. Their ranks broke, falling back away from the rails.

A group of Shriekers made for the helm and Tallis braced herself to meet them. A great wordless bellow rose above even the shrieks of the monsters and the wild and a great axe swung out, taking off one head cleanly and burying into the shoulder of its neighbor. Alleto yanked the axe free and swung again, the force of his blow knocking a Shrieker overboard. Jayim sprang after him, as quick and limber where Alleto relied on brute force. He held a sword in each hand, catching a Shrieker between the teeth with one as it lunged to bite, and taking the head off another with the second blade.

"Keep your eyes on the water, Commander!" Alleto shouted. "We'll keep them off you."

Tallis longed to go help them, but knew if she didn't keep an eye on what was ahead of them, they risked colliding with another ship or sailing over another wreck and getting swarmed with more Shriekers. Reluctantly, she sheathed her sword and turned her focus back to steering the ship. Alleto took up guard on one set of stairs and Jayim the other.

On the deck, Shriekers clashed with soldiers. The sharp clang of metal echoed the clashes of thunder overhead, and it was nearly impossible to distinguish between the shrieks of their assailants and the wailing of the winds.

A human scream cut through the din as sharp as a blade. Jayim collapsed, and Tallis had no time to assess if he was alive, dead, or worse before she found herself surrounded. She dodged a swinging blade and slashed the Shrieker across the gut in the same motion as she drew her sword. It stumbled back, giving her space for a swing at the neck. The Shriekers tried to knock her back to tamper with the wheel system, attacking with blades rather than leaning in to strike with their teeth and so give her an opening to strike at their one weak point.

"Turn her round!" Eiran was shouting over the din. "Tallis! Get her out of here!"

With only one hand on the wheel, and her sword in the other, parrying blow after blow until her shoulder felt like it would crack under the strain, Tallis didn't have the strength to do anything more than hold the wheel steady.

"Tallis, hard to port!" Eiran's voice was more urgent now.

Tallis managed to knock one Shrieker to the deck with a blow to its knees. She kicked it back, but the blow she'd dealt meant almost nothing to it. Its hands scrabbled on the slick deck, dragging it back toward her despite maimed legs, mouth wide in a shriek of rage.

"We'll cover you, Commander!" Harrin, Cara, and a few others fought their way up to the helm and pushed back the group harrying Tallis. Alleto remained below, now covering both sets of stairs alone, but the wide swings of his great axe kept more Shriekers from ascending to the helm. She could no longer see Jayim, and prayed he'd taken a survivable blow from a blade and not a Shrieker's jaws.

Tallis sheathed her sword, wiped rain from her eyes, and peered through the gloom. The sea glowed red, reflecting the flickering flames consuming enemy and ally ships alike. Somewhere ahead, a warship that dwarfed the *Storm Ghost* was careening toward a Shrieker ship. The warship was blazing, flames leaping high up into the dark sky. A giant boom echoed across the water. It took a moment for Tallis to realize it wasn't more thunder, but the mast had cracked and was crashing onto the warship's deck. She was lost and was going to take the Shrieker ship with her, and the *Storm Ghost* was being blown straight for the point where the two would collide.

"Now, Tallis!"

Tallis wrenched the wheel, and it spun. Slowly, the prow of the ship began to turn away from the inevitable collision. The wind fought against the *Storm Ghost* and blew her closer to the two ships.

"Turn her aside!"

With a shout, Tallis threw her whole weight on the wheel and turned it as far as it would go.

A cacophony of shattering wood and screams of both people and Shriekers louder than any thunder burst as the two ships crashed into each other directly in the *Storm Ghost*'s path. A blast of heat preceded the explosion. Flames leaped up the Shrieker ship, devouring both ship and monster.

The prow was turning too slowly. Tallis watched, helpless, as they sped toward the burning ships. On the deck below, the crew stood inert, the last of the Shriekers having been thrown overboard. Eiran was barking orders and the sails started to go up again. They billowed in the wind and the prow turned faster, the wind carrying them beyond the two ships.

At last, the *Storm Ghost* pulled out of the collision path and toward open water. They passed at a safe distance, but

Tallis could feel the heat of the flames on her face. There were people in the water, fighting the current to stay afloat. Some had noticed the *Storm Ghost* passing and were shouting and waving. Eiran ascended the stairs and took over control of the ship again.

"Should we help them?" Tallis asked, unable to turn away from the people in the water.

"They're dead already," Eiran said, eyes fixed ahead. "Look closer."

Tallis looked again. It wasn't just people in the water, and they weren't just screaming because they were drowning. Some had changed already, some were changing.

"There must be some that could be saved," Tallis protested.

"And risk our own crew?" Eiran glared at her. "They knew what they were doing when they went to ram that ship. We'd lose more than we'd save if we attempted a rescue."

Tallis took one last look at the people drowning in the water before turning to gaze back the way they'd come. Behind, all she could see was the outlines of broken ships burning. If there were any survivors like them, they'd fled or gotten lost in the storm. Above, the sky was still dark with clouds, but for now, the rain had slowed and the lightning ceased.

"What are your orders, Captain?" Tallis asked.

"We try to outrun this storm," Eiran stated. "Search for shelter on one of the islets around here perhaps. If we can't find shelter, then we worry about surviving. If this is the sort of autumn tempest I expect, this is just the herald of the storm, and the worst is yet to come."

As if to confirm Eiran's suspicions, another clap of thunder rumbled, for a moment drowning out the screams of the dying soldiers.

"What about following the *Lady's Kiss*?" Tallis asked, wondering where Finn was in all this chaos, stomach clenching as she swallowed down a rising fear she'd never see him again.

"Do you see her?"

Tallis looked around. Through the rain and the wreckage, it was nearly impossible to tell friend from foe. Black water faded into the horizon, and it was nearly impossible to tell where the sea ended, and sky began. As she watched, several more ships destroyed themselves to stay out of enemy hands. The flames shot toward the sky, and reflections distorted by the roiling waves stained the water below with flickering orange. Grayston's ship was nowhere in sight. Either she'd fled or sunk, but regardless, they were on their own now.

"It seems we were right. The Lady doesn't approve of these abominations sailing her waters," Eiran said. "But if we can't escape this storm or find shelter, we'll go down too."

"As you say, Captain."

Tallis bowed her head and turned away from the ruins of the fleet behind them.

"Waves take their bones," the captain whispered.

As they sailed on, the storm grew steadily worse. Waves near as tall as the ship rolled her back and forth, water sloshing on the deck. Anything not tied down slid with the tilt of the ship. The crew seemed more concerned with staying aboard than on whatever their duties were. The bodies of the dead were forgotten. Most were tossed overboard with the heaving of the deck.

Tallis struggled to keep her footing on the slick wood. The largest wave she'd ever seen made the *Storm Ghost* buck like her horse had the first time she'd ridden. Her father had laughed and laughed when she'd landed with a plop in the mud. No one laughed when Tallis landed with a thud on the deck of the *Storm Ghost*.

Somewhere, Eiran was shouting, "The cove, make for the cove!"

Tallis scrambled to her feet and squinted through the rain and darkness. Off in the distance, a black shape loomed up out of the roiling sea before them. At its base the waves crashed higher than the ship itself.

She's gone mad, Tallis thought. The island before them seemed little more than a spit of rock, perhaps smaller even than the Giant's Hands. Surely, they'd dash to pieces upon its shore. Then she saw it, a small strip of white out of the storm. There was a beach. Protected there from the wind, perhaps they could survive.

Tallis grabbed a hold of a rope that had come loose and tied it down. The center sail was rising and the ship nearly rocked her off her feet again. The *Storm Ghost*'s nose was turning, pointing toward their salvation, but Tallis could tell they were coming in too fast.

"Eiran!" Tallis shouted as she dragged herself up toward where the captain stood at the wheel. "Eiran we can't make it. She'll break on the shore!"

"Better start praying the anchor won't snap then," Eiran kept the wheel steady, a wild gleam in her eye. "The Lady will see us safe to shore, or she'll take us in. If you have a better idea, speak quickly, or hold on to something and wait."

Tallis knew better than to question Eiran's judgment. She grabbed onto the rail and cast a wary eye toward the quickly widening stretch of sand.

The ship jolted as it ran over some unseen sandbar or rock. Tallis slipped on the wet deck and lost her hold on the rail. Another jolt knocked her off her feet. She thought she could hear Eiran shouting something as the ship reeled to one side.

Suddenly, there was no more deck beneath her feet. Tallis tried to scream but only tasted salt. The cold faded with the light as the Lady of the Waters took her into her embrace.

CHAPTER TWENTY-FOUR

The Tempest

"Turn her about," Admiral Grayston sighed. "This storm is too much. The battle is over. Turn her about and get out of here."

"What about the rest of the fleet, sir?" Commander Bevan protested.

Grayston cast his gaze across the chaos of burning ships and churning waters. Finn did too, hoping to catch a glimpse of the *Storm Ghost*. He hadn't seen any sign of her since she'd come to their rescue. At least he knew Tallis was alive then, but the *Storm Ghost* was nowhere in sight. There was no way of knowing for certain what happened to Tallis.

Everywhere, Finn could see the wreckage of the battle. Flashes of lightning illuminated the silhouettes of ships, though in the dark it was almost impossible to tell which ships belonged to which fleet. Many ships were burning: either Shrieker ships destroyed by the fleet's guns, or fleet ships blown apart by Tallis' failsafe to keep them out of enemy hands. Flames reached up toward the sky as lightning flashed down, as though the Lady was trying to reach her hands up to the Protector.

"The fleet is either dead or dying," Grayston said grimly. "If the surviving captains have any sense, they'll be running too. Set a course east. There's nothing more that can be done here. Go, turn her about!"

The order was carried across the ship. Finn sheathed his sword and dashed to help in the process of turning the ship around. The *Lady's Kiss* fought back against them, spurred by the wind. Finn could hardly see through the pelting rain. A rope was in his hand, but he only knew by instinct what it was for, because the other end was lost in darkness. It struggled to wrench itself from his grasp, and the wet cord slipped in his tired hands. But he held on anyways, dragging it down and tying it off securely.

The night was lit by an eerie orange and white glow. The *Lady's Kiss* passed between the wreckage of broken and burning ships. There were bodies in the water. Finn tried not to look, but the screams of drowning soldiers tugged at him with a force he couldn't ignore. There were survivors in the water, swimming desperately toward the *Lady's Kiss*, but the harsh winds of the storm filled the sails, driving her past them. The waves rose up, tossing the ship and dooming the people in the water to a dark grave in the depths.

"Waves take their bones," Finn whispered, wondering who they were and whether those they'd loved would ever know what happened to them.

The *Lady's Kiss* passed beyond the chaos of the battle and into open water. Their only enemy now was the sea herself. The storm did its best to drown them, but the *Lady's Kiss* was built to drown others. She would not be bested by the tempest.

Finn found himself praying. Praying to the Lady to bear them away from the battle and the Shriekers, and to do the same for the *Storm Ghost*. Praying to the Protector that they would ride out this storm. Praying that another lost battle didn't mean Okaesa was doomed.

The storm raged on through the night and no one aboard the *Lady's Kiss* could pause to rest. The wind sounded like screams. The rain and salt spray stung Finn's eyes and the flashes of lightning revealed only high waves and dead bodies on the deck that would not be dealt with until the storm quieted. Finn had not seen Cori either among the living or the dead, and fear at his fate nagged at the back of his mind along with his worry for Tallis.

"We need to shed weight!" Grayston's voice rang out over the storm. "Any supplies we don't need and the dead should be thrown in the sea. Let the Lady have the sacrifice she desires."

Finn shivered and cast his eyes across the deck. Others were hesitating as well, not wanting to rob the dead of a proper funeral.

"Now!" Grayston called out. "Or the depths will be the grave for all of us!"

Finn grabbed the wrists of a Shrieker's body first, not ready to face the crew they'd lost. The body didn't want to move. Finn's boots slipped on the wet wood of the deck and the Shrieker had been a bigger man than him. But slowly, he reached the edge of the deck and hoisted the body up and over the rail. It disappeared beneath the waves almost instantly.

After the first, Finn moved to grab the nearest body, knowing it didn't matter if it was a Shrieker or a fellow crew member. Funerals were for the living, not the dead, and there would be no funerals and fewer living if the *Lady's Kiss* sank.

The arm he grabbed was a girl, younger than him. *Kerryn.* Finn promised himself to remember the names of every person he had to drag overboard. Someone had to remember them. Not everyone had people waiting for them back in Giant's Isle, but Finn knew those who did would want them to know what had happened.

Bernt, Hyval, Tarsi, Rohya...

Finn paused, panting as he leaned against the railing that separated him from drowning. Grayston was shouting, but he couldn't hear the words. It felt like someone had wrapped his body in thick layers of wool blankets. He could barely see or hear, and his arms felt weighed down by an invisible force.

The wood hit Finn's knees with a blunt force that almost shook him out of his exhaustion. Looking down at the water, Finn saw the faces of the dead staring up at him. Tallis glared at him with black eyes, reaching an arm up toward him.

"Finn!"

His uncle was down there too. Finn could see that look on his face, the one that meant he'd had too much to drink and was coming to take it out on Finn.

"Get up!"

A sharp pain spread across Finn's face. He pulled his gaze up from the water to see Cori kneeling at his side.

"Did you just hit me?" Finn asked.

"Have you been bit?"

Cori had a sword in his hand.

"What?"

"Tell me!"

"I don't think so."

Cori looked him over, searching for any sign of injury, then grabbed Finn's face and examined his eyes. The boy put his sword away with a sigh of relief.

"I was worried. I just found you slumped over here. Took you a while to respond to me."

"Sorry," Finn said. "I'm just tired."

"We're all tired," Cori offered Finn a hand to help him up. "But we have to keep working through this storm."

"It's good to see you too, Cori."

"I'm glad you're not dead."

Finn had lost track of time. All he knew was that it was still night and the storm had been raging for hours. He and Cori worked side by side, encouraging each other to keep going and keep working. Finn wondered if he would ever be dry again, or if he would be drenched for the rest of his life.

Imperceptibly, the winds began to die down. Little by little, the waves grew smaller, and the ship swayed less. It began to feel more like they were sailing the ocean, not that they were an unwitting victim of its whims. The navigator began shouting orders to get them on course to Giant's Isle.

It felt like an eternity before the horizon to the east began to brighten. A pink light spread through the sky, illuminating the retreating clouds and reflecting in the sea. It looked as though the sky and water were stained with the blood of those who had been lost during the night.

The ocean was empty from horizon to horizon. No sails could be seen of either fleet or enemy ships. They were alone, adrift in a bloody sea. Finn could see Grayston standing at the helm, his face unreadable as he took in the night's destruction. The deck was a mess, there were sails torn. Anything that hadn't been tied down was strewn across the deck or had been lost to the sea. The crew had paused, watching the dawn, and waiting for the admiral's orders.

"We return to Giant's Isle," Grayston said after a long moment.

Grayston and Bevan disappeared into Grayston's cabin. The navigator took over the helm and sails were raised. The *Lady's Kiss* turned in the water and began to make her way back home.

"Do you think anyone else survived?" Cori asked.

Finn immediately thought of Tallis. He wondered if he'd ever know what happened to her, or if she'd just disappeared from his life forever.

"Finn?"

"If no one else survived, I'm not sure how long the rest of us will survive."

"Maybe the others will also go back to Giant's Isle to regroup," Cori said with forced optimism. "We can't be the only ones that made it through. There's a lot of experienced captains out there. If they couldn't survive a storm, they wouldn't have become captains anyways."

"I hope you're right."

"I mean, one of them's even named the *Storm Ghost*," Cori pointed out, knowing that's where Finn's mind would be. "That ship got its name for a reason. If any of the fleet lasted the night, the *Storm Ghost* did."

"Yeah," Finn nodded, and hope began to rekindle in his heart. "You're right. Captain Eiran and Commander Tallis are survivors."

"So are we," Cori pointed out. "We're still standing and the *Lady's Kiss* is still sailing."

"If we survived, then some of the Shrieker fleet could have too. This isn't over."

Finn gazed out at the western horizon. The sun hadn't risen high enough yet to illuminate the whole sky. They sailed toward the light of dawn, and away from the dark of the night and the storm. In that darkness, the Nightmare Bridge stood with its Guardian. Finn guessed the Guardian knew more about this crisis than what it had allowed him to see. Visions he'd seen there kept coming to pass: the riots at the Serpent's Mouth, and now the burning sea.

Finn remembered seeing Shriekers swarming the walls of Giant's Isle, and a chill deeper than that of the rain and seawater drenching him settled in his bones. For now, the danger still lurked in the slowly fading dark in their wake, but Finn knew it was coming for Giant's Isle.

Withering Rose

I'm dead, was Tallis' first thought upon waking. Her second was to wonder why her head hurt so much if she was dead. She opened her eyes to blinding light.

"Captain!" someone shouted. "She's awake!"

Dimly, Tallis remembered dreaming of someone dragging her out of the water and onto the sand. Pounding on her chest until she coughed and spluttered up what seemed like half the ocean before she could breathe in real air again.

The blinding light turned into Eiran's concerned face and gray-blue sky above. The captain brought a flask to Tallis' lips and she sucked greedily at the fresh water. Eiran pulled the flask away sooner than Tallis would have liked. Her tongue felt like it was made of crusted salt.

"I don't suppose this is what you meant when you said I should learn to be like the sea," Tallis groaned as her mouth began to feel real again.

The concern melted off of Eiran's face to be replaced by the familiar grin. "No, I had something a bit different in mind."

The captain stood and turned to one of the crew. "I want *Storm Ghost* ready to sail as soon as she's able. Send someone to explore those cliffs over there. See if there's anything we could use for shelter if another storm comes through. There's got to be fresh water somewhere on this island so soon after rain. Find it. If you find anything we can eat, even better. Now go."

"What happened?" Tallis asked as she sat up.

They'd placed her in the meager shelter beneath a gnarled, weather-beaten tree. The beach was as small as it had seemed from out at sea. On either side rose steep white stone cliffs. But between them a steep hill covered in dense forest promised more than the bare rock could. The *Storm Ghost* sat upon the sand, the low-tide waves barely licking at her stern.

"We made it," Eiran sighed, sitting down on the outstretched root of the tree beside Tallis. "Though you almost didn't."

"I thought I drowned," Tallis squinted out at the waves. They were rough and gray beneath the still cloudy sky, but at least they were calmer than before.

"You nearly did," Eiran looked down at her. "Though it seems like the Lady didn't want you yet. The waves washed you toward shore. I spotted you in the shallows and dragged you out. At first I thought... well, you weren't gone yet."

Tallis noticed that Eiran's coat was missing, and the white shirt she wore beneath was as sodden as Tallis felt. Eiran began unlacing the leather bracers around her wrists. She dropped them on the hard packed sand at their feet and rolled up her sleeves to wring them out.

Using the gnarled roots of the tree as support, Tallis pulled herself back to her feet. Her head swam and it took a few moments for her vision to clear. All she wanted was to sink into a warm bed and sleep for maybe a decade or two. It felt like every muscle in her body ached from fighting the storm to steer the ship through the battle. Her insides felt like they'd been dashed upon a rocky shore like seaweed and she had to swallow and take deep breaths to quell a rising nausea.

"Easy," Eiran steadied her with a hand on her arm. "You need to rest."

Tallis coughed again, her lungs still burning from the sea she'd inhaled. "It sounds like we can't rest yet. What about the rest of the fleet?"

Eiran chuckled softly. "Now you're starting to sound like me. Take care you don't follow too close to my footsteps. I've taken many wrong steps in my lifetime."

Eiran pushed the water flask back into her hands.

"I think I've had enough of water," Tallis joked, but drank eagerly. After the bitter sting of salt in her mouth, lungs, and stomach, fresh water had never tasted so sweet. Gradually, the dizziness began to fade, replaced by a dull ache in her skull.

"Now let's get you back to the *Storm Ghost*," Eiran said. "You need—"

Eiran's words were cut off by a scream that was quickly smothered. The captain's sword leapt to her hand. The crew all stopped what they were doing and looked up. Tallis felt a surge of panic as she grasped for her sword hilt and found it missing from its place. She must have had it when she fell, and she felt a pang of loss that her father's sword was likely somewhere on the bottom of the ocean.

They heard them before seeing them. The sound they'd all learned to dread and fear spread across the beach. Shriekers were pouring out of holes in the bottom of the cliffs on the opposite side of the beach from where the *Storm Ghost* sat. A man bearing the rose upon his bloodstained uniform ran at the head of the horde.

"It seems my scout found the caves," Eiran turned to Tallis and gripped her arm tightly enough it almost hurt. "Go! Rally the crew by the ship and find yourself a weapon!"

Tallis looked on, wide-eyed as the monsters approached with their jolting, shambling strides. Hadn't they survived enough yet without this?

"Tallis! Go!"

The desperate urgency in Eiran's voice broke through Tallis' shock. She shook herself and nodded, unable to bring herself to speak. Eiran's stormy eyes bored into hers, blazing with fierce rage. The captain released her arm and turned to face the oncoming Shriekers.

"For the king!" Eiran cried as she charged, sword raised high, the few crew that had still been on the beach with them close behind.

Tallis wrenched her gaze from the captain and dashed down the beach toward the *Storm Ghost*. Each footfall in the sand made her head throb, but she kept moving. She reached the crew that were gathered around the ship and saw that many hesitated. *Where do the fools think they can run?* Tallis wondered.

"The Captain needs us!" Tallis shouted to them. "To arms!"

Those that hesitated looked abashed and got to their feet. Jayim waved to her from where he sat in the sand, back to the hull of the ship, and relief nearly overwhelmed Tallis' fear. His usually copper skin was almost as pale as the sand, and bandages were wrapped around his middle, but he was alive.

"I won't be any good in a fight, I'm afraid," Jayim said, grimacing. "Take one of my swords. It'll be more use in your hands than mine."

Jayim offered her the hilt of his sword with a trembling arm. Tallis took it and raised it above her head.

"For the Rose!" she shouted.

Tallis charged across the sand. Ahead, Eiran had already taken the head off the man she'd sent to search the cliffs. A Shrieker ship must have crashed upon the island in the storm as the *Storm Ghost* had and, disliking daylight, they'd taken shelter in the sea caves. The soldier must have awoken them with his search.

Tallis didn't have time to guess at the Shriekers' numbers before she reached the pack. She lifted Jayim's sword to bury it in a monster's neck. A Shrieker grabbed her from behind, and Tallis wheeled to put her steel between its teeth and her flesh just in time. It had once been a large man, and its strength nearly bowled her over. For a moment, she feared it'd get the best of her before an axe came out of nowhere and sent its head flying. The body fell to show Hemma standing behind.

"Thanks," Tallis panted quickly.

"S'nothing, Commander," she replied.

The two stood back-to-back and faced the oncoming mass of Shriekers together. They danced around each other, slashing and hacking, always careful to leave no opening for a Shrieker to come up behind the other.

"Harrin!" the girl behind her screamed suddenly.

Tallis turned to see the other twin surrounded. Hemma was already running, trying to cut her way to her brother's side. Tallis followed and together they broke through the ring surrounding Harrin.

"There!" Tallis pointed, seeing another knot of the crew forming on the open area of beach between the cliff and the ship. "We must defend the ship!"

The three fought their way to the small group holding the beach around the ship against the Shriekers. Someone had found torches that had somehow stayed dry and was lighting and handing them out. Tallis took one and thrust the fire into the belly of a Shrieker.

"Torches in front, blades behind!" Tallis shouted. "Form a line. Drive them back to the cliffs!"

For once, the crew listened to her immediately and without question. *Where's Eiran?* Tallis wondered and briefly scanned the beach but saw no sign of the captain.

Tallis gritted her teeth and pushed onward, torch in her left hand and sword in her right. Soon, most of the Shriekers she saw were blazing and falling. Putrid smoke filled the air and stung her eyes. Her legs soon began to ache with the effort of running on the sand. It was still wet and hard from the storm, but despite that, it slipped and collapsed beneath her feet. Tallis ignored it and carried on, boots sinking into the bloodstained sand seemingly deeper with each step.

At last, Tallis relieved a final Shrieker of its head and the body crumpled, oozing its pool of black blood onto the white sand. She looked around. Across the beach, other soldiers were taking care of the last handful of Shriekers. The once pristine beach was now streaked with black and red, and the bodies of Shriekers and soldiers alike. Some of the bodies still smoldered, sending tendrils of thick black smoke up toward the sky. Tallis looked around for any sign of Eiran.

"Tallis, come here."

Tallis heard the captain's calm voice. Tallis turned quickly, relieved Eiran had not been lost. The captain stood at the end of the beach near the cliffs, where the Shriekers had first appeared. She leaned against a large boulder of the same rough stone as the cliffs, her sword lying in the sand before her. The sand around her was piled with headless bodies. Tallis rushed to her captain's side, dropping her burnt out torch onto the sand.

For a moment, Tallis caught a glimpse of child-like fear on Eiran's face. The look was replaced by her normal stony expression almost as soon as Tallis looked, but it had most definitely been there. Eiran held her right forearm in a vice-like grip with her left hand. Her skin was almost too stained with blood to see, but the bite mark still stood out, stark red tinged with black, against the captain's pale skin.

"Captain—"

"You lot!" Eiran shouted to the soldiers, the ones closest turned and got the attention of the rest. She raised her arm for them all to see. "I'm still captain, so you listen up. If ever you respected me, you listen to Tallis, you hear? She'll be your captain before long, so obey her orders or so help you, I will rise from the grave to haunt your filthy hides 'til you're running for your mothers. Now go clean up this beach. I want the heads off all the dead, theirs and ours."

The soldiers stood in stunned silence for a moment, most staring in disbelief at the bite on their captain's arm. Tallis watched, struck dumb from the moment she'd seen what was wrong, unable to wrench her eyes from the black blood oozing from Eiran's forearm. Tallis thought of the bracers which Eiran had left forgotten in the sand, thick leather that might have saved her, removed to wring out her soaked shirt.

"You heard me, go!" Eiran barked her final command.

Alleto was the first to raise a salute and the rest of them followed suit without a word. Eiran stared them down with blank eyes and nodded back. Then one-by-one they shuffled off to carry out her final order. Tallis drew a deep breath and snapped back to the moment. She hesitated, not sure whether Eiran wanted her to stay, or if she should join the others.

"You stay here," Eiran said, sensing Tallis' confusion.

"Captain." Tallis stood at attention, but her voice faltered and the same thought echoed in her mind over and over. *My fault. My fault. My fault.* If she hadn't fallen overboard, if Eiran hadn't dove in after her, if Eiran had gone into the fight still wearing her bracers and the thick jacket of her uniform, this wouldn't be happening.

Eiran smiled and sank down into the sand. She leaned back against the boulder and stared up at the sky. For the first time, Tallis thought the captain looked tired, and old. Somehow Tallis had managed to forget that Eiran was old enough to be her mother. Gazing down at Eiran, Tallis suddenly remembered her vision from the Nightmare Bridge of herself on a beach, beheading a black-haired woman. She shuddered, no doubt left in her mind now that the Guardian's visions were somehow prophetic

"Take this," Eiran reached up and unclasped the shell locket from around her neck, beside it hung a ring of gold. She held out the chain and Tallis stepped forward to take it, kneeling in the sand at Eiran's side. "Give the ring to Leander. He'll understand. But the locket's for you. You can have my standard too, the Rose. I don't have any children of my own to pass it onto. The *Storm Ghost* is yours, may as well have the flag and the titles too."

"Thank you," Tallis couldn't think of anything else to say. She clutched the locket so tight in her fist that the links of the chain bit into the skin of her palm.

"You remember me, eh?" Eiran looked up at her with damp eyes. But she didn't let any tears fall. "Don't let those fool men who follow you walk all over you. Always remember, you want them to respect you, you must be as strong as the sea."

"I don't feel as strong as the sea," Tallis choked. The sea had almost taken her, and in taking her back, Eiran had incurred a debt, one that she was now paying in full. Tallis would never have the strength of that sea.

Eiran chuckled. "I'll tell you a secret. Neither have I, but just never let them know it."

"What if I can't do it without you?"

Eiran was silent for a moment and stared her down. Tallis squirmed as nervously as she had on the day she'd first met the captain. Finally, Eiran shook her head and smiled.

"You'll do fine, Tallis," Eiran said. "I'm sure—"

With a shout of pain Eiran convulsed, shrinking away from Tallis. She held her bitten arm close to her chest. When the moment passed and she looked up, Tallis saw again the childish fear in Eiran's eyes. Though still the gray-green of a stormy sea, black veins were seeping into the corners. One tear escaped and slid down the ridges of her scar.

"You do it quick, you hear," Eiran glanced at the sword that hung forgotten from Tallis' hand. "I don't want to find out what it's like to be one of them. Let me die while I'm still me. And I want you to do it. Do it so the crew can see. Do it so they can see you're not too weak to do what needs to be done."

Tallis shook her head and opened her mouth to protest.

"Do it!" Eiran's jaw clenched and Tallis knew that she must be fighting the disease and the pain. Most didn't even last this long. "Please."

Eiran took hold of the boulder and pulled herself up to her feet to face Tallis. She did her best to stand up tall, but she still hunched over her bitten arm. Trails of black blood now flowed from the wound and spread out in spirals through the veins beneath her skin. The captain's body trembled like a leaf in the wind.

"Do it now, Tallis," Eiran begged.

"Thank you, Eiran, for everything" Tallis managed to choke out through her tightening throat. She raised a hand in a final salute. "You'll always be my captain."

"Goodbye, my friend," Eiran nodded with a grin that almost looked like her usual smirk, but Tallis could see the venom starting to drip from Eiran's teeth.

Tallis raised her sword and swung. The captain didn't look away until the moment of impact, so neither did Tallis. Sinew split and bone crunched as her sword bit through Eiran's neck and spine. The captain's body dropped like a puppet with its strings cut. The head bounced and rolled down toward the water, leaving a trail of red in its path.

Tallis turned away from the captain's body before the reality of what she'd done could sink in. Forcing bile and tears down, Tallis clasped Eiran's locket around her neck and hid it beneath her shirt alongside her mother's ring. She strode off down the beach toward the *Storm Ghost*. She paused to wipe Jayim's sword clean on the shirt of a fallen man, trying not to look at the red blood mixed in with the black. This was the second time she'd ended the life of someone she loved, and Tallis wondered how many more she would be forced to take before this all was over.

Some of the soldiers had stopped what they were doing and stared at her. Tallis met their gazes with her best recreation of Eiran's unfaltering stare. For the first time, she could see respect in their eyes. Eiran had been right. She'd done what needed to be done. The crew could see that at last. But doing one thing right wouldn't be enough. The threat had not cleared with the storm. The *Storm Ghost* had survived, so other ships, both Shrieker and Okaesan, must have as well. Tallis prayed the *Lady's Kiss* was one of those survivors. Desperate to leave the horror of the Nightmare Bridge behind, she and Finn had never discussed what they'd seen. Now she was certain the visions were more than just illusions, Tallis had to know if Finn had seen anything she hadn't.

Tallis gazed out at the water, the tide coming in to lap at the *Storm Ghost*'s hull. It was time to ready the ship, *her* ship, to be put back out to sail. The constancy of the tides would not wait for her to deliberate on next steps or mourn the fallen, and Tallis finally understood Eiran's words. *You must be as strong as the sea.*

ship, to be put back out to sail. The constancy of the tides would not wait for her to deliberate on next steps or mourn the fallen, and Tallis finally understood Eiran's words. *You must be as strong as the sea.*

ABOUT THE AUTHOR

Athena Giles grew up adventuring in the woods of Seacoast New Hampshire, wooden sword in hand. They graduated from Hampshire College, where they studied creative writing and children's literature, before running away to join the circus for 5 years. Athena is now a Special Education Teacher living in Arlington, Massachusetts. Their work with middle school and upper elementary students has inspired them to expand the books available for children and adolescents to see themselves in, especially for those identifying as trans and non-binary. For updates on their work, visit www.athenagiles.com.

Please take a moment to review this book at your favorite retailer's website, Goodreads, or simply tell your friends!